Praise for Sharon Ward

Sharon Ward's IN DEEP is a stellar, pulse-pounding debut novel featuring a female underwater photographer. A heady mix of underwater adventure, mystery, and romance.

— Hallie Ephron, New York Times bestselling author

Pack your SCUBA fins for a wild trip to the Cayman Islands. *In Deep* delivers on twists and turns while introducing a phenomenal new protagonist in underwater photographer Fin Fleming, tough, perceptive and fearless.

— Edwin Hill, author of *The Secrets We Share*

How much did I love In Deep? Let me count the ways. Fin Fleming, underwater photographer, is a courageous yet vulnerable protagonist I want to sip Margaritas with. The Cayman Islands are exotic and alluring, yet tinged with danger. The underwater scenes and SCUBA diving details are rendered in stunning detail. Wrap that all into a thrilling mystery and you'll be left as breathless as - well, no spoilers here. You must read it to find out!

— C. Michele Dorsey, Author of the Sabrina Salter Mysteries: No Virgin Island, Permanent Sunset, and Tropical Depression

Breathtaking on two levels, Sharon Ward's debut novel IN DEEP will captivate experienced divers as well as those who've only dreamed of exploring the beauty beneath the sea. The underwater world off the Cayman Islands is stunningly rendered, and the complex mystery involving underwater photographer Fin Fleming, especially the electrifying dive scenes, will have readers holding their breath. Brava!

— Brenda Buchanan Author of the Joe Gale Mystery Series

In Deep is a smart and original story that sucks you in from page one. Edge-of-your-seat suspense, a hauntingly realistic villain, and a jaw-dropping twist make this pacy read unputdownable until the very last word.

— Stephanie Scott-Snyder, Author of When Women Offend: Crime and the Female Perpetrator

Hidden Depths

Hidden Depths

A Fin Fleming Scuba Diving Mystery
Book 5

Sharon Ward

Published by Penster Press, LLC

For permissions contact: Editor@PensterPress.com

Printed in the United States of America First Printing, 2023.

Cover design by Cover2Book.com

Hidden Depths, Fin Fleming Scuba Diving Mysteries Book 5

eBook ISBN: 978-1-958478-06-6

Trade Paperback ISBN: 978-1-958478-09-7

Hardcover: 978-1-958478-23-3

For the real Carl Duchette. Thanks for letting me use your name.
Rest in Peace, Buddy.

And as always, for Jack, the best husband in the entire universe

Foreword

Thank you for reading the Fin Fleming Scuba Diving Mysteries. Fin and I are grateful for your support.

Once again I'd like to remind readers that I know that Rosie has already greatly surpassed the reasonable lifespan of an Atlantic Pygmy Octopus. Rather than upset readers who have come to love her, I have chosen to ignore this inconvenient fact. Rosie will be here forever. Hey, it could happen. There's a lot we don't know about the octopus world.

And if you must, you can assume that with each book, Fin has adopted a new octopus, named her Rosie, and trained her to perform the same types of intellectual feats.

I do a lot of fact checking, with the Navy Diving Manual and the NOAA Diving Manual, AIDA training documents, and multiple respected sources on the sport of freediving.

As always, please don't try to emulate Fin's diving feats. She is a trained professional, with every certification and professional credential possible. And while it may look like she's doing crazy stuff sometimes, rest assured that she always knows it's well within her capabilities and if someday she can't do what she thought she could...Well, trust me on this. She'll feel the risk was worth it to accomplish her goal.

Most stuff in my books is possible, even if hazardous. But remember this is fiction, and I do occasionally take liberties in service of the story. But you, Dear Reader, should stay within the bounds of your training and capabilities, and do not assume this is a scuba diving or freediving training manual, because it most assuredly is not.

Chapter 1
The Hammock

THE NOISE from the larger-than-life-size poster flapping in the pre-dawn breeze woke me up from a light doze. I opened my eyes and glared at my own face staring back at me. The sign proclaimed "Grand Opening Celebration at Ray's Place Tiki Bar and Restaurant. Location: The Madelyn Anderson Russo Institute of Oceanography (RIO) on Grand Cayman. Free Continental Breakfast 7:30 to 9 AM. Have your photograph taken by world-famous underwater photographer Fin Fleming."

The world-famous part was a bit of an exaggeration, but it was all part of the institute's marketing. It would be the free breakfast that drew in the crowds, not my name or the opportunity to have me take someone's picture. I sighed and gave Liam a poke in the ribs to awaken him.

He and I were lying in one of the two-person hammocks that we'd recently installed in RIO's recreation area. We'd been planning to go for a pre-dawn dive, but then we'd taken a moment to watch the big yellow Cayman Islands' sun rise. I must have fallen asleep, but now that I was awake again, I wanted to complete the dive before my day went sideways.

I started to work my way out of the hammock, but he nuzzled my neck and pulled me closer. "Stay a little while," he said. "You never get a chance to relax and sleep in."

But instead of relaxing, I went right back to what I'd been doing before I fell asleep—which was brooding about the secrets between us. I never could seem to let my questions go for very long. "Are you ever going to tell me the truth?"

He sighed softly. "Fin, I always tell you the truth. I'd never lie to you."

"Yes, I agree. You always tell me the truth, but you don't always tell me the whole story. So, let me rephrase. Are you ever going to tell me the whole truth?"

"You know I love you completely, but you pick the oddest times to ask the hardest questions. Can't we just stay here and watch the sun come up? Or go for that dive? Your day will go off the rails soon enough without looking for trouble so early."

He was right about that. I had a ton of competing demands on my time. My life never goes according to plan. Thanks to the annual documentaries produced by RIO, I am a well-known scuba diving pro. I'm also the VP of marketing and chief underwater photographer at RIO. I'm on the board of directors of my father's company, Fleming Environmental Investments. And I'm the Editor in Chief of *Ecosphere*, a high-end photography magazine focused on environmental issues.

Liam Lawton, my hammock-mate, was the magazine's creator. A few years ago, he'd founded Quokka Media, *Ecosphere*'s publisher, with a small chunk of the payout from selling his first company, the originator of the super-popular *Oh! Possum* game app.

Scowling, I turned over to see him eye-to-eye. "It's the one thing that drives me nuts. I always feel like you're hiding something."

He sighed again, not quite as softly this time. "I've told you before. I am one hundred percent open and honest with you about everything that matters. There's just one part of my life that I can't discuss."

Even I could hear the frustration in my voice. "Why not? Are you a secret agent? An assassin? An undercover narc? Or maybe you're still married to another wife you forgot to mention. Whatever it is, I should know about it, or this relationship will never go anywhere." I sat up, almost spilling both of us to the soft white sand below the hammock. I curled my fingers into the hammock's rope loops so I wouldn't tumble out.

Luckily, Liam was able to put a foot to the ground and stop our spin before the hammock dumped us. We settled back and continued our discussion.

His tone was infuriatingly reasonable. "I'm not at liberty to tell you what you want to know. But Newton and Maddy both trust me. Can't that be enough for you?" he said.

That statement was true. My father, investment guru Newton Fleming, had taken to Liam right away. They spent hours chatting about business and all sorts of other boring topics. Maddy Russo, my mother, had once hired Liam to be the CFO of the oceanographic institute she'd founded without so much as a single interview. In fact, Maddy liked him so much that she'd recently asked him to step back in again as interim CFO while she looked for a permanent replacement.

A few years ago, after I'd been hanging out with Liam for ages, we'd all been shocked when he told us he still had a wife in his native Australia. When he returned to RIO months later with his divorce papers in hand, my parents had found it a lot easier to forgive him than I had. Even though Liam had kept our relationship at the friendship stage before telling me about his wife, the unspoken deception still hurt.

I tried to cover up the depth of my pain, but it came through clearly in my voice. "We'll see if my parents have any questions when you propose to one of them. In the meantime, it's just me…"

Candy, the newest addition to the RIO menagerie, squawked. "What a pretty girl." She was a young Cayman parrot, just learning to imitate words and sounds. So far, her favorite phrases were "What a pretty girl" and "Give us a kiss." Her perch was across the RIO grounds, inside Ray's Place, the open air restaurant and bar we'd built after Hurricane Willard destroyed all our previous outbuildings.

Liam smiled at Candy's pronouncement. "She's got that right. You are a very pretty girl indeed." He kissed my forehead. "Now let's get going. I need to get all the RIO work taken care of by lunch since I have Quokka Media projects to attend to this afternoon. And I'd like to get a dive in today if we can." He looked at me with a questioning expression.

3

I nodded. "At least one dive a day is a requirement of my job. I'm up for it. Maybe we should go now before the day gets away from us."

Liam and I turned back-to-back to get out of the hammock simultaneously so neither one of us would fall if the hammock spun.

Before we'd counted to three, I heard my best friend Theresa's voice calling from across the recreation area.

"Morning, you two. Did you spend the night in that hammock?"

We both waved to her. She had her daughter Angelica, called Angel, in her arms. She put the toddler down and fumbled with the keypad to unlock the sliding doors that enclosed Ray's Place overnight. I jumped up, forgetting about Liam. Fortunately, his reflexes were fast enough that he managed to avoid taking a tumble.

"Here, I'll get Angel," I said, racewalking across the lawn to hold my goddaughter while her mother opened the restaurant.

Angel's blue eyes lit up and she toddled toward me on her chubby little legs. I smiled happily, but I was chagrinned when she tottered right by me and threw herself into Liam's waiting arms. "Reem," she said, which is as close as she could come to pronouncing his name.

Liam scooped Angel up and swung her around. Her happy squeals pierced the early morning air, and Candy joined in the merriment with "Give us a kiss." Obediently, Angel planted a big wet smooch on Liam's cheek.

We all laughed. Theresa finally opened the electronic lock and slid the doors back on their runners. She quickly walked over to the control panel to turn off the security system alarm.

"That's odd. The alarm's not on. I know I set it when I closed the bar last night. I'm sure I did, because Gus was waiting to take me home and he helped me slide the doors shut afterwards so I wouldn't get caught by the two second delay. By the way, we really need to extend that time. It takes a while to get all the doors in place."

"I'll speak to Chaun about it." Chaun was my friend Chaunsey, a tech genius who had sort of adopted RIO as a pet project. Nobody knew whether Chaunsey was Chaun's first or last name. He was very private, a little antisocial, but extremely helpful and loyal. He talked incessantly when he was nervous, but once Chaun decided you were his friend, you were friends for life.

4

Theresa finished fastening the last tie that held the sliding doors open to the soft ocean breezes off the nearby cove. "Thanks."

As a non-profit research organization, RIO is always looking for new sources of funding. Liam, Newton, and Maddy had all pooled their money to cover the cost of rebuilding the dive shack after Hurricane Willard, but they'd agreed there was no reason to stop with just a small dive shop like the one we'd lost.

We opened Ray's Place to attract everyone—experienced divers, tourists who came to visit our aquarium, the people who took dive classes with us, and of course, the local population. We hoped the nearby ocean, RIO's marina full of carefully maintained boats, the glorious Cayman sunsets, and the easy shore diving, along with great food and drinks would make our new restaurant popular.

Now, to attract those precious tourist dollars, in addition to the new, larger dive operations facility, we had Ray's Place and an assortment of open air tables and hammocks shaded by tiki umbrellas or vine-and-flower covered pergolas.

A lone car pulled into RIO's parking lot. My adopted adult brother Oliver Russo and his girlfriend Genevra Blackthorne waved as they emerged from the vehicle. Holding hands and smiling brightly, they walked toward us. You could almost see the cloud of bliss they floated on.

They were only a few feet away from Oliver's car when the stillness was broken by Candy's screeching. "Uh-oh. Uh-oh. Uh-oh. Uh-oh."

"Sounds like Candy learned a new word," I said, just before Theresa's scream shredded what was left of the peaceful morning.

Chapter 2
Discovery

THERESA WAS DEATHLY afraid of spiders, so I hoped the scream simply meant she had an unwelcome arachnid visitor this morning. "Hang on, Theresa. I'm coming." I looked at Liam, happily bouncing Angel in his arms. "Please keep Angel away from whatever it is that has her mother so upset." I raced barefoot across the sand to the lawn, and then on to the flagstone patio that surrounded Ray's Place.

I rounded the corner of the bar and skidded to a stop. A bright red high-top canvas sneaker stuck out from under a lumpy pile of colorful striped awnings, snowy white napkins, and other assorted bar linens. I knew those kicks. That had to be Chaun under the mess.

Candy kept screeching, so I yelled over to Liam. "Call DS Scott. Ask him to come right away. There's been an accident. And keep Angel as far away as you can. Oliver, please find Doc and bring her here. Genevra, if you could track down Stewie, I'd appreciate it."

I pulled my phone out of the pocket of my cargo shorts and snapped a few pictures so Dane Scott would have at least a few crime scene photos. Those two quick clicks were all the time I was willing to wait before starting first aid. Chaun needed help, and every second could count.

Theresa and I burrowed through the mountain of cloth to reach him, tossing each piece aside. By now we had nearly made it to the bottom of the pile of fabric, but as I reached for a crumpled tablecloth, my hand encountered what felt like another shoe. I pulled it out. It was a black patent leather stiletto sandal with a bright red sole. I knew beyond the shadow of a doubt that this shoe didn't belong to Chaun.

Sure enough, when I heaved the last heavy canvas tarp aside, two people were revealed. As I'd suspected, one was my friend Chaun. The other was a young woman I'd seen at the bar last night. Both of them were ashy pale and as still as death.

I reached over to test their vitals and check their breathing. Chaun had a faint heartbeat and a trickle of blood on his temple. I couldn't find a pulse on the woman's throat or wrist, so I bent over and put my ear to her face to check for breath sounds. My heart sank when I neither heard nor felt any signs that she was breathing.

Candy shouted, "Oh, what a pretty girl."

I glared at the blameless bird, and for a quick moment I was torn. Should I work on Chaun, my friend, who I knew was barely alive, or should I work on the stranger just in case there was a lingering whisper of life in her? She was obviously farther gone than he was. Forgive me, Chaun. Hoping I could work a miracle for her and that you'd be able to pull through the next few minutes on your own, I chose to work on the woman until more help arrived.

I'd only done a few chest compressions on her when Doc ran into the bar, followed closely by Oliver.

Oliver leaned over to put his hands on his knees while he caught his breath. "Stewie's on his way. He and Genevra should be right behind me," he said.

Doc was carrying her medical bag. She knelt beside me and tested the woman's pulse, just as I had. Then she pulled a syringe out of her bag and drew some blood. "Theresa, please take this to the lab in the infirmary. Ask whoever is on duty to test it for drugs along with the usual metabolic panel. Stat. And please stay there to get the results."

Once Theresa was on her way, Doc took over the compressions. "How's Chaun doing?"

I'd jumped up as soon as she'd started compressions on the woman and grabbed the AED—a portable defibrillator—from the wall. I

8

placed it next to Doc before answering. "Faint pulse. Breathing shallow."

She nodded. "Got oxygen handy?"

Since she already knew the answer, I took it as a request. We're a diving facility, so RIO had supplementary oxygen all over the place. She glanced at what I was doing to see that I had just finished placing the oxygen cannula on Chaun.

She smiled and gave a quick nod of approval. "Collar him." She meant she wanted me to stabilize his neck because of the head injury. When I finished, she said. "Good work. Can you draw blood?"

I'd had some medic training, so I nodded and reached into her bag for an empty vial.

Meanwhile, Doc pushed aside the top of the woman's dress and connected the AED, hoping the shock would revive her. "Clear," she shouted.

I'd just finished the draw of Chaun's blood and capped the syringe when DS Dane Scott and Roland Kerwin, his second in command at the RCIP, strode into Ray's Place.

"Roland, please take that." He pointed at the tube of blood in my hand.

Roland took the vial of Chaun's blood, labeled it, and dropped it into an evidence bag before putting the bag into the large case of forensic equipment that went with him everywhere. "EMS is on the way. Meanwhile, how can I help?" he said when the vial was secure.

I checked Chaun's pulse again. It had gotten stronger since he'd been on the oxygen. "I think Chaun is stable for now. There's another vial of blood from the second victim on its way to the lab."

"No good. Tainted chain of custody. I'll need a fresh draw." He pulled a syringe from his kit and filled a vial with the woman's blood. "What are you thinking, Doc?" he said when he'd secured the new sample in his case.

The unresponsive woman had been wearing a bright red sundress with cutouts over her hips and ribs. Doc sat back on her heels and pointed to two tiny, nearly invisible points on the woman's ribcage. "Drugs," she said. "Needle spikes."

I noticed the look that passed between Roland and Dane, but I said

9

nothing. We'd had a rash of needle spikes on the island a few years ago, but the problem had faded away as quickly as it had begun. I'd hoped it was gone forever.

The sound of the approaching ambulance drowned out any response from Dane. EMTs rushed across RIO's grounds to the open air bar. Doc gave them a quick status on each of the unconscious people. They loaded the patients on gurneys and were gone as quickly and noisily as they'd arrived.

Dane turned to Roland. "Send Morey to the hospital. I want him to question both of them as soon as they wake up." Roland nodded and walked away a few steps to call his partner.

"Who found them?" he asked me.

"Theresa found them when she opened up this morning. Liam and I were over there." I pointed to the hammock, swaying serenely in the cool morning air. "Liam took Angel for a walk so she wouldn't see anything scary. Theresa took the woman's blood to the infirmary."

He pulled out his notebook and a pen. "How long were you and Liam in the hammock? Did you see anyone around when you arrived this morning?"

I shook my head. "We got here before sunrise, but nobody was around. We were going to do an early morning dive but then we got to talking…"

"It's okay. You don't need an alibi. I'm pretty sure neither one of you had anything to do with this. I'm just trying to get an idea of the timeline."

I drew in a deep breath to gather my thoughts. "Right. We left here a little before ten P.M. last night. We went to my place to get our stuff for work today and to catch a few hours of sleep. We got back here an hour or so before dawn. I didn't see any cars in the parking lot, and no one was around. The security lights back here were still on. When we walked by, the hammock was calling to us, and we must have dozed off. We woke up with the rising sun in our eyes. We chatted for a few minutes, then Theresa came in so she could open Ray's Place for breakfast."

He clicked the point of his pen. "If you were talking for about ten minutes after the sun rose that means it must have been around 6:15 to

10

6:30 or so when you found them. What time did everybody clear out last night?"

"You'd have to check with Theresa, Brian Walker, or Noah Gibb. They were working the bar last night, and it was still going strong when Liam and I left."

He wrote their names in his notebook. "Got it. What time are the bartenders due in today?"

"Sorry. No idea. Theresa would know. She's the bar's manager."

He flipped the notebook shut. "I'll go talk to Theresa. You can stay back here and if you don't mind, keep people away while Roland works."

Genevra and Stewie Belcher, RIO's dive operations manager, trotted up from the direction of our boathouse. "What do you need?" Stewie shouted when he was still ten or fifteen feet away.

I put up a hand to stop their approach. "Morning, Stewie. Hang on a second."

I was worried we'd have an influx of people looking for the free breakfast and coffee we'd promised. We were celebrating the grand opening of Ray's Place all week, and we'd put up the advertising signs around town and at many of the major resorts along Seven Mile Beach. "Roland, will you need to do your forensic thing in the parking lot, or can I direct any breakfast customers that show up to a buffet station near the front entrance?"

He looked around. "I don't think that'll be a problem. I'll set up a twenty-five foot perimeter, and unless I find something suspicious along its border, you should be fine. But try to keep them on the other side of the parking lot anyway, just in case."

I nodded. "Stewie, I need you to help me set up some tables in the parking lot. I'll explain while we work."

He was already on his way to carry out his task. "No worries. Doc already told me what's going on. I'll meet you out front," he said.

Stewie and Doc were in a relationship, and it had been good for them both. I should have known that if Doc was in this early, Stewie would be around somewhere too.

Genevra, Stewie and I trotted across the recreation area to the dive shop. I logged into the computer and printed several signs that read

"This Way to Free Coffee and Breakfast Pastries." While the printer was running, I explained to Genevra where I wanted her to post them.

Stewie gathered several rolls of duct tape, a hammer, and some nails. He dumped them all into a heavy canvas bag, then he loaded a couple of sawhorses on a hand truck.

He trundled everything to the parking lot while I rushed into RIO's café to talk to Marianna, the kitchen staff manager, to let her know about the change in plans. She was just finishing her daily team meeting, so I asked her to hold her staff back for a minute while I told them about the change in the location of the breakfast, carefully avoiding the reason for modifying our meticulously worked out plans.

Marianna took the switch in stride. "No problem. Here, there, or out back—it's all the same to us."

Then I raced to RIO's front entry to help Stewie. He'd already set up the sawhorses to keep traffic away from the section of the parking lot nearest Ray's Place. I set up the folding tables and chairs. Oliver and Stewie lugged market umbrellas out of our maintenance shed and from the rear picnic area and set them up around the tables. They'd raised the last few umbrellas by the time Genevra returned from posting the signs directing guests to the free food and coffee.

Marianna and her team came out carrying large baskets of breakfast pastries still hot from the oven, pitchers of fresh fruit juice, along with urns of coffee and tea. The first cars started rolling in, and Stewie directed them to the far side of the parking lot, away from the bar and Roland's forensics operation.

I unfurled a portable background and set up the lights for the photo ops and placed my camera on a nearby table. Some people would want their pictures taken by me, and some would want me in the photo with them, so Oliver was on tap to help take the pictures. He and I would print out the photos and put them in commemorative folders for the guests to pick up at their leisure.

A steady stream of people lined up for photographs, and I tried to smile, but it felt more like a grimace. Oliver and I had taken dozens of photos before the crowd dissipated and we could shut down the picture-taking operation.

I'd been on the run since I woke up this morning, and even though it was still early, I was about ready to collapse. I put a "Sorry you missed us" sign on the photography table and went off in search of my own breakfast.

But before I could grab a coffee, a muffin, and a chair, my cellphone rang.

Chapter 3
A Sad Announcement

I GLANCED at the caller ID before I answered. The display showed it was Carl Duchette, managing director of Liam's company Quokka Media, and my nominal boss for my job at *Ecosphere*. "Good morning, Carl. I thought you'd be here for the free breakfast at RIO today."

He sighed. "I wish. I'm actually already on a plane to the states awaiting takeoff. I've been putting off telling you this, but it can't wait any longer. I'm retiring."

My heart thudded. "What? You can't retire. I need you." Carl had been close friends with my late stepfather Ray Russo, and he and my biological parents were also good friends. Carl had offered me my first big break as an underwater photographer when he'd been editor-in-chief at *Your World*, and now that he was the head of publishing at Quokka Media, I relied on him for both advice and friendship.

He sighed again. "It's not my choice. I had a health scare a few weeks ago. The doctors say I can't take this much stress and I need to change my lifestyle. I bought a fifty acre plot of undeveloped land in the middle of Maine, USA. A little cabin on the edge of a lake. Nobody and nothing around for miles except the wind in the trees and the call of the loons. No phone service. No deadlines, and no pressure. I'm looking forward to spending my time there."

I swallowed my sorrow. It was time for me to return the support.

Carl had always been there for me, and it seemed like his health would be in jeopardy if he didn't take this step. "Sounds wonderful. Maybe I'll stop by for a visit next time I'm in the states."

"Don't wait too long," he said. "I'll miss you."

"I'll miss you too," I said. "Do you know yet who will be replacing you at Quokka Media? Genevra maybe?" Genevra is my assistant, and she pretty much takes care of all my responsibilities as editor of *Ecosphere* along with all the minutiae of my job at RIO, but she'd been an editor at Quokka Media for several years before that. Although I'd be lost without her, she deserved her chance to shine.

Carl was silent for a moment. "I'm not quite sure who will be replacing me. You should talk to Liam about it. You know he values your input on the business."

I knew this ploy. Carl used it to deflect the conversation whenever he had bad news. I immediately assumed that Carl didn't want to talk about his replacement because Liam had already made a choice and hadn't sought my input at all—or even bothered to let me know about an upcoming change that would affect me. I bit my lip. Although I hate conflict almost as much as Carl so obviously does, I knew I'd have to confront Liam about this slight.

I took a deep breath to keep my voice steady. "Okay then. I'll discuss it with Liam as soon as he's done talking to Dane. Or minding Angel for Theresa. I don't know which one he's currently involved in."

I heard Liam's approaching footsteps. "Here he is now. Have a safe trip and let me know when you've arrived. I've loved working with you."

"Likewise," Carl said before disconnecting.

Liam's happy smile turned serious when he saw me. "What's the matter? What's going on?"

"Let's get some coffee and go to my office. It seems we have some additional things to discuss." I stalked off toward the coffee station Marianna had set up near RIO's main entrance.

After grabbing a mug of coffee and a gigantic blueberry muffin, I went back through the front door at a brisk pace. Liam was behind me, so I couldn't see his face, but we were so attuned to each other that I sensed his puzzled hesitation.

I was so upset I hadn't yet taken the lid off my coffee when he walked into my office.

He paused in the doorway. "May I join you?"

I waved toward the table in the corner. "Be my guest."

Liam opened his coffee and the heavenly aroma wafted across the small space. My stomach growled. I took the lid off my own cup and sighed with pleasure at my first sip.

Liam drank from his stainless steel RIO-branded mug before speaking. "Okay. Let me have it. What'd I do now?"

"Had you planned to tell me Carl was having health issues? That he was retiring—today? That I have a new boss at Quokka Media and that you didn't even show me the courtesy of letting me meet him or her? Where does all the secrecy end, Liam?"

He paused for another sip of coffee. "I was hoping I could talk you into taking the job. You'd be fantastic at it, and Genevra could still be your assistant and handle the details you don't enjoy. I put off asking you because I was afraid that you'd say no. But now that it's all out on the table, what do you think of my idea?"

I broke off a tiny bit of muffin and stared at it. "I'd say you know better than that. I'm committed to RIO, and the ocean is my life's passion, not the magazine biz. Running your media company is not a job for me." I popped the muffin morsel into my mouth.

Liam looked sad. "I knew that's what you'd say. But if that's the case, you can't have any objection to my hiring someone else into the role. I confess I do have someone in mind."

"Quelle surprise," I said, in a lousy fake French accent, dripping with sarcasm. "Who is it?"

"You may have heard me mention him. Gary Graydon. We hung out together at uni. He was running a small indie press back in Sydney, but I hear he's looking for something new. If it's okay with you, I'll call him today and see what he thinks."

"What are you going to do in the meantime? Carl's leaving today, and it will take this guy Graydon a while to put his affairs in order to leave Australia—if he's even interested in the role."

Liam looked up at the ceiling. "Actually, he's already here on Grand Cayman, and he's interested. We could all have dinner together tonight if you'd like to meet him. But I won't hire him if you don't think you'll get along."

My lips tightened with annoyance. "Sorry. I already have a very busy day planned. I need to work with Dane to find out more about the woman we found in the bar, go see Chaun at the hospital, and Christophe is due to arrive today." It seemed obvious to me that Liam had already made up his mind and decided not to discuss it with me. I'd bet he'd already promised Gary the job and then set up this dinner meeting as an afterthought in hopes of staving off my anger. Well, it wasn't going to work.

There was sincere concern in his eyes. "No time to dive with me? No running together? Are you overdoing work? I'd hoped Gary coming aboard would help you free up some time to relax. You seem very stressed lately."

"I am."

"I hope you're not too stressed to make it to a fancy dinner with the man I hope will be the new editor-in-chief of Quokka Media. If you squeeze it in, I'll tell Gary to meet us at Ristorante Pappagallo tonight. Are you up for it? If not, we can wait until you're ready."

I love Ristorante Pappagallo, and Liam knew it. I bit my lip and thought it over for a moment. "Okay. Bring it on. I'm up for anything you can dish out."

Chapter 4

Christophe

A DEEPLY MELODIC voice with a very authentic and extremely alluring French accent came from the open door. "Christophe is here, but I have a bad habit of always being early. Should I come back later? Perhaps go for a café au lait while you finish your meeting?"

I looked up and sucked in a breath. The man peering in through my open door was undoubtedly one of the most attractive men I'd ever seen. He had dark cocoa-colored hair, chocolaty dark brown eyes with a merry twinkle, a full sensual mouth, and a slim build.

I rose from my desk and walked over to welcome Christophe, trying not to gawk too obviously. "Welcome. And you're right on time. Liam and I got a late start this morning, but we're just finishing up. Liam, this is Christophe Poisson, the world champion free diver. Newton hired him to be my trainer for the deep freedive in this year's documentary."

Liam rose and extended his hand. "Nice to meet you, Christophe. I'm Liam Lawton. Poisson—that means 'fish' in French, right? Great last name for a diver. Did you change it?"

Christophe shook Liam's hand and smiled wryly. "You're not the first person to ask me that, but I assure you I was born with it."

I took Liam's arm and subtly walked him to the door of my office before he could start drilling into Christophe's life story. "I'll see you later. Maybe we can do a sunset dive?"

He smiled. "Sure. I'll pick you up at quitting time."

Christophe sat at the table. "I fear you will be too tired to dive with your boyfriend later. Our training will be full time and very rigorous." His accent made every word a seduction, even though I didn't like what I heard.

"I'm not sure what you mean by full-time, but I can't spend more than a few hours a day, and only a few days a week on training. I already have several full-time jobs."

Clearly surprised by my response, Christophe looked at me in silence for a moment before he spoke. "How do you expect to become an expert if you don't work at it? My understanding was that you wanted to be a champion like Ray Russo. He was one of the greats, but he didn't get that way without dedication to his sport."

I sighed. We clearly had different goals for this gig. "I agree that Ray was a superlative diver, and he worked hard at it while he was competing. But when he retired from competitive freediving, he had other ways of filling his time. For one thing, he worked here full time. Like I do."

I saw Christophe nodding along with my words, so I kept going. "I'm already an accomplished scuba diver, and I have no intention of ever freediving competitively. My father hired you because he wants to be sure I'm safe during the filming of our annual documentary. I just need a few tips. Maybe a few practice dives. That's all."

Christophe narrowed his eyes. "Freediving is my passion. I don't do tips and practice dives. I only take on divers interested in serious training. If you want to work with me, it's all or nothing."

I shook my head. "Then I'm afraid it's nothing, Christophe. I'm sorry we brought you out here before making our needs clear to you. Of course, we'll pay you for your time and take care of your travel expenses, but I simply don't have the time you were expecting."

Genevra walked by my door on the way to her office, and I called out to her. "Genevra, would you please see that Monsieur Poisson gets a cab to his hotel? And set up his travel arrangements to get him back home or to wherever he wants to go."

She stopped outside the door to wait for Christophe to join her. He turned away from me to leave. Their eyes met.

She looked at him.

He looked at her.

You could almost hear the thunder roll.

He took Genevra's hand, lifted it to his mouth for a kiss, and introduced himself.

I'd never seen my usually unflappable assistant so awestruck. Her cheeks were flushed, and her eyes were wide as she stared at Christophe's exquisitely sculpted face.

She stammered. "I'm a big fan. I've heard so much about you that it's nice to finally meet you in person."

When I rose to shake his hand and say goodbye, I was startled when he put his hands on my shoulders and air kissed me on both cheeks.

"Not necessary to say au revoir. I gave my word to Newton that I would keep you safe on your dive, and I never go back on my word. I will work within your boundaries."

"Excellent," I said, surprised by the rapid change in his position.

Christophe smiled, and it was like the most glorious sunrise I'd ever seen. He turned to Genevra. "Will you show me around this beautiful facility? I'm especially interested in the marina and the training pool."

She pointed down the hall. "This way."

Chapter 5
Security Footage

I WAS STILL in the hall when Dane Scott came around the corner.

He watched them leave. "Who's that with Genevra?"

"Christophe Poisson, a champion freediver. Newton hired him to be my trainer for the documentary dive," I said. "He's pretty intense."

"Don't take this the wrong way, but I'm glad he's here and I'm glad everyone is taking the dive seriously. I don't want anything to happen to you, and after what happened to Ray, we know even the best-trained diver…"

I held up my hand to stop him from continuing. "I know." My voice cracked. "It can be dangerous. Let's not go there."

He grimaced. "Sorry. Got time for a coffee?"

"Sure. I was just about to call you to check in. What do we know so far?"

His scowl deepened. "Chaun got hit on the head with a blunt object. He has a concussion. Both of them were drugged. Spiked with a mix of Fentanyl and Ketamine. Unfortunately, the woman got hit twice, and she ODed. Luckily, Chaun will pull through okay. He should be coherent enough for us to question later this afternoon."

I broke in. "I should be there when you question him. Chaun is pretty skittish with people he doesn't know well. He trusts me. I can help to keep him calm."

Dane nodded. "I agree you're a stabilizing influence on Chaun. I'm hoping he knows who the woman is. There haven't been any reports of missing persons and identifying her is the first step in the investigation. I actually came by to ask if you're free to accompany me. Do you have some time today?"

Chaun was a dear friend. He was shy and sensitive, and he usually found it hard to connect with people. If they'd been friends, he'd be devastated by the woman's death. My heart broke for him and the beautiful young woman who'd died. "I'll make the time. Whenever you need me."

"Good," he said. "On another note, can you pull the security video from last night? Even though your surveillance system always seems to be down when anything happens, maybe this time we'll get lucky. You may have caught something on camera that will help us."

"Hang on a sec. I think I can do it from here."

I opened the security monitoring app and streamed the video to the computer on my desk. Dane stood behind me, looking over my shoulder. The cameras were working perfectly, clearly showing throngs of people enjoying the opening night music and dancing. I recognized many of the local people in the crowd, but as you'd expect, there were a lot more people I didn't know. The film showed Liam and me leaving a few minutes before ten, just as I'd told Dane.

When the time stamp in the corner of the video showed a few minutes after ten, two men entered Ray's Place. They were both of medium build. Both wore generic gray hoodies, completely zipped up, and they kept their chins snuggled down into the fabric. They had dark blue ball caps pulled low over their faces. Neither cap had a logo. Nothing to help identify them.

They paused inside the entry and looked around for a few minutes, then they split up. On each of the film feeds that covered the bar, I saw one of the men approach a corner where a camera was mounted. They both kept their heads down and turned away from the cameras. Almost simultaneously, they each pulled something from the hoodie's pocket. Still with their heads turned away and their faces shaded by the ball caps, they raised their arms. The camera views immediately went blank.

I turned to Dane in puzzlement. "What happened? The system was working fine."

He grunted. "It probably still is, but I think they sprayed the camera lenses with black paint. Let's go see."

When we approached Ray's Place, Roland was just packing his forensics case. He'd already taken down the crime scene barrier tape, and the bright yellow ends sticking out of the trash barrel fluttered gaily in the breeze, belying the seriousness of their purpose. He'd also removed the security cameras from their mounts in the dim corners of the thatch roof and left them on the bar.

He scowled when he saw us approach. "I don't think we'll find anything conclusive. There must have been hundreds of people through here last night, and the guys with the needles weren't kind enough to leave their calling cards behind. This CSI stuff will take a lot of effort but provide little or no insight into the crime."

The wrath in his voice was apparent, but I knew he wasn't angry at us. He was furious at whoever had ended the life of that beautiful— and still unknown—young woman.

He slammed the lid on his case. "And you're going to need new security cameras. Again. I wouldn't wait too long. They'll probably be back." He stalked away, lugging his bulky case with one hand.

Dane watched him depart. "Don't mind him. He really hates when the bad guys manage to get away with their misdeeds."

I was incensed that Dane seemed ready to give up before he'd even started trying to find the people who had hurt Chaun and the unknown woman. "Get away? You mean you don't think you'll be able to find out who did this? You are going to investigate thoroughly, aren't you?"

Dane held up his hands in a conciliatory gesture. "Slow down, Fin. We'll investigate, and we'll be looking hard. But there's a lot of ground to cover on this island. And a lot of tourists who come and go. We may find that just like last time when we had that rash of needle spikes, the crimes are hot and heavy for a week or so. Then the guys who are responsible go home, taking their drugs and their needles with them. We'll have to wait and see what happens."

"I get it," I said sadly. "Isn't there any way to check names? See if anyone who's on the island now was here the last time this happened?

It wasn't that long ago. Can you compare hotel registries or airline manifests?"

"Already in process. Morey is working on that angle. I'll see if he's found anything yet." He whipped out his phone and turned away to call the other detective on his team.

While he was on the phone, I went over to Candy's perch to give her a treat.

She hopped from foot to foot when I approached with a palmful of seeds I'd scooped from the small dish we kept under the bar to hold her day's allotment of treats. Left to herself, she'd keep eating until she made herself sick, so we kept her on a strict ration. "Uh-oh. What a pretty girl," she said.

Dane finished his call and joined me in front of Candy's perch. "Too bad she couldn't tell us what happened here last night."

She flapped her wings when she saw him. "Give us a kiss," she said, leaning toward him.

He smiled at her. "Maybe another time. I'm working right now."

"You know she's not really talking, right? Not like having a conversation. She just mimics sounds she's heard."

Candy let out a blood curdling scream. She yelled, "No, Chaun. No. No. No."

She paused a moment, and then she said, "Uh-oh."

"Uh-oh, indeed," said Dane. "Let's go pay Chaun that visit we discussed."

Chapter 6
At the Hospital

DANE and I walked across RIO's recreation area to the parking lot. There were still a few stragglers who had come for the free food this morning, and since we were both pretty well-known, we tried to look anonymous and casual as we crossed to where his unmarked police car was parked. He unlocked the doors, and I slid in on the passenger side. After he put the car in gear, we drove sedately out of the lot.

Once we were out of view of the civilians who had been lingering over their coffee or just enjoying the sunny day, Dane really stepped on the gas. He didn't speak, and his face looked grim. Within a few minutes, we'd pulled into the parking lot of the Cayman Islands Hospital in Georgetown.

The attendant at the hospital's front desk knew Dane from his frequent business there, so she immediately sent him to Chaun's room. The shades were drawn when we walked in, and Chaun appeared to be sleeping. There was a white bandage wrapped around his head.

"Maybe we should come back later when he's awake," I whispered.

Chaun sat up and rubbed his eyes. "I'm awake."

Dane motioned me to the comfy visitors' chair next to the bed, then he used his foot to pull over a rolling stool that stood under a small wall-mounted folding desk where I assumed the medical team stopped to make notes and update patient charts. We both sat down.

For a moment, nobody spoke. At last, I broke the ice. "How are you feeling?"

His voice was a croak. "Awful. I got whacked in the head pretty hard. They said I have a concussion. And I was drugged. But that poor woman. It's all my fault."

I cringed. His words sounded way too much like a confession to be said in front of the police. "I'm sure that's not true. Can you tell us what happened? And who was that woman you were with?"

He shrugged. "I met her at the bar. She said her name was Polly, but I think she probably just made that up when she saw Candy." He looked at me, misery on his face. "She was trying to teach Candy to say, 'Polly wants a cracker.' I guess she thought it was funny to say her name was Polly. She was so beautiful, and she wasn't stuck up like so many pretty women are. We were chatting and having fun. It was the best time I've ever had with someone I don't know well."

Dane broke in. "Did you drug her? Try to keep the good time rolling?"

I glared at him. I didn't think that was the best way to keep Chaun talking.

But maybe I was wrong, because Chaun took a deep breath and went on with his story. "No, it wasn't me who drugged her. A couple of men came in. Gray hoodies and ball caps," he said, looking at us to make sure Dane knew he was giving a description of the men who had drugged him. "Tall."

Chaun calling them tall didn't mean much, since he was barely four-foot eight himself, but I nodded encouragingly. "Then what happened?"

He was pleating the sheet between his fingers; clearly upset by his inability to protect the woman he'd been with. "They walked around the bar for a little bit, then they left. A half hour or so before closing, they came back. One of them asked Polly to dance, but she told him she was with me and didn't want to dance. They went away. Polly and I left the bar together at closing time. We were in the hammock when they came back and asked her if she wanted to go to their hotel for another drink. She said she didn't, and one of the men grabbed her. I saw he had a needle hidden in his hand, and I pushed it away from her. That's when I felt the sting. The drugs hit me like a punch in the

28

gut, but I still tried to fight back. I saw one of them leading Polly toward the dive shop, but there was nothing I could do. When I started to follow them, the other one hit me in the head with something. I was down and couldn't get back up. The next thing I knew, I woke up here. Where is Polly? Is she okay?"

I reached over and took his hand. "Polly didn't make it, Chaun. I'm sorry."

Dane broke in. "Do you have any idea of her real name, Chaun? Or where she was staying?'

Chaun shook his head sadly. "No. She just called herself Polly. And I don't have any idea where she was staying."

Dane's gaze met mine over Chaun's head before he asked the next question. "When did Candy learn to say 'No, Chaun?' She said it several times this morning."

Chaun didn't seem to find any significance in Dane's question, because he answered without hesitation. "I taught her to say my name. She's really smart. She catches on quick." He thought a moment. "And Polly kept saying "No" to those guys. Maybe Candy just put the phrases together on her own."

"Why didn't anyone hear her shouting at those men? The bar was packed," Dane said.

Chaun scrunched up his face. "This all happened later. The bar was already closed by then. The lights were off, and the doors were shut. We were pretty far away from the bar anyway. Over on the hammocks."

"What were you doing between the time the men first arrived and closing time?" Dane's voice was grim, and the harsh sound made Chaun shrivel.

"We were just sitting at the bar. Talking and having fun getting to know each other. Then when Theresa said she was closing, we walked across the lawn to grab the hammock. I can't remember anything else that I haven't already told you," he said meekly.

Dane stared intently at Chaun for what felt like an age. Then he turned and walked toward the door. "Coming?"

I patted Chaun's hand. "We'll be back later. Try to get some rest in the meantime. Everything will be okay."

Chapter 7
A Surprise at Lunch

DANE and I walked out of the hospital together and got into his car. "Do you have time to stop for lunch before I drop you back at RIO? I'd like to kick around some ideas with you."

"Sure. If we're quick. I've got a million things on my plate today."

He was looking straight ahead, but I could see his half-smile. "You always have a million things to do. I'll be quick."

He pulled into the parking lot of the Paradise Restaurant by the Sea, a small oceanfront place with a tiny but terrific outdoor deck that overlooked the ocean. When we went inside, the hostess showed us to an outside table near the rail. The sparkling waves of the Caribbean Sea were only a few feet away. We both ordered sodas, burgers, and fries.

While we waited for our food, we watched a group of people snorkeling at the nearby site. They could wade into the ocean from the beach, so the entrance here was easy. I knew it was an interesting site for both snorkeling and diving, and I hoped they were enjoying themselves. I love seeing people appreciating the ocean.

Our food came quickly, and after I took my first bite, Dane said, "This needle spiking bothers me. The last time we had this happen was over at Nelson's, right in front of you and Liam. Now it happens at your new restaurant. Do you think there's a connection?"

I nearly choked. "Between me and the needle stick guys? Not a chance. You know me better than that."

He nodded. "I do know you better than that. I didn't mean you. Maybe Liam? Or someone else at RIO? The younger Gibb boys have been working at RIO, and their brother owns Nelson's. Could that be the connection?"

I thought about it for a minute. "You know I'm no fan of Stefan Gibb, but I don't think he'd tolerate drugs at his place. He's worked too hard to make a good home for his younger brothers. They're orphans, you know."

Dane sipped the last of his soda. "I notice you didn't say anything about Liam."

"Because that's just too crazy an idea, even for you. Remember, Seb Lukin, the big drug kingpin, nearly killed Liam not that long ago. He wouldn't have done that if Liam had been part of his inner circle."

He threw some money down on the table. "True, very true. Ready?"

I stood up and followed Dane off the deck, but then I saw the hostess seating my father at a table under the big red awning. "Hold on, Dane. I want to say hello to Newton."

Newton saw me approach, and he stood to kiss my cheek. "What a nice surprise. Let me introduce you to Joely Wentworth. Joely used to work with me years ago at Fleming Environmental Investments. She's interviewing for the CFO position at RIO this afternoon, and I was just giving her a few pointers. Joely, this is my daughter, the famous Fin Fleming."

"I'm a big fan," she said. "So nice to finally meet you.'

Joely appeared to be in her late forties. Highlighted brown hair curled softly over her shoulders in a very chic style. Bright blue eyes. Tall, fit, and strong looking. She wore an elegant dark blue linen suit with a silky white shirt and sky-high heels of matching dark blue suede. Her only jewelry was a pair of small gold hoop earrings, a simple gold bracelet, and a Rolex watch. Her hands were perfectly manicured; her makeup was understated and polished. Her looks were not conventionally pretty, but she had an almost palpable presence.

There was something about Joely I liked immediately. I hoped she got the job, so we'd have a chance to become friends. "Pleased to meet you, Joely. And this is my friend DS Dane Scott of the RCIP. We have to rush off, but I wish you good luck with your interview."

Dane and Newton had a complicated relationship. They were sort of friends, but since they were both in love with my mother, they were also intense rivals.

"Fin, why don't you join us? I can drop you off at RIO when I bring Joely over." said Newton. "That way Dane can get back to work faster. I know how busy he is."

Dane responded for us both. "Thank you, but I'm headed that way anyway. Sadly, today my work is at RIO. I take it you haven't heard what happened."

"Nope. You can fill me in when I bring Joely to her appointment. I'll see you there later." He kissed my cheek again, and he and Joely sat back down.

Chapter 8
Diving with Maddy and Doc

I LEFT Dane conferring with Roland under the thatched roof at Ray's Place and headed along the crushed shell path to RIO's back door. Before I got there, the door popped open and Maddy and Doc came out.

"Oh good. You're back. We're going for a dive. Want to join us?" Maddy said.

I was delighted by the invitation. "Love to. Let me just grab some tanks."

Doc shook her head. "No need. We've already loaded enough tanks for an army on the *Sea Princess*. Just grab your gear bag on the way to the boat."

Maddy put her hand on my arm. "I'm glad we're taking the *Princess*. I'll captain and you can relax for a change. It's been a tough day for you."

"Thanks, it has been a hard day. I'll see you on board." I hurried over to the row of large wooden lockers where the staff kept their personal dive gear. I grabbed my bag, a dive suit, and my favorite camera. Stewie Belcher, RIO's dive operations manager and Doc's significant other, saw me as I passed the dive shop, and he came outside and walked along beside me.

The *Sea Princess* was in its usual slip next to my boat. I stowed my gear under one of the benches that lined her gunwales and sat down. Maddy climbed the ladder to the flying bridge and started the engines. Stewie unfastened the line and tossed it to me as Maddy expertly backed out of the slip and headed out to sea.

"Where are we going?" I asked Doc, raising my voice to be heard over the engine noise.

Doc's eyes glowed with anticipation. "Sentinel Rock."

It didn't take us long to reach the site's mooring. Maddy pulled the *Sea Princess* up close, and I used a long handled gaff to grab the loop and then ran the bow line through it. When I was sure we were secure, I raised my arm so Maddy would know it was okay to cut the engines.

By the time she'd climbed down from the flying bridge, Doc and I were already getting into our dive suits and setting up our gear on the port side. Maddy's gear was on the starboard side. She quickly doffed the outer layer of her clothes and put on the thin dive skin she'd be wearing over her bathing suit.

We all finished gearing up about the same time, so we walked over to the dive platform. I offered Maddy a steadying arm while she slid her fins on, then I checked her tank. She thanked me and put the second stage regulator in her mouth. She covered her mask and her regulator with one hand and held her BCD inflator hose with the other. One step, and she was in the water. She quickly bobbed to the surface and made the okay sign.

I repeated the spotting and checkout procedure for Doc, and she did the same for me. Then she too was in the ocean.

My turn. I handed my camera down to Doc for safekeeping before I slipped on my fins. Then I stepped off the platform. As soon as I rose to the surface, Maddy turned her thumb down, the diver's signal to descend, and we all sank beneath the waves.

Sentinel rock has a massive coral pinnacle that starts at about seventy-five feet of depth, and we swam directly to it. I took a few shots of Maddy and Doc as they hovered over the abyss, admiring the pinnacle's lush corals. The orange and yellow tube corals extended out six or eight feet from the main reef, and the delicate purple sea fans, wafting gently in the current, were even bigger.

A large green moray eel stuck his head out of his nearby lair. He flexed his jaws in a way that looks menacing but is really just the eel's way of getting enough oxygen from the water. That doesn't mean an eel won't bite someone foolish enough to try to touch them though. Moray eels are notoriously nearsighted, and they can easily mistake an unwary diver's hand or finger for a delicious fish.

Doc and Maddy were experienced enough to know this, and anyway, we all adhered strictly to a 'don't touch the wildlife' policy when diving. We had no need to worry about an attack from a renegade eel.

Doc gave me a little poke, and we turned to look out into the blue, just as a pair of large eagle rays swam by. They paid no attention to us and gracefully swept past in an instant.

Diving never gets old for me. The sense of oneness and sharing with other divers stimulates peace and wonder, and my favorite dives are made with the people I love. It was a special treat to be diving with my two favorite women, and to just float along, enjoying the water, the serenity, and the unique view into a whole different world.

We continued swimming and came to one of the many swim-throughs at this site. This one was inhabited by about fifteen large silvery tarpon. We let them be rather than chase them out by entering the swim-through. After all, they were there first.

We ascended slightly and came across a huge tiger grouper hovering close to the wall. I estimated his weight at about twenty pounds and his length to be about three feet, much larger than divers usually see at the most frequented dive sites. I snapped a picture of him, managing to get Doc in the same frame to act as a reference for his extraordinary size.

We continued our ascent and passed several rainbow parrotfish pecking at the coral with their funny beaks. They floated easily in the current's mild surge. As always, time underwater passed in a blur, and too soon, we had to head back to the boat. After a leisurely ascent using the mooring line as a guide, we stopped below the *Sea Princess*'s stern and hovered effortlessly at fifteen feet for the required three minute safety stop. When the necessary off-gassing time had elapsed, one by one, we climbed the ladder to get back on the boat.

When I crested the top rung, Maddy was standing near the cabin with her back to me. She had pulled her silver dive skin down to her waist, and her long blonde hair hung down her back. She reached behind her and pulled it over her left shoulder to braid it.

A large mottled red, brown, and black raised mark on her right shoulder marred the perfection of her skin, and the sight of it made me uneasy. I didn't know what it was, but I knew it didn't look like anything good. I racked my tank and walked quickly across the deck, motioning to Doc to join me as I passed her.

When we reached her, I said, "What's that on your back, Maddy? Have you had it looked at?"

She spun around, confused. "What? Where?"

Doc said, "Let me give it a quick exam."

Maddy sighed. "I don't know what you're talking about, and you two are probably overreacting, as usual. But go ahead, Doc. If it will set your mind at rest, take a look."

Her tone of voice said that Maddy truly thought we were making a big deal over nothing, but before I could take reassurance from her confidence, Doc's eyelids twitched.

But Doc's voice was calm and soothing when she spoke. "Mads, I'm not a dermatologist or an oncologist, but I want you to see someone about this right away."

Maddy's voice didn't quaver a bit. "No need. I'm sure I'm fine. I always use sunscreen. I wear sun-protective clothing and a hat when I'm outdoors. There's no way."

"Nonetheless, we are done diving for today and I am taking you to see a friend of mine who's a specialist. Right now. No argument."

We all knew better than to argue with Doc when it came to medicine anyway, so I was surprised when Maddy said, "No. I don't want to see anyone about this. I'm sure it's nothing."

I was shocked. My mother was sticking her head in the sand about something that could easily be put to rest. She was usually so confident about facing down her fears—even to the point of going nose-to-nose with a great white shark. And if this turned out to be skin cancer, the sooner Maddy received treatment the better.

Doc pulled her cell out of her gear bag. She turned her back to us and stepped away before speaking quietly into the phone.

I tried to reassure Maddy. "You're one of the luckiest people in the world, and we've always said it's better to be lucky than good. Have faith your luck will hold. Everything will turn out just fine."

Doc came back and held the phone down by her side. "Okay if I take a picture to send to my friend? That may clear this whole thing up without any need for a visit to a doctor."

Maddy nodded, but it was easy to see the stress in her eyes.

Doc's face was carefully nonchalant as she focused her phone's camera on Maddy's back. When she took my hand and had me extend my thumb next to the growth to give the photo a metric of its scale, I realized she was worried.

She sent the picture and moved to the stern of the boat to finish her conversation with her friend.

Maddy was shaking. I put my arms around her. "It'll be okay. It may be nothing, but whatever it is, you'll beat it because we'll all be fighting it together. Don't worry until you know for sure you have something to worry about."

Maddy's huge turquoise eyes were red, like she was trying hard to hold back tears, but she didn't cry. "My father," she said. "Cancer." Then she buried her head in my shoulder while I patted her back.

Doc removed the keys to the *Sea Princess* from the outer pocket of Maddy's gear bag. "He wants to see you in person. I'll take you." She climbed the ladder to the flying bridge and started the engines.

I led Maddy to one of the benches and gave her a cup of water drawn from the cooler, then I released the boat from its mooring. Doc took off gently, but we picked up speed as we traveled.

Chapter 9
Health News

WHEN WE ARRIVED BACK at RIO, Doc walked Maddy to the locker room so she could shower before her doctor's visit, while I cleaned all our gear in the huge freshwater rinse tank, hung our dive skins in the employee drying area, returned our tanks to the dive shop for refilling, and stowed our gear bags in our respective lockers. By the time I finished with the cleanup, Doc and Maddy were dressed and ready to go.

Doc's car keys were in her hand. "My friend knows exactly what to do. He'll probably want to do a needle biopsy. A simple in-office procedure."

The word 'biopsy' made me cringe, but I hid my terror. "Great. I'll come along in case Maddy needs me."

Maddy shook her head. "That's not necessary. I know how busy you are, and Doc will be there if I need anything. Anyway, I'll want to take some time alone to process it if there's bad news."

She gave me a hug, and I clung to her for a moment. "No bad news. Remember your luck, and please call me as soon as you know anything."

I'd spoken to Maddy, but Doc was the one who replied. "We'll call you."

I watched as they walked across RIO's grounds. Doc drove a baby blue Volvo EV, and I watched with trepidation as it left the lot. I should have gone into the office to work, but I knew I wouldn't be able to concentrate. Between Chaun in the hospital suspected of murder and my worries about the growth on Maddy's back, I didn't have a single spare brain cell to devote to office tasks.

I sent a text to Genevra.

Heading Home. C U tomorrow?

She replied with a smiley emoji, so I figured all was good. Then a longer text came through.

Christophe 6:30 AM

Yikes. In my worry about Maddy and Chaun, I'd forgotten about Christophe. Our first session was tomorrow.

I sighed. This freedive training was one more thing on my already overloaded plate. I was exhausted, but I sent Genevra a thumbs up, then I stopped by my office to pick up the canvas tote I used instead of a purse. Head down, I walked slowly out of RIO.

I was exiting the front door when Newton pulled up in his dark blue Mercedes. The electric vehicle was a handsome machine, and it had all the bells and whistles available. Even so, I still preferred my own by-now ancient Prius. In my opinion, a car's purpose is to get you between two points in the most efficient manner, and the Prius still did that for me just fine.

Newton and Joely got out of the vehicle, and I slapped my forehead. Maddy was supposed to be interviewing Joely for the CFO position this afternoon, but of course, she wouldn't be around to take care of it. I walked over to let them know that Maddy had been called away.

It wasn't like Maddy to forget an appointment, and Newton could tell by my voice that something was wrong. "What's the problem?" he asked.

"Doc took her to see a friend, Dr. LaFontaine. Nothing to worry about yet." I cringed when I realized I'd said yet. Newton was too sharp to let that slip by. I continued speaking hoping he'd forget I'd

42

said that ominous word by the time I finished. "I'm sorry, Joely. The appointment must have slipped her mind. I'll check with her to reschedule."

Newton had been staring at the front door, clearly not listening to my exchange with Joely. "She went to see Dr. LaFontaine? He's an oncol...." Newton broke off in the middle of the word and held up a hand, like he thought saying the word oncologist out loud would bring bad luck. "Let me check with Maddy before you do anything else." He pulled his phone out of the pocket of his precisely tailored and well-pressed cargo shorts, turned his back, and walked away a few steps. Meanwhile, Joely and I stood awkwardly smiling at each other.

Newton's call didn't take long, and he took me aside when he disconnected. "Maddy is leaving the decision on the new CFO in our hands. If you and I agree on a candidate, then we have the green light to go ahead and make an offer. Joely already has my vote. I need to leave right away—a personal emergency—so why don't you talk to Joely now if you can. And if you wouldn't mind, would you please see that she gets to the airport on time for her flight?"

Newton, who normally has flawlessly polished manners, walked away without a thank you or a goodbye. I realized Maddy must have told him about Doc's concerns. He was upset and wanted to be with her.

"Sure thing," I said to his back. Then I smiled at Joely.

She must have read the exhaustion in my face. "It sounds like you've put in at least a day and a half already today. Why don't I come back early in the morning? We can talk then, and as long as I get to the airport on time for my flight, it's all good."

I breathed a sigh of relief. "Thank you. I appreciate your flexibility. It really has been a tough day, and it's still not over." We went inside and I called a cab to take her to a hotel.

After Joely left, I checked my phone. There was a text from Doc. I was chagrined that I'd missed it.

> Needle biopsy. Results day or 2. She's asleep.
> Down 4 the night.

43

Chapter 10
A Dinner Meeting

I WAS TOO tired to drive all the way out to Rum Point to get ready for the dinner meeting Liam had arranged, and besides, I only had cargo shorts, polo shirts, and bathing suits in my wardrobe at home. I called Liam and asked him to pick me up at Newton's condo.

Several years ago, Newton had hired a stylist for me as a surprise before an event. Since then, he'd kept the stylist on retainer, and he'd taken to sending me the designer clothes she selected whenever he traveled to New York. I stored most of those clothes in the massive walk-in closet in the room he kept for me at his place, so I had a lot of unworn clothing to choose from for tonight's dinner with Gary Graydon. I surveyed the racks of fancy gowns, elegant business suits, and chic little black dresses.

I probably should have chosen one of the business suits, but I hate being dressed up. I chose a simple black silk shift with cut-in shoulders. I accessorized with a string of large freshwater pearls Ray had given me and a pair of high-heeled designer sandals that I was sure would give me blisters by the end of the evening. Unfortunately, even I couldn't justify wearing my usual rubber flip-flops with the chic dress, so my feet would have to pay the price of fashion. I finished getting ready just as Liam rang the door chime, and I hurried out to greet him.

He drew in a deep breath when he saw me. "You are stunning." He took my hand, and we rode the elevator to the underground garage.

Liam drove his new electric car, and since it was a beautiful evening, he opened the moonroof. The slight breeze carried the scent of the ocean as well as the fragrance of the abundant flowers that grew everywhere on Grand Cayman. I leaned back against the headrest and relaxed. The evening would be fun simply because I was with Liam.

We walked into Ristorante Pappagallo, an elegant, tropical-themed restaurant, and the host immediately recognized Liam. "Your guest is already here, Mr. Lawton," he said before leading us across the room.

The man seated at the table stood up when he saw Liam approaching, and they did the man hug thing—part handshake, part subtle chest bump, and a little bit of back patting. As soon as they finished the ritual, Liam stepped back and took my arm. "Fin, this is my old friend Gary Graydon. Gary, this is the famous Fin Fleming."

Gary's dark brown hair curled slightly around the nape of his neck, and his large brown eyes gleamed with intelligence behind the tortoise-framed glasses he wore. On his wrist was an expensive looking analog watch with a brown leather strap. He wore light colored linen pants and a white button-front collarless shirt tucked in at the waist. Gary was a good looking man. Not in the same class with Liam, but close.

He smiled. "I'm so pleased to meet you. I've been a big fan for years, and this guy can't stop talking about you."

I smiled back and held out my hand. "Liam has told me a lot about you too. I'm glad we were finally able to meet."

We sat down, and the waiter immediately came over to take our drink orders. We all ordered gin and tonics, and then we smiled uncomfortably at each other before picking up our menus. The first few minutes felt awkward, and then the resident parrot started squawking from his perch in the corner. That reminded me of Candy asking Dane for a kiss, and I told the story, exaggerating slightly to imply the bird had a crush on Dane. Both men laughed heartily at the idea of the parrot having a crush on the soft-hearted cop.

The laugh broke the ice, and after that the conversation flowed smoothly, with topics ranging from their time together at university to some of our favorite dives. Before we knew it, dinner was over, and the restaurant was closing. Liam paid the bill, and we walked out to our cars.

Gary waved as he got into his rental. "I'll see you both tomorrow."

Chapter 11
The Ride Home

LIAM HELD the car door for me. I sat down and immediately kicked off my shoes, wiggling my toes in relief. Liam laughed when he saw what I was doing.

Once we were on the move, he asked," What did you think? Could you see yourself working with Gary?"

"I liked him very much. If you think he's the right man to take over Quokka Media, then he must be. I'm sure we'll get along fine."

Liam smiled. "Good. Now I can get started on my next big project."

I reached over to hold his hand. "And what will that be? It's very quiet here in this car. Perfect for conversation."

He laughed. "Yes, it is." He drew in a deep breath. "Since I've been working with you and the folks at RIO—and Newton—I've become more and more interested in finding ways to help the environment. My next company is going to be focused on that. I plan to identify places that need help, and travel there with a team to help clean things up. I also want to increase awareness, educate big corporations, and do whatever needs doing to make things better. And I plan to invest in technology that can help with cleanup—like reducing emissions, removing pollutants, breaking down forever chemicals. Stuff like that. What do you think?"

I thought a moment. "I like the sound of it, but I have several questions, if you don't mind."

"Shoot," he said.

"Do you have a way to monetize the work you plan to do, or will this be a non-profit?" I asked.

"Some of each," he said. "The part that travels to various sites to do cleanup will be a non-profit foundation. The technology to invent new methods of cleanup will be commercial. I'd license our inventions to other companies or countries that need it. I have enough money to fund a lot of the work myself, and Newton has promised to partially support the company through Fleming Environmental Investments."

"Okay. Sounds good. You said your company would travel to locations that need help. Does that mean you will personally be doing all this travel? You won't be living here full-time anymore?"

"I'll be doing a lot of it myself. The travel probably won't ever go away completely, but as the company grows, I'll be able to delegate more to my team. I promise I'll always come back to you. You should know by now that wherever you are, that's my home. Grand Cayman will be my permanent address."

"Uh-huh. And will you be incommunicado the whole time you're away, like when you went to Australia to finalize your divorce from Amelia?"

He sighed. "No, that was different. And I am so sorry about that. It kills me that I hurt you, but I'll try to do better. I can't guarantee that I'll always be able to communicate from wherever I am in the world, but I will do my best to talk to you every day. I promise."

"Why won't you tell me what you were really doing for that year you were gone? It couldn't have taken the whole year to track down Amelia and get your divorce finalized."

He tightened his lips. "It didn't, but I think you know what I was doing. I can't tell you exactly what it is, but it involves taking down bad guys. You already know that since you saw me undercover that time on Seb Lukin's mega-yacht."

I nodded. "And you knew Newton long before you worked at the Ritz while he was staying there, didn't you?"

"Yes, but that's all I can say about that. If you want more information, you can try to get it from Newton."

"Nope. I'm good for now. Besides, it's late. Let's just go to bed and continue this discussion after I've had some time to think things over."

He cleared his throat. "There's something else I wanted to talk to you about."

I was beyond exhausted. This was no time to start discussing another one of Liam's bombshells. "Sounds heavy. I'm tired and I've got training with Christophe tomorrow at dawn. Can it wait?"

"It could, but I've been putting it off for a while and it's time I confessed."

My heart plummeted. I didn't think I could deal with a confession right now considering everything else going on in my life. "Go ahead," I said in a small voice.

Liam read my tone and glanced over at me. "It's nothing bad. In fact, I hope it will make you happy."

He took a few seconds to navigate a dark stretch of road. "I've bought a house."

Maybe this really was good news, as long as the house was on Grand Cayman. "Congratulations," I said. "Where is it?'

"Rum Point," he said. "It's very close to your place." He paused. "In fact, it's right next door."

I was so giddy with relief to hear he wasn't leaving the island that I laughed. "So, you're my noisy new neighbor?"

"'Fraid so," he said. "Are you good with me living right next door?"

I rested my head against the back of the cushy seat. "Very good. In fact, it's wonderful. I want to hear more, but I'm just so tired." I couldn't control it. My eyes shut of their own volition, and I slept the rest of the way home, secure in the knowledge that my life was going well.

Chapter 12
An Interview

Bᴜᴛ ᴏɴᴄᴇ I was home in bed, I couldn't get back to sleep. I tossed and turned all night, worried about the change in leadership at *Ecosphere*. I liked Gary, but I'd loved Carl. I'd never even considered he might leave someday. And as for Gary taking over, I trusted Liam's judgment, but still…

I was exhausted when I arrived at my office at 6 the next morning. I really had to find a way to cut down on my workload. Newton still relied on me at Fleming Environmental Investments, even though I'd relinquished a lot of my duties to Oliver when he came aboard. I didn't want to let my father down. I couldn't ease back on my responsibilities at RIO, especially with Maddy sick. I loved my work at *Ecosphere* and didn't want to give it up. I put my head down on my desk in despair.

The office intercom chirped. "Dr. Fleming, this is Fred in lobby security. Joely Wentworth is here to see you. She said she has an appointment."

I pushed the button on the phone to reply to Fred. "Yes, we have an appointment. I'll be right down to collect her." Then I sent a text to Christophe pushing back our training until tomorrow.

When I walked into the lobby, Joely was intently watching a video playing on one of the overhead monitors. We had something running on the screens all the time to highlight the work we do here and also to give people something to entertain them while they're waiting in line for aquarium tickets. I glanced up at the screen. My documentary on Harry the stingray was playing.

Joely looked fabulous, and extremely professional. Today she was wearing a dark gray skirted suit, a silky blouse, and gray suede pumps. I was wearing my usual tan cargo shorts and a faded red RIO-branded polo shirt, with matching flip-flops. I sighed, until I remembered that Joely was going to be sitting at a desk every day, while my job required me to be on and off boats, working in the aquarium and research lab, and in and out of the ocean. I was drenched in sea water multiple times a day. I squared my shoulders and crossed the lobby to greet her.

When I approached her, Joely said, "This movie is fascinating. Is that the kind of thing you do?"

I smiled. "That's exactly the kind of thing I do. In fact, I wrote, produced, scored, and shot that entire film."

"I'm stunned. The film is incredible, and the fact that you did everything yourself is amazing.

"Well, I'm impressed that you can do finance and accounting, so we're even."

We both laughed.

"C'mon. We can talk while I show you around." Joely and I walked down the hallway on the atrium's left toward the gift shop and the aquarium. Joely admired a display of graceful glass dolphins, so I quietly asked the store's manager to include one along with the usual T-shirts and mug when she brought a VIP visitor packet for Joely to my office.

When we'd seen enough of the gift shop, we walked down the long dim corridor to the aquarium. I waved to the attendant as we went through the gate, and we took a quick walk through the exhibits. We visited the public café, the gym, the locker rooms, and RIO's huge training pool.

"This place is incredible. I never realized what a large and varied operation you have," Joely said.

I smiled. "Wait until you see the research labs. That's the real heart of RIO." I wanted to show her the labs, but even more, I wanted a chance to show off Rosie, my Atlantic pygmy octopus.

I pointed out some of the more interesting specimens in the lab, and explained at a high level the research they were used in. Finally, I brought Joely over to Rosie's tank.

After washing and thoroughly rinsing my own hands at the nearby sink, I stroked lightly on the glass. Rosie peeked out of her shell home. When she recognized it was me, she shot across the tank and rose to the surface. She stuck one tiny pink tentacle out of the water, clearly telling me she wanted to hold hands.

I put my hand in the tank. Rosie immediately wrapped two tentacles around my fingers. Rosie is tiny—her entire body would fit easily in my palm, even with her tentacles fully extended.

Joely watched, fascinated. "Wow! She obviously loves you, and she's so cute."

I smiled. "Yes, she is, but Rosie's not just a pretty face. Watch this."

I gently disentangled my hand from Rosie's tentacles. Then I picked up a card with a picture of two red balls and held it to the glass. Rosie slinked over to her pile of treasures in the far corner of her tank. She brought first one, then a second red ball to the edge of the tank and placed them directly under the card.

"But wait. There's more," I said after Joely exclaimed in amazement.

I held up a new card, with 5 blue squares on it. Rosie brought five blue boxes from her pile and lined them up under the card.

"She can count!" Joely said.

"That's not all she can do," I said. I held up a card with five objects, a mix of balls, blocks, and jacks, all in different colors. Once again, Rosie performed flawlessly in matching objects to the images on the card.

"I can't believe this," said Joey. "Are all octopuses this smart?"

"They're all pretty intelligent, but I believe Rosie is exceptional," I said.

"You should publish a paper on this. I bet it would win some kind of an award," she said with a touch of respect in her voice.

"I have, and it did."

Then we headed along the back hallway toward the executive offices. She asked several pertinent questions about the business, and I liked her more with each passing minute. She had a quick mind, and she instantly understood many of the nuances of RIO's business. She had my vote for the CFO position.

I opened the door to the office reserved for our CFO and was surprised to see Liam sitting at the desk.

"I'm sorry," I said. "I didn't realize you were working here today."

He smiled that devastating smile of his. "No problem. What's up? Can I help you with something?"

I introduced him to Joely, and then I had an idea. I'm pretty good at a lot of stuff—diving photography, and marketing—but numbers, spreadsheets, and accounting bore me silly. And while I knew that Newton wouldn't have put Joely's name forward if she hadn't been more than qualified for the role, Liam would be able to gauge her abilities in the finance area far better than me. He could show her some of the systems and procedures we used, so she'd know what she was getting into.

I put my idea into action. "Would you have a few minutes to talk to Joely about what it's like to be the CFO here at RIO? When you're done, let me know and I'll drive her to the airport."

"Not necessary. I have a rental car today," said Joely.

I tried to keep my sigh of relief inaudible.

I saw Liam's lips twitch as he held back a grin. "I'd be happy to talk to Joely. But why don't you head out? It's been a long tough week. I'll see you at home later."

"Thanks. I am pretty beat. I have another couple of hours of work to do, but I may leave early."

As if.

Chapter 13
Waiting

BACK IN MY OFFICE, I checked my messages to see if I'd missed a call from Maddy or Doc, but my message queue was frustratingly empty. I sent a text to Doc.

> ??? Should I come?

> No news yet. I'll call. Maddy fine. N and D here."

I realized Newton must have contacted Dane and told him about Maddy's health scare, and I was impressed at Newton's love and consideration for his wife. It was obvious he still loved her, and probably always would. He knew her feelings for Dane ran deep, even though she and Dane weren't together right now, and Newton was willing to put his own happiness aside for Maddy's sake.

I sent Newton a text.

> ⸱ on Joely. You?

He responded immediately.

> ⸱

That cleared the way to offer Joely the CFO position. RIO needed someone right away, so I stopped by HR and had them start on the paperwork for Joely's job offer. Then I went back to Liam's office. "Joely, would you mind stopping by my office when you finish here?"

Liam looked up and smiled. "We're just about finished, and I know Joely has a flight to catch. We can pick this up anytime. It's probably more important that she talk to you right now."

Joely nodded and thanked Liam for his time. We walked back to my office, where HR had already placed the offer letter in a folder on my desk. All I had to do was offer her the job.

She beamed at me. "Thank you. I'm so excited. When do you want me to start?"

"As soon as you possibly can. Things are hectic here."

Her eyes were shining. "I'll only need a few days to clear out my place in Boston. Let's say late next week? Does that work for you?"

"It does. I'm excited that we'll be working together."

Liam rapped on the door frame. "If you're done here, Joely should leave for the airport. I wouldn't want her to miss her flight."

Joely placed the envelope with her offer letter in her shoulder bag, and I presented her with the VIP goody bag from the gift shop. She thanked me and then Liam walked her to the lobby.

I breathed a sigh of relief. One problem solved. But my message queue was still frustratingly empty, with no news from Doc.

Chapter 14
Meeting Henrietta

My feelings had been slightly hurt that Maddy hadn't wanted me with her, but she had Newton and Dane, as well as her best friend Doc by her side. I could respect her wishes, at least until she was feeling better, and we knew what she'd be dealing with.

At 5:00, I put my car in drive and took off. After stopping at the convenience store to pick up a sandwich for dinner, I headed to my home on Rum Point. The house had been a twenty-first birthday present from Newton, and it was perfect for me in every way. Even though we'd recently been through a killer of a storm, unlike the house next door, my home hadn't suffered so much as a scratch.

But the people who owned the neighboring house had taken one look at the devastation of their vacation home and put the wreckage on the market. They'd left the island, abandoning Chico, their free-range rooster. Chico was smart enough to come to my door every day for a handful of seeds and a bowl of water, but after he ate, he always went back to the yard he'd called home his whole life.

This was the house that Liam had bought, and renovations had started over a week ago. I sighed in frustration when I realized he'd just gotten around to telling me.

The constant noise from the renovations must have unsettled Chico because he was standing on my walk when I pulled into my driveway. A striking, sleek red chicken I'd never seen before stood next to him.

I left my car in the garage and went through the gate to my fenced-in backyard, holding the gate for Chico and his friend. They waited patiently while I opened the sliding glass doors. Chico followed me in, but the hen stayed outside on the patio, making soft clucking sounds.

I dropped my sandwich on the counter and stuck a small scoop into the jar of seeds I kept handy for Chico's visits. I filled two bowls with seeds and a slightly larger bowl with water, placing all three bowls on the floor near the door.

Chico walked over and stood near the food, calling to his friend with a noise that sounded like "tuk, tuk, tuk." She entered slowly and approached the nearest bowl of seeds cautiously while Chico chivalrously stood guard until she finished eating. Then she sipped some water and sat down to wait for Chico.

When he too had eaten his fill, I grabbed my sandwich and a glass of lemonade. I sat outside at my glass-topped table while I ate, willing the phone to ring with news about Maddy with every bite. I was so on edge I could barely sit still. Normally, I'd have gone diving to calm down, but I didn't want to be away from my phone in case Maddy called.

Because Liam was hoping to get back into Ironman competitions, I had recently taken up running to be able to spend a little extra time with him. And if I went for a run instead of a dive, I could keep my phone with me so I wouldn't miss a call from Maddy. I went inside to change into my running clothes. Just as I stepped outside my front door, Liam's jet black electric car pulled into the other lane of my driveway.

He hopped out of the car and then reached back in to remove a large grocery bag. "You just starting out or just getting back?"

"Just leaving. Wanna come?"

"Nope. I already finished my run for the day. But you go ahead. I'll wait here if that's okay with you."

Chico and the hen walked out through my open gate. Chico was fond of Liam, and he went over to get a pat. The hen followed shyly behind him.

"Hey, Chico," said Liam when he bent to ruffle the bird's feathers. "Who's your friend?"

"That's Henrietta," I said, making up her name on the spot.

Henrietta murmured softly, so I assumed that meant she liked her new name.

When Liam and I stopped laughing, I said, "I'll be back in twenty minutes. I don't need to go far."

"Take your time. I'll have a surprise for you when you get back," he said.

I wiggled my eyebrows at him. "Oooh. Maybe I should skip the run."

He laughed. "Sorry. Not that kind of surprise. Go run." He walked through the gate, followed by Chico and Henrietta.

I took off slowly, heading toward the nearby beach at Rum Point. When I reached the shore, instead of swimming or wading in the shallows as I usually would, I turned around and ran home.

Although it was not quite dusk when I arrived, Liam had turned on the twinkling outdoor fairy lights that festooned the palm trees and the fence. I smiled and walked through the gate.

On the patio table, there was a small chocolate fountain bubbling away next to a covered bowl of fresh strawberries. A bottle of champagne cooled in a nearby ice bucket. Liam was sitting on the edge of the pool with his feet dangling in the water. I kicked off my running shoes and sat down beside him. We sat, shoulder to shoulder, watching the light fade.

When it was fully dark, Liam stood and took my hand to help me up. We walked over to the table, and he poured champagne into two plastic flutes. Then he took a fat, luscious strawberry and swirled it in the chocolate bath. When he judged it was sufficiently covered, he popped it in my mouth. I was still chewing when my phone rang. Caller ID said it was Doc, and I almost choked in my haste to swallow the mouthful of strawberry so I could take the call.

I pushed the answer button. Before I could say anything, Doc spoke up. "Don't worry. She'll be fine."

I sighed with relief, and it was a moment before I could speak. "It wasn't melanoma?'

"Oh. Sorry. It is melanoma. But Dr. LaFontaine says it's early, so it might be easily treatable. He'll be doing some staging tests and an excision tomorrow, and then we'll decide what to do. In the meantime, try not to worry."

I snorted. "Fat chance. Is she home now?"

"Yes, she's here. Newton and Dane are both with her. She'd like to see you. I'll be calling Oliver next. You're probably upset. Maybe you shouldn't be driving right now. Do you want me to send Stewie to pick you up?"

I blew out a breath. "Naturally I'm upset. You just told me my mother has a deadly form of cancer. But Liam's here. I'm sure he'll drive me. We'll see you in a few minutes." I clicked the button to disconnect the call.

Liam stood and put his arms around me. "Get your things together. I'll clean up here." He was already disconnecting the chocolate fountain.

I went inside to pack an overnight bag. Rather than have him drive me back to Rum Point after I'd seen Maddy, I'd either stay the night at Liam's condo downtown or on the *Tranquility*.

Chapter 15
At Maddy's Condo

WHEN WE ARRIVED at Maddy's, she was on her couch, surrounded by the people who love her—Newton, Dane, Doc, Oliver, Genevra, Liam, and me. She was more subdued than usual, but otherwise, she seemed to be holding up well.

I walked over and gave her a hug. "How are you doing?"

She shrugged. "A little nervous, but I'm sure everything will be okay."

"What can I do to help? Are you hungry?"

"No, but I would like some tea if it's no trouble." Her voice sounded tired, lacking its usual vibrancy.

Oliver jumped up. "I'll get it." It was obvious he felt as helpless as I did.

He went to the kitchen to make a cup of her favorite tea, and I went to help him. I wanted to be sure he included a couple of her much-loved lemon cookies, just as Ray had always done for her when she was stressed.

Maddy smiled when Oliver handed her the delicate Villeroy and Boch Marie Fleur patterned teacup with the two lemon cookies balanced on the saucer. "Thank you. How did you know to include the cookies?"

He blushed. "Fin told me. Otherwise, I wouldn't have had any idea."

She smiled at me. "Thank goodness for Fin. She takes care of everything."

Now it was my turn to blush.

She sipped her tea. "I need you all to hear this. If anything happens to me, I want Fin to take my place at RIO. And I want all of you to pitch in to give her any help she needs."

I put my hand on her shoulder and looked her straight in the eye. "Nothing bad is going to happen to you, so you don't need to worry about it. Remember, we're the luckiest people in the world."

She put her hand over mine and squeezed. I bit my lip and tried to smile.

Oliver crossed the room quickly and sat in the chair across from her. "Maddy. Mom." His voice cracked and he didn't say anything else.

Maddy touched his hand. "I know, Oliver. But it will be fine."

He looked at Newton. "I know it's short notice since I'm supposed to leave tomorrow, but I have to cancel that business trip. I don't want to be away right now."

Newton nodded. "No problem. We'll rearrange the schedule."

But Maddy shook her head. "Nothing doing. Oliver will be going as planned. It took months to get the itinerary arranged and to align the schedules of all the key investors. It's crucial to his career. I can't let him cancel when we all know I'll be fine."

Oliver looked to Newton. "I can't ..."

"Maddy has spoken," Newton said. "You'll be leaving in the morning as planned. It's only for a few days, and anyway, you'll have the company jet at your disposal if you need to get back quickly. Which you won't have to do, since we all know Maddy will be fine."

With that settled, Maddy yawned, and looked pointedly at Doc.

"Everybody out," Doc said. "She needs her rest. I'll call you after the procedure tomorrow. In the meantime, don't worry."

Maddy's smile was worn. "I'll see you all later. Don't worry."

We took her not-so-subtle hint, kissed her goodbye, and left.

As we walked through the door, Dane took me aside. "I want to give you a heads up. I asked Roland to spend every evening at Ray's place, pretending to drink while keeping an eye on things. So don't get nervous if you see him there a lot. Morey's doing the same at Nelson's."

"Good idea," I said. "That should help keep everyone safe." Liam was holding the elevator for us, so Dane and I hurried across the hall.

Before we reached the garage level, Oliver whispered in my ear. "I don't want to go home yet. Can we have dinner together? Just you, me, Genevra, and Liam. Maybe at Ray's Place?"

"Sure," I said. "I'd like that."

Chapter 16
Genevra's Proposal

LUCKILY, when we arrived at Ray's Place, the bar wasn't crowded enough to make it impossible to have a conversation, but it was just crowded enough to make it hard for others to overhear what we were saying to each other. When we walked in, I waved to Brian Walker, the bartender on duty, and he pointed to a table for four in a distant corner away from the bar. I gave him the okay sign, and we walked over to claim it. There were soft murmurs of recognition as we passed through the crowd, but nobody said anything or stopped us. Liam and I sat facing the bar while Oliver and Genevra sat opposite us.

Oliver slung his arm across the back of Genevra's chair, and she turned her face up to smile at him. They were so cute together. I was happy my brother had found someone as perfect for him as Genevra seemed to be. He'd had a difficult life until my parents adopted him a short time ago, and in a way, this newfound happiness made up for some of what had come before.

Brian brought over menus and small bowls of mixed nuts and tiny fish-shaped crackers. He took our drink orders while we perused the menus. By the time he was back with the drinks, we'd decided on our entrees. Now we could focus on our worries about Maddy and Chaun.

We knew Maddy was in good hands with Dr. LaFontaine and Doc, and we agreed that she wouldn't welcome our attention if we hovered over her. We had to respect her wishes, so all we could do was let her know we loved her.

The conversation turned to Chaun. We were pretty sure he wouldn't be held responsible for Polly's murder. For one thing, he'd never conk himself on the head, and anyway, everyone knows he's too smart to stick Polly twice or to stick himself at all. No, if Chaun had been involved, the event would have been meticulously planned and carefully calibrated.

But still, we were worried. Chaun wouldn't do well in jail. He is intensely private—so much so that if anyone is around, he won't undress to put on his dive skin even when he's wearing his bathing suit under his clothes. He needs a lot of alone time to be at his best, because too much interaction with people makes him anxious. Alone time is in short supply in hospitals and jails.

We loved Dane, but he didn't have a big team and he was distracted by Maddy's illness, so we couldn't sit around and wait for the police to find the needle spikers. By the time they figured it out, Chaun might have already lost it for good from the stress of being under constant surveillance.

We were tossing around ideas that we would probably never be able to carry out, when I noticed a woman sitting at the bar alone. She was dressed in a hot pink halter top sundress, her tanned shoulders peeking out between strands of the wavy long blonde hair that lifted gently in the slight ocean breeze. A mass of gold chains hung around her neck. A big straw hat with a broad brim shaded her features, and a pair of oversized sunglasses with gradient lenses sat low on her nose, the rims covering her cheekbones as well as her eyes. A tropical cocktail stood in front of her, and she absently twirled the tiny paper parasol while gazing into the darkness beyond the dim glow from the tiki torches.

Something about her stirred a wisp of memory, but I couldn't place her. Maybe she'd been a student in a dive class at one time or another.

I brought my attention back to my own group when Genevra cleared her throat. "I have an idea about what we can do to solve the crime. I don't think you'll like it at first but hear me out. I look small and helpless, even though I'm not. I know martial arts, and I'm a good shot with a gun. I just mean, I may look defenseless, but I can take care of myself. So why don't we use me as a decoy? I can sit alone in the bar and maybe that will draw the bad guys out. You guys can take turns keeping an eye on me from your boats. I'll be perfectly safe."

Oliver was shaking his head violently. "No. No. No. We can't risk it. In fact, please don't go anywhere alone until we catch them." He tightened his arm around her shoulder. "I don't want to take the chance that anything might happen to you."

Liam nodded. "I agree with Oliver on this one. It's way too dangerous."

I was in total agreement with them. "Besides, I need you available to keep Christophe occupied when I'm not training. Otherwise, he'll be hounding me to do more, and I don't have the time."

By now we'd finished our dinner, but we were no closer to finding a way to solve the mystery. Liam rose. "Let's continue the discussion on one of the boats. Maybe the moonlight will give us some fresh thoughts."

Oliver held out his hand to Genevra. "Good idea. Let's use the *Flemingo*. I have some new IPAs in the fridge I think you'll like. And white wine and lemonade." He knew I rarely drank alcohol the night before a heavy dive day.

I paid the bill on the way out, and while I was waiting for Brian to cash me out, I noticed the woman who'd been staring at me had left. As I'd thought, she must simply have been a former student or a curious fan.

We walked down the dock to the *Flemingo*, which was in the slip next to Maddy's *Sea Princess*. We'd set aside several of the slips closest to the beach for people who arrived at Ray's Place by boat, and as we passed, I noticed every slip was filled. That was another good sign for the success of our newest venture.

When we reached the *Flemingo*, Genevra and I went straight to the bow. We sat with our backs against the transom so we could enjoy the moonlight glistening on the gentle wavelets. Oliver and Liam joined us a few minutes later, carrying our drinks in chilled stainless steel RIO-branded mugs. We sipped quietly for a few minutes and continued discussing ideas for identifying the needle spike crew. The only realistic way we could think of to solve the crime was to take Genevra up on her offer to go undercover, but except for Genevra herself, none of us were willing to put her at risk like that.

Chapter 17
First Freedive Training

THE SUN WAS BARELY UP the next morning when Liam gently touched my shoulder. He waved a cup of hot coffee near my nose. The heavenly aroma was the only reason I opened my eyes. I yawned and stretched my arms over my head.

He wrapped my hand around the stainless steel RIO mug. "Hey, Sleepyhead. Get a move on. You can't blow Christophe off again, and it's after six."

I groaned. After Oliver and Genevra had yawned hugely and tactfully ushered us off the *Flemingo*, Liam and I had sat up chatting aboard the *Tranquility* until quite late. We hadn't gone to sleep until we saw Theresa shut off the lights at Ray's Place. At the time, I wasn't thinking about the fact I'd promised to meet Christophe at six-thirty.

I gulped the coffee, burning my tongue in the process. "Thank you. You're a life saver."

He handed me a fully stuffed gym bag. "I packed your stuff. You've got everything you need. Run along to the locker room to get ready, and I'll meet you by the pool with a muffin. If you hurry, you'll have just about enough time to gulp it down."

I took another slurp of the coffee, kissed his cheek, grabbed the bag, and raced down the dock and across RIO's expansive lawn. I was

71

searching through the bag for my keys to open the back door when I was saved by Stewie's arrival from the inside. He opened the door and held it while I ran past him with a hasty hello.

He carried his own cup of fresh coffee, and he laughed at my frantic pace. "Good morning to you too, Dr. Fleming," he called to my rapidly fleeing back.

"Sorry, Stewie. I'm late." I said as I careened around the corner and headed to the pool-house locker room. Once there, I rushed through a quick shower, brushed my teeth, and threw on the bathing suit and zip front sweatshirt Liam had packed. I stepped into my flip-flops and raced toward the exit that led to the pool.

As I tore through the locker room door, Liam handed me a warm blueberry muffin. "I believe you just set a new world's record," he said with a grin.

I sat on a nearby bench and devoured the muffin. I had just finished the last bite when Christophe entered the pool house. He wore a whistle around his neck and carried a large white board and a timer.

"Good. You're here," he said.

He inspected the pool, which isn't like a typical backyard pool or even the usual gym pool. It's 164 feet long and twenty-five feet wide. For the first hundred twenty-five feet of its length, it's shallow, starting at three feet and gradually sloping to four feet deep. A line of red tiles in the floor marks the point where the depth changes abruptly to twenty-five feet. We use the deepest part for advanced skills training in our scuba classes.

He turned his back and started setting up his whiteboard easel. "Let's get started."

I was taken aback by his abruptness, but I rose and followed him to the deep end of the pool. I stared at the whiteboard. It was divided into two columns. One was labeled depth, the other time. At the top it read Today's Goal. The numeral 7 was filled in.

"I already know you're an accomplished scuba diver, but you've never done competitive freediving. Is that correct?"

"Right. I've done some freediving, but mostly spearfishing or ocean research. Never competitively."

"Okay," he said. "We'll probably have to break some bad habits, but at least you're not a complete novice. Give me your dive watch, then jump in, sit cross-legged on the bottom, and stay down as long as you can."

So much for getting to know each other or putting together a collaborative plan. I took off my sweatshirt and placed it on a nearby bench. Then I stepped off the pool edge and let myself plunge to the bottom of the twenty-five foot deep end. I sat on the bottom, assuming the cross-legged position he'd requested, and placed my palms on my knees. I shut my eyes, straightened my spine, and thought happy thoughts.

The first time my body tried to force me to breathe, I swallowed the urge. I did the same the second time. The third time, I headed to the surface. As soon as my head was fully out of the water, I exhaled and then took in a deep breath. "How long?"

Christophe wrote a number on the white board. Six minutes and fifteen seconds. "Not bad for a beginner," he said grudgingly. "Now try it with the timer." He handed me back my watch.

I strapped it to my wrist and waited for him to tell me to go.

He watched me closely, and when he judged my breathing was back to normal, he said, "Whenever you're ready."

Once again, I stepped into the pool, sat on the bottom with my legs crossed, and closed my eyes. I thought happy thoughts. After what felt like a long time, I peeked at my watch. Three minutes.

I went back to thinking more happy thoughts, before peeking again. Four minutes.

Eyes closed, I tried for serenity, but the temptation to check the breath hold time on my watch was even more overwhelming than the need to breathe. Five minutes.

This time, as soon as I'd seen the duration of my dive, I felt an irresistibly urgent need to breathe. I shot to the surface.

Christophe wrote the time on his board while I exited the pool. Five minutes, thirty-seven seconds. He turned to face me. "So now we know. You do much better without a timer. In future, leave your watch on the surface while we're training."

I put my watch on the bench where I'd left my sweatshirt. "Now what?"

"I want you to swim laps. Six strokes breathing normally, three without breathing, and repeat. As many times and as many laps as you can or until I tell you to stop."

I dove into the deep end and began swimming, synchronizing my breathing and not breathing periods as he'd outlined. The laps were easy for me. When Ray taught me to swim and dive, he'd made sure I could swim long distances without breathing. After I'd swum the length of the pool and back several times, Christophe blew his whistle, signaling the end of the exercise.

At this point, I was in the shallow part of the pool, so I stood up. I could see that Christophe noticed I wasn't breathing hard, but he didn't say anything about my performance.

All he said was, "Do it again. This time three strokes breathing, six strokes not breathing." He folded his arms and stared, like he was challenging me to complete a dare.

I started swimming. After ten times up and back, I heard the shrill sound of the whistle. I stood up and then climbed out of the pool.

"Next time we'll do twelve and three, but you're good for now. Let's practice equalization."

We spent a few more hours on various training exercises before I called a halt. "I'm sorry, but I have other work to do. I need to stop training for the day."

He frowned, but said, "Okay." He handed me a list of training exercises I should do on my own as I had time. After handing me the paper, he picked up his easel and walked away toward the men's locker room.

I looked over the list and noticed one of the prescribed exercises was running using intermittent breathing. It sounded awful, but the rest probably wouldn't challenge me because it was mostly all water based.

I walked into the women's locker room to get ready for my workday. I showered again, changed into a dry two-piece bathing suit, and put on shorts and a t-shirt over it. I combed my hair back, stepped into my flip-flops, and I was good to go for a full day of work.

I wanted a moment to myself to gather my thoughts, so instead of walking through the RIO building's corridors, I went outside to take the long way around.

I was surprised to see Genevra and Christophe seated together on the patio at Ray's Place, drinking from RIO's ubiquitous stainless steel mugs. They were so deeply engrossed in their conversation they didn't notice me passing.

Chapter 18
A Breakup

LIAM and I went for a run at the end of the workday, and I tried running without breathing for a few steps at a time as Christophe had said I should. I'd thought I disliked running before, but not breathing added a whole new level of misery to the practice. I quit after the first mile and a half. Liam continued his run, and I knew he'd be gone for at least another hour.

We weren't far from my house, so I started walking, justifying my slow pace by calling it recovery time. But I almost turned around and started running in the opposite direction when I saw the familiar red open air SUV.

Yup. There he was. My ex-husband, Alec Stone, leaning against the car and watching my approach. He waved when he saw me.

Alec was persistent. He'd keep trying to hunt me down until I listened to his latest scheme. He'd never go away until he'd said his piece. He might even try to follow me into my house right now if I didn't speak to him outside.

I might as well get it over with. "What?" The word was as cold and rude as I could make it.

"You're so beautiful," he said. "I always forget when I haven't seen you for a while."

"Stuff it. What do you want?"

He shrugged. "Lily left me. She's gone. I don't know what to do. Can you talk to her for me? Help her see that we belong together. Please?"

I wasn't totally sure, but I thought that might have been the first time Alec had ever said please to me. Even so, it wasn't going to help him win his case. I had no intention of intervening in his relationship with Lily Flores Russo, Oliver's nut-job twin sister.

"I'm sorry you and Lily are having problems, but I really don't see how I can help. You know she hates me." That was an understatement. She'd tried to kill me multiple times.

He licked his lips.

I blinked. Was his tongue actually forked or was I still oxygen deprived? I shook my head and looked back at him.

"She doesn't hate you. She looks up to you." He was using his weasel voice, so I would have known that what he said was a lie even if Lily herself hadn't already made her loathing for me abundantly clear.

"There's not a chance in the world I'll help you. Separately, you two are each toxic, but together, you're absolutely lethal. Now go away." I started walking up the crushed shell path to my front door, but Alec wasn't taking the hint.

"Please, Fin. I love her. Just talk to her."

This time he sounded sincere, but I knew faking sincerity was his superpower. And even if his words had been truly heartfelt, I knew better than to get involved in his problems.

I took another step toward my door. "Go away."

Alec reached out and grabbed my arm to hold me back. Unshed tears glistened in his eyes.

Too bad I knew that producing tears on demand was another talent of his. "Give it up, Alec. You're better off without her."

He raised his voice. "Help me, please. I need her. You have to help."

Chico and Henrietta had been pecking at the dirt in the yard at Liam's new house, but they poked their beaks around the hedge to see what was going on when they heard Alec's shouting. Chico crowed out a warning, which Alec ignored. He didn't let go of my arm.

Both Henrietta and Chico raced over to us, both making loud

noises, flapping their wings, and hissing. Startled, Alec took a step back and dropped my arm. The birds kept coming at him. He turned, jumped in his car, and sped off in a cloud of dust.

"Good job, Guys," I said. "But I could have handled him myself." The thought that I had my very own chicken protection detail made me laugh. It felt good to laugh.

I went through the gate into the backyard to give Henrietta and Chico an extra treat. By the time they'd eaten their seeds, Liam had finished his run. He went inside and filled a glass with water and joined me on the patio.

"You look beat. Christophe must have worked you hard today," he said.

"Not so bad. I'm used to this kind of drill. Today was actually nothing compared to the training Ray put me through, and it was Ray's training that made me strong. It made me who I am. Thanks to Ray, I can take anything Christophe—or Alec—can throw my way."

Chapter 19
Ocean Training

THE NEXT MORNING, I groaned as I slammed the door of my locker. I was having a hard time psyching myself up for Christophe's training regimen, and I was emotionally as well as physically exhausted. I wanted to be with Maddy, check on Chaun, and help Dane solve the murder. All of which seemed more important than time spent holding my breath underwater. I was frustrated.

I dragged my weary carcass out to the pool deck. Christophe was already there, holding a large monofin, a specialized type of swim fin used in some freediving competitive events. A monofin looks a little bit the way people imagine a mermaid's tail would. The diver inserts both feet into the pocket, and uses a special kick called a dolphin kick for propulsion. Using a monofin can propel the wearer up to twenty-five percent faster than someone using bare feet or even regular fins. I'd never used one before, and it was one of the few diving related things I'd never done. Instantly, my enthusiasm for the training came back.

Christophe and I sat on the bench while he showed me how to insert my feet in the special pocket and explained the construction of the fin and the best place to position the foot straps. "Ready to try it?"

"Sure thing," I said, reaching out for the device.

He moved it out of my grasp. "Show me your dolphin kick first."

I got up, dove into the pool, and swam a few laps without using any of the conventional swimmer's kicks. Instead, I held my arms forward over my head and my feet close together, so my body was as straight and hydrodynamic as it could be. Then using my abs, hip flexors and glutes on the upstroke and my lower back, glutes, and hamstrings on the downstroke, I zoomed through the water. When I reached the pool wall, I did an underwater somersault and went back. I made a few laps up and back before I stopped in the shallow end.

Christophe was smiling. "Let's take this to the ocean. Can you get a boat?"

"We'll take mine. The *Tranquility*. What gear do we need?"

"Dive suit for warmth, freediving mask, and a nose plug. I have my stuff already." He held up a small black bag that I guessed held his equipment.

"I have a dive suit onboard, but on the way to the boat we can stop by the dive shop so I can pick up the other stuff." I was elated to be heading to the ocean, my happy place. We left through RIO's rear entrance.

Stewie was sitting outside the dive shop sipping his coffee and enjoying the morning sun. "Whaddya need?" he said when he saw us approach.

We went inside and Christophe selected the nose plug and low volume mask he thought would be most suitable for my training, and then we walked down the pier to the *Tranquility*. "Nice boat," he said.

"Thanks. Where do you want to go?"

"Someplace not too far away, with very little current, where there aren't any other boats, and at least three to four hundred meters deep. Other than that, you choose. You know the island."

"We don't have to go far," I told him. "We have a site like that right here in our cove. Training Site Two." Saturday is always a slow day for us because the tourists usually went home on Saturday or Sunday, so there were few off-island divers on weekends. And we weren't running any classes or events today.

I started the *Tranquility*'s engines for the short cruise to Training Site Two. When I pulled up to the mooring, Christophe secured the boat. I climbed down from the flying bridge and put on my dive suit.

Christophe had donned his during the short hop we'd just made. He tied a rope around one of *Tranquility*'s life preservers and attached one end of another heavily weighted line to it.

This special line had fluorescent markings every meter, with larger, more visible markings every tenth meter, so a diver could monitor their depth. He attached the whole thing to a cleat on *Tranquility*'s hull and used a D-clip to secure the monofin's case to the life preserver. Then after letting out a long line so he could move the life preserver away from the boat, he stepped off the rear dive platform, put an arm over the nearby float, and swam to the farthest reaches of the tether. "Coming?" he asked.

I jumped in and swam to join him.

"Dive to thirty meters," he said. "No fins. Any strokes you want except dolphin. I'll time you. Whenever you're ready." When he was in instructor mode, this man wasted no words.

I took a deep breath and swam as fast as I could to the thirty meter mark—just a hair under 100 feet. I wasn't wearing fins, so I only had my hands and feet for propulsion.

When I surfaced, Christophe gave me a few seconds to catch my breath, then he said, "Again. Dolphin kick."

The dolphin kick shaved a few seconds off my time.

After he'd recorded my time on his waterproof slate he said, "Now the monofin." He helped me get my feet in the pockets. I took some deep breaths and once again did the round trip. He clicked his timer. "Again."

He had made me make the trip several more times, then suggested I try forty meters, slightly less than the length of RIO's pool. Before the dive, he taught me to equalize my ears using both the "mouth fill" method and the Frenzel Maneuver while wearing my new metal nose plug.

I already knew the Frenzel Maneuver because it's a common scuba technique, but "mouth fill" was new to me. It requires pushing air from the lungs to the mouth with a tensing and then relaxing of the abdominal muscles, so the air pushed up from the lungs naturally fills the ears and sinuses.

Both techniques were easy for me to master. I dove several times both with and without the monofin, and alternating equalization methods until he was satisfied with my time. "Fifty meters," he said when he thought I'd rested enough to dive again.

This time he taught me to wet equalize. Instead of filling the ears and sinus cavities with air, in wet equalizing the diver uses the tongue to block the throat and lets water fill the sinuses and ear canals. Because the water inside the diver's head is always at the same pressure as the ocean, there's no need to equalize air spaces and no pain from pressure differentials.

It didn't take too long for me to catch on, but it felt weird to let my nasal cavities flood after years of scuba diving where wet equalization is impossible. After several dives to fifty meters, he suggested we return to the boat. As soon as we were aboard, I handed him a towel and he handed me a small canister of oxygen.

He dried his face, then sat on the bench with the towel draped over his shoulders. He gave me a long look. "You are already quite good at this."

I passed him a RIO cup full of water drawn from the portable dispenser lashed just inside the cabin. "Thanks. I've had some experience." I grinned at him.

He nodded. "It shows. Where did you learn all this?"

Obviously, he had no idea of who I was or of the wealth of experience I already had. Which was actually nice for a change and made me smile. "I learned from my father, Ray Russo."

He goggled. "*The* Ray Russo? Champion freediver? Are you telling me Ray Russo was your father? I thought Newton Fleming was your father."

I shrugged. "Newton Fleming is my biological father, but Ray Russo—yes, that Ray Russo—was my stepfather, and he raised me. I started diving with him before I could walk."

Now he looked at me almost with awe. "No wonder you're so good at this. You want my advice?"

"That's what Newton's paying you for," I said.

"This isn't swimming advice. It's about your documentary. Ray's planned dive got a lot of publicity, and people still remember the tragedy. I suggest you use the monofin to differentiate your dive from his. The monofin and the dolphin kick will be more dramatic underwater anyway. We'll film the whole dive. I'll help."

I nodded along as he spoke. "I like it. I'll talk to the production team about it. And now, if we can call it quits for the day, I have a lot of obligations I need to take care of."

Chapter 20
An Unexpected Arrival

BACK AT RIO, I showered, dressed, and then sat down in my office. Not five minutes later, my phone buzzed.

Surgery over. Went gr8.

I called Liam to let him know and started rummaging through my desk to find my tote so I could leave.

"Knock. Knock."

I looked up at the sound of the soft voice. "Joely, I wasn't expecting you until next week. I thought you'd need at least a few days to move. And today's Saturday."

She smiled and lifted her shoulders in an ironic shrug. "I know. But you said you work every day, and you wanted me to start ASAP, so I booked turn-around flights, packed enough clothes for a week, and here I am. Since I was renting a furnished apartment, I had very little to pack back in Boston anyway. I shipped the rest of my clothes and my books and stuff, but I'm here now and ready to go to work whenever you need me."

"Terrific," I said. "Liam isn't around today, and I have to leave in a minute, but maybe I can get you started."

I walked her down to her office and cleared Liam's stuff off the desk and out of the drawers, before piling everything on the table for him to pick up later. I handed her a requisition pad and told her to take her time getting settled and to make a list of questions and anything she thought she'd need. "You can stick around or take off whenever you want. I'll drop in later to answer any questions."

She smiled. "Perfect. Sounds good."

I left Joely setting up her office and drove to Quokka Media head-quarters to pick up Liam. We bumped into Dane in the parking garage at Maddy's building, so we all took the elevator together.

When we walked in, Maddy was sitting on her couch dressed in blue sweats. Her face was pale, but her eyes shone with their usual liveliness. Newton sat on the other end of the couch, and Doc was in the armchair beside her.

Maddy held out her arms, and Liam, Dane, and I each took a turn hugging her.

Maddy put her tea down on the table next to her and then she yawned. "I'm going to take a nap."

Doc helped Maddy up and started walking down the hall to her room, but she paused after a few steps. "I'll stay here with her. You guys should leave. You can come back later after she's had time to rest. Or better yet, tomorrow morning after she's had a full night's sleep. I'll call you if we need anything or if there's any change in her condition."

Since we all knew there was no one in the world who could care for her better than her best friend Doc, and no one in the world Maddy would want by her side more, we shuffled out obediently, albeit reluctantly.

"Joely's all alone at RIO, so I'd better get back there and make sure she's okay," I said. "I don't want to make her feel abandoned her first day."

Newton gave a wry smile. "Joely will be fine. She's almost as self-reliant as you."

"Even so, I'm leaving. Call me if you hear anything, okay?"

"Will do," said Newton.

Chapter 21
A Consultant Comes Aboard

WHEN I ARRIVED AT RIO, Joely wasn't in her new office. I walked outside through the back door to see if she might be on the dock or at Ray's Place.

She was sitting at one of the umbrella tables, having lunch with Benjamin Brooks, RIO's most-recent former CFO. I stopped by the bar and picked up a lemonade before strolling over to their table.

Joely smiled. "Hi, Fin. I came outside to get something to eat, and I bumped into Benjamin. We got to talking, and he offered to help me get up to speed since you and Liam are both busy today."

"I should have thought of asking Benjamin to show you the ropes. He's brilliant with numbers. It's so nice to see you, Benjamin. How have you been?"

"Not diving as much as I used to while I worked here," he said. "Chaun and I are pretty busy with the new company. You know how it is with startups. I came by because Chaun is supposed to be released today and Roland was going to drop him off here. We were going to have lunch and swap out your security cameras before I took him home. But then Roland got tied up with work, and I met Joely at the bar while I was waiting for them, and she and I started talking."

Benjamin was a deep thinker and he rarely spoke unless it was important, but when he was nervous, just like his best friend Chaun, he talked a blue streak. He'd left his role as CFO at RIO a few months ago when it became apparent that our tepid romance wasn't going anywhere—especially with Liam back in the picture.

"Thanks for stepping in to help Joely out," I said. "Say, would you be interested in a temporary consultant role to help with Joely's training? Liam is tied up with a major transition at Quokka Media, and as you know, I am not good with numbers. It would be a big help, and we'd pay you for your time."

He went quiet for a minute while peeking at Joely from under his long eyelashes. "Sure. Why not? But Chaun and I have something on the calendar Monday. Is Tuesday soon enough to start?"

Theresa and I were planning to play hooky on Monday, and I intended to bring Joely along. "Perfect. Joely doesn't know it yet, but she has something on her calendar for Monday too." I grinned at her.

Benjamin smiled. "Thanks. I can't wait to get started."

"Great. I'll leave you to continue your conversation, and I'll see both of you later." I breathed a sigh of relief. That was one dreaded task off my plate.

Chapter 22
A Fun Day

A LOT of people think my jobs are all fun, and to be honest, most of the time they are. I'm an avid underwater photographer. I love the ocean and I love to dive, so that part is great. And it's no hardship to bring a camera along on a few dives a month to get whatever images I need for my monthly column at *Ecosphere*. And although my title at *Ecosphere* is editor-in-chief, Genevra does most of the routine stuff. My role on the board of directors at Newton's company, Fleming Environmental Investments, only comes into play when Newton is away or there's a quarterly board meeting. And now that Oliver works there full-time, he has taken over all the routine approvals and administrative stuff I used to do, so it doesn't take up as much of my time as it used to.

But still, I work seven days a week, from before dawn until sometimes late at night. I don't have a lot of free time to socialize, so last week, when Genevra and Theresa cornered me and insisted that we take a day to go shopping or to the spa, I'd agreed.

We were all so busy that Theresa and I hadn't had much time together now that she was managing Ray's Place along with raising Angel. And although I was her boss, Genevra and I rarely needed to interact during working hours because she's so efficient. The excursion would be fun, and only a couple of hours away from work. I earned my occasional time off. And now that she was here, I wanted to include Joely so I could get to know her better.

After I'd finished my training with Christophe for the day, Joely, Theresa, Genevra, and I jumped in my Prius for the ride to Camana Bay, Grand Cayman's premier shopping district. We strolled along the cobblestone walkways, ducking into all the boutiques we passed. I bought a bathing suit, a new pair of sunglasses, and some hairbands and bracelets for Angel, but that was nothing compared to what my friends bought. They were all lugging several heavy shopping bags.

By now we were starving, so we stopped for a late lunch at one of the many restaurants with outdoor seating. Before we decided on our entrees, we ordered several appetizers to share and lots of fruity drinks that came adorned with paper parasols.

Joely took a sip of her drink. "How did you and Theresa meet? You're so comfortable together you must have known each other forever."

Theresa laughed. "I'll tell the story, Fin. You always leave out the good parts."

Theresa entered her story-telling mode. "I grew up on the island, and I'd always heard about the girl who lived at RIO and spent half the year on the big boat. She didn't go to school with us, and because nobody knew her or ever even saw her around town, she was like a myth."

"Now flash forward. When I turned twenty-one, I got a job wait-ressing at one of the bars downtown. It was a good job. I was making what I thought was good money, and meeting lots of people. One day, I was working the afternoon shift, and Ray Russo came in with another man and a young woman. Of course I recognized Ray. Everyone knew him, so I guessed the man with him was Gus Simmons because, according to the stories, they were always together. Gus was so hot. But I thought Gus was with that woman, and it killed me that he was taken. I didn't realize it, but Gus thought I was pretty hot too…"

I smiled at her. "You are pretty hot. Did you really think Gus wouldn't have noticed?"

She laughed. "No. I mean, you were sitting right there with him. I thought you were his girlfriend. But still, I took special care of your table, going out of my way to make sure you got great service. You guys had finished lunch, and Ray ordered another round of drinks. I put the drinks on a tray and headed to your table. Some idiot diver had his gear bag on the floor, and the strap was sticking out into the aisle. I was holding the tray, so I didn't see the strap and I tripped. The drinks went flying. Drenched everyone at your table."

She giggled. "But the worst part was, when I fell, I landed right on Gus. Knocked his chair over, and we both ended up on the floor, with me on top of him. I was sure he'd be mad, but when I dared to look, he was laughing. And he said, 'I wanted to ask you to have a drink with me, but I would have preferred the bar to the floor.' I was so embarrassed."

"Here it comes..." I said.

She winked at me. "I asked him about his girlfriend, and he had no idea what I was talking about. When he realized I meant Fin, he couldn't stop laughing. He told me then who you really were."

"I didn't want to miss out on the chance to spend time with him, so I handed him a pile of napkins to dry off with and told him my shift ended at five. He was at the bar waiting for me on the dot of five. Gus and I have been a couple ever since, and Fin and I became good friends."

"And Genevra? Tell me about yourself," said Joely.

Genevra shook her head. "I'm not very interesting."

"Yes, she is," I said. "She's amazing. Not only is she super smart and competent, but she saved my life one time when a crazy person was trying to drag me away to kill me."

"We don't know if that was actually his intention," Genevra said.

"I'm certain it was. And you were very brave."

Genevra looked scornful. "I could have disabled him with a single kick. But he was such a chicken he ran away before I could."

We all laughed at the image of pint-sized Genevra scaring a cold-blooded killer.

But then I shivered, remembering the feeling of being trapped in that secluded hallway with a very, very bad man. Genevra had no idea how glad I'd been to see her when she rounded the corner, and how scared I was that he'd kill us both. I reached out and patted her hand, and she smiled at me.

"I know," she said softly.

Eager to change the subject, I turned to the newest member of the group. "Now tell us about you, Joely."

She shrugged. "Not much to tell. I grew up in New England. A good family, but not much money. I worked my way through college and interned my last year at Fleming Environmental where Newton taught me how to invest. I worked there for a few years after I graduated and made a lot of money. I moved to the West Coast to become an angel investor. Then I realized I didn't have anywhere near enough capital to compete with the big boys, and I didn't enjoy it much anyway. I moved to Boston to look for my next challenge, and I called Newton. He suggested I talk to Maddy about joining RIO. So here I am."

We continued talking, swapping stories, and getting to know each other. We laughed a lot. I really liked Joely, and I could tell Theresa and Genevra did too.

When lunch was over, Theresa suggested we go to a salon to get mani/pedis. The closest nail salon was able to take us right away, and the receptionist directed us to pick out our polish colors. Genevra quickly chose a delicate soft shell pink, while Theresa and Joely spent several minutes selecting their perfect colors. I didn't even bother looking. I knew from past experience that whatever polish they applied would soak right off after a dive or two, so I asked to have my nails buffed instead of polished.

When we exited the salon a couple of hours later, the sun was heading toward the horizon. With a guilty start I realized I'd spent most of the day having fun instead of working, and I hadn't even called to check in with Maddy. "I've got to get back," I said. "I'm sure my desk is piled high with work, and I want to drop by her place to see how Maddy's doing."

"Okay by me," said Theresa. "I bet Gus is ready for a break from Angel by now anyway." We walked to my car, and I drove us back to RIO.

I was on my way to my office when my phone rang. Caller ID said it was Dane. "What? Is Maddy all right?" I asked breathlessly.

"Yes. Sorry. I didn't mean to scare you. This is about the needle spikes. There's been an incident at Nelson's. Can you meet me there?

I'd like you to talk to Stefan and his brothers with me, and then look at their surveillance video. See if you recognize anyone."

"Of course," I said. "Is the victim okay?"

"Missing," he replied tersely. "Happened last night. Her roommate called it in this morning. Hurry. Bring Liam if he's around."

I called Liam from my car before I left the parking lot. He and Gary were working at the Quokka Media offices, but Liam agreed to break off for the day and meet me at Nelson's. He and I had been the first to notice the needle spiking events there a few years ago, and I figured that's why Dane wanted him to come along.

Chapter 23
Diana

NELSON'S IS a fun waterfront restaurant and bar, owned by Stefan Gibb. Stefan and I had gotten off to a bad start when we met a few years ago because I blamed him, at least partially, for my stepfather Ray Russo's death. But since then, we'd managed to call a truce, and Stefan had gone on to purchase Nelson's. His place is popular, and he has a nice little business going.

Nelson's claim to fame is that it shows reruns of the old Sea Hunt TV show pretty much full time. That's where the name of the bar comes from—the lead character in the show is named Mike Nelson. The only time there isn't a Sea Hunt rerun playing on the television over the bar is when Stefan puts on reruns of the RIO documentaries.

I usually leave when those come on. I hate being there when the RIO reruns are playing because the older ones show me in my most awkward years. I guess Stefan thought I liked seeing them though because he always puts the RIO documentaries on when I come in. I tend to avoid Nelson's whenever possible, partly because of this habit of his.

Dane was already seated at a table with Stefan, who was swiping through an array of mugshots on an iPad. Dane rose when he saw me. He took me aside. "Noah and Austin said they left last night before the dinner rush to put in a shift at Ray's Place. That true?"

I nodded. "It's true." Noah and Austin, Stefan's younger brothers, were friends with my stepbrother Oliver, and they worked odd jobs at RIO whenever we had any work for them. They'd both been giving Theresa a hand by carrying ice, slicing limes, and bussing tables during peak hours.

Liam came racing in. "Are you okay? I was scared to death something awful had happened to you.

"Relax. I'm fine. I'm not the one who was injured here," I said.

Dane drew us both away from the bar, out of earshot of a small group of restaurant patrons that had come in just behind Liam. "Stefan has offered to let us use his office to watch the security video. If you see anyone you recognize or anything that looks suspicious, let me know. I'll be especially interested if you recognize the missing woman or anyone from the needle spiking problem we had a while ago—or from the other night at Ray's Place."

Liam nodded. "Let's get to it then."

Dane led the way to Stefan's office, a cramped windowless room behind the bar. Stefan had left the video queued up for Dane. Before he clicked the button to start it, Dane showed us the missing woman's picture. She was beautiful, with dark hair in tiny, beaded braids and big, intelligent brown eyes. "Her name is Diana Hayward. Ring any bells?"

Liam and I studied the picture, but neither the name nor the image was familiar. "Sorry. I don't think I've ever seen her."

"Me either," said Liam.

"Okay. It was worth a shot." Dane looked haunted as he moved on to the security footage. His face was gray, and his hands shook as he pointed out where Diana Hayward was sitting alone at the bar. Once we'd seen her, he began moving the video forward slowly, practically frame by frame. After a half hour or so, I said, "Stop. Freeze it there."

The blonde woman who had been staring at me the other evening at Ray's Place was sitting at the bar. Exactly like the situation the other day, she wore a wide brimmed straw hat and sunglasses. Her face was turned partly away from the camera, so it was hard to see her features clearly. As before, she had a tropical drink with an umbrella in it sitting in front of her, and she was alone.

I pointed her out "Probably doesn't mean anything, but she was at

Ray's Place the other night. I only noticed her because she was staring at me."

Dane didn't seem particularly interested in this woman. "She had a drink in two bars where women have disappeared, but that doesn't mean anything. She's not the missing woman, and there's no law against drinking alone at a bar. Or staring."

Since Dane wasn't concerned about the woman, I let it drop. We continued watching the video frame by frame.

A few minutes later, I pointed at a man who had just entered the bar. He was standing on the edge of the crowd, his face partially turned away from the camera. "I think that's one of the guys involved in the needle spiking incidents before." I paused a moment. "Or maybe I saw him on the *Golden Kelp*."

The *Golden Kelp* is a mega-yacht owned by Seb Lukin, a nasty oligarch with both feet in the drug trade. In the past, Liam and I had each spent some time on the *Golden Kelp*, but for different reasons.

Oddly enough, Seb seemed to have a soft spot for me. He'd caught me spying and let me go anyway, and then he made a gift of a $35-million personal submarine I'd admired. Of course, later he'd tried to kill Liam, so I wouldn't say he'd turned away from his life of crime.

Liam squinted at the screen, trying to sharpen the details of the man's appearance. "Can you enlarge it?"

Dane adjusted the controls, and the picture grew larger but no sharper. We all stared at the full-screen image, but we still couldn't be sure about this man or where we'd seen him.

I turned to Dane. "Let's see if there's a clearer shot later on in the recording."

He continued slowly advancing the video. We watched as the man I might have recognized turned away from the camera and went out the main entrance. He'd only been inside for a few minutes. We watched the video right up to closing time, when Diana Hayward paid her tab and walked out of the bar alone, but the suspicious-looking man never reappeared.

Disheartened because we hadn't found any real clues, I asked, "Isn't it odd that he only stayed a few minutes? Could he have been there looking for someone to take?"

Dane closed the video file and emailed it to his office. "Maybe.

Maybe not. Could be he was just looking for a friend, or he didn't like the vibe at Nelson's. They'll enhance the images at the station and then we'll see if we can identify that guy. Meanwhile, you two keep trying to remember where you saw him—if you actually saw him."

I took a deep breath before I spoke. "What if we saw that man in both places—here and aboard the mega-yacht. That might mean that Seb Lukin is back in the area."

Dane nodded. "Could be. I'll ask the Coast Guard to keep a sharp eye out for him and the *Golden Kelp*. Even if he is around, we can't do anything about it yet, but I'd feel better knowing either way."

Chapter 24
Thank You

AT SUNSET A FEW DAYS LATER, Liam and I were just pulling into RIO's parking lot after a meeting at Quokka Media. I looked toward the recreation area and saw Benjamin and Joely heading toward Ray's Place. "Wanna join them? I owe them a dinner, and I'd really like it if you were there too."

"Sure. Let me park the car and I'll meet you at the bar."

I strolled over to the open air restaurant. "I'm so glad I ran in to you two. I haven't had a chance to touch base. How are things going?"

"She's completely up to speed," Benjamin said. "She even showed me a couple of things I didn't know. I guess my work here is done. Again."

"Thank you," I said.

Benjamin looked at Joely when he spoke. "It was my pleasure."

"Well, you were a lifesaver, and I appreciate it. If you're free, I'd like to take you both to dinner tonight. Sort of a joint thank you slash welcome aboard celebration. If you're up for it, would Ray's Place work?"

They both nodded, just as Liam walked up to join us.

I took his hand. "We're having dinner with Joely and Benjamin here. Let's see if I can get us a table."

Theresa was seating the crowds of people arriving for dinner. She shook her head at my request. "The place is hopping. There's a forty-five minute wait for a table. And before you ask, no, you can't pull rank. What kind of impression would that make?"

"I'm starving," I said. "It's been a long day and I missed lunch. How about some snacks?"

"Sure," she said, handing Liam and me each a bowl of nuts. "And if you're that hungry, why don't you place a 'to go' order and eat on your boat instead of waiting for a table? It's a beautiful evening, and you can keep an eye on people coming and going while you eat."

"Great idea," I said. "Let me check with the gang."

She gave me a menu and the list of dinner specials.

I took it to the end of the bar and asked the others in the party if they were okay with eating dinner on the *Tranquility*.

"How exciting!" Joely said. "That's a great idea. I was hoping to get a chance to see your famous boat. I'm in."

"Me too," said Benjamin.

I had a feeling he'd have agreed with any plan as long as it included Joely. It made me very happy to see he'd moved on after our failed romance, and I hoped the nascent relationship with Joely worked out for him. He was a nice man and a good friend. With a pang, I realized I'd missed him—just not romantically. There's never really been anyone else for me since the first time I saw Liam.

We all checked out the menus and Liam made a list of everybody's dinner and drink orders. I brought it over to Theresa.

She looked at our selections and nodded. "Good choices. Hang on a sec for the drinks. I'll text you when the food is ready."

I waved my friends over to collect their drinks, and we strolled through the last of the golden sunshine to my boat, berthed in her usual slip at the end of the pier. I handed Liam my drink and stepped aboard, still holding the bowl of nuts in one hand. I put the nuts on the bench so I could hold both our drinks while he came aboard. He stepped down to the deck before turning to offer a helping hand to Joely.

Benjamin was the last one to step onto the deck. "Nice to be back on the *Tranquility*. Doesn't look like anything much has changed."

"Nope," I agreed. "The *Tranquility* is perfect exactly as she is."

I led them below into the cabin where we all took seats in the captain's chairs that surrounded the table.

Joely looked around with interest. "It's beautiful," she said. "You're so lucky."

Benjamin laughed and took a small handful of nuts from the bowl. "Luck is practically Fin's middle name. And if you're working at RIO, chances are you'll be spending a fair amount of time aboard this boat."

We made small talk until my phone buzzed with an incoming text from Theresa.

Food ready

I texted back.

Thx nother round plz

"You stay here and enjoy yourselves. I'll be back before you know it." Liam rose to pick up our order.

By the time he returned with the food, Benjamin, Joely, and I had set the table with napkins, condiments, and utensils from *Tranquility's* well-stocked cupboards. I passed out the drinks while Liam handed out the food, making sure everyone got the right items.

We were all more than ready to eat, so we were silent for the first few minutes. Once the worst hunger pains had been satisfied, we started chatting again. I was surprised at how easily the conversation flowed, and I took it as another sign that any awkwardness between Benjamin and me was over.

When we'd finished eating, Liam said, "Anybody want another drink? Some dessert?"

Everybody groaned.

"Couldn't eat another bite," said Joely.

"Great. Then let's go up on the flying bridge and watch the moon rise," I said. "It's full tonight."

We climbed the ladder, settled ourselves and then chatted companionably while the moon put on her nightly show for us.

A few minutes later, the stars were twinkling, and the silvery moon was shining brightly when I heard Chaun's voice from the dock.

"Permission to come aboard, Captain," he called.

We hadn't heard him approach, but Benjamin, Liam and I raced down the ladder to greet him, with Joely following at a slightly slower pace. Benjamin and I both hugged him hard.

Benjamin clapped him on the back. "Good to see you, Buddy."

Then we stepped back, giving Chaun room to breathe. He disliked being touched, and I was worried that in our excitement at his return we might have made him uncomfortable.

Chaun did look a little shaken, although that was understandable given what he'd been through in the last few days. "Thanks. It's good to be back. Benjamin, can you take me home now please?"

Benjamin nodded. "Of course. Let me just say goodnight…"

Tactfully, I grabbed Liam's hand. "Let's walk Chaun to the car. Benjamin can catch up in a minute."

Chaun turned and walked along beside me without comment. I looked over at Ray's Place when we passed, and it was still packed with happy looking people. Roland was sitting at the bar, doing a credible imitation of a guy intent on getting seriously drunk.

We stopped beside Benjamin's car to wait for him. In a few minutes, he came hurrying toward us with his keys in his hand. He was still several feet away when he pushed the button to unlock the doors.

As soon as he heard the chirp, Chaun climbed into the passenger's seat. "See ya," he said, with his head down.

Liam and I waved goodbye to them, then we turned to rejoin Joely. We met up with her walking along the shell path toward Ray's Place.

"Do you need a ride home?" I asked her.

She shook her head. "No thanks. I've got a car, and I know the way. I think I'll just stay here and enjoy the evening. It's beautiful here."

"Want some company?" Liam asked.

She smiled. "Thank you, but that's not necessary. I'll only stay a minute or two. I had a wonderful evening, and I really appreciate your kindness and the warm reception, but I need a little alone time. You two go on and do whatever you would normally do. You don't need to babysit me."

I smiled at her. "We're happy to have you here. I hope you'll be around for a long time."

"Me too," she said. "Well, goodnight." She turned and walked toward Ray's Place.

I was uneasy leaving her here alone with everything going on, but Roland was at the bar keeping an eye on things.

She'd be fine.

Chapter 25
Night Dive

"You up for a night dive?" asked Liam.

"Sure thing," I said. "You read my mind."

We started walking toward the dive shop, and after a few steps, Liam stopped with his hands in his pockets, watching the carefree revelers having fun. "Looks like you've got a hit on your hands. Opening Ray's Place was a great idea."

"Maybe," I said. "If Dane can stop the needle spikers. If he can't identify them soon, I'm going to shut it down. I don't like feeling as though we've made their dirty work easier."

We continued on our way to pick up our gear and some tanks. "It would be a shame to shut the restaurant down," he said. "People seem to be enjoying it. Maybe the incident with Polly and Chaun was just a one-time thing."

I looked at Liam with disbelief. He was too smart to actually think this was over. The bad guys were still around. The incident at Nelson's had proven that. Then I realized Liam was trying to cheer me up. It wasn't working, but at least he'd tried.

We approached the bright lights of the dive shop. Stewie had agreed it made sense to keep the shop open for tank rentals a little later now that we had Ray's Place. That way people could do a sunset or early night dive and then stop afterward for a casual dinner. The additional profits would all go back into our research, and even after just a few days, Ray's Place was bringing in a lot of revenue.

Stewie had the dive shop's Dutch-door open, and he was leaning on the shelf of the bottom half, watching the goings on at Ray's Place. He smiled when he saw us. "Night dive?"

"Yup. How's business?" I said.

He shrugged. "Very brisk for a while, but now everybody's across the way having a great time. I was going to close up a half hour ago, but then I figured I'd stick around for a bit and give Roland a break. I've been keeping an eye open for anything suspicious. So far nothing."

"That's good news. Thanks for standing watch." I said.

"No problem. Doc's with Maddy now, so there's no sense in going home anyway." He opened the door and put two tanks on the cement pad and a handful of glow sticks on the shelf.

I put the glow sticks in my pocket. "Maddy was still tired after the surgery, so she went to bed early."

Stewie perked up. "Doc's there all alone? I'd like to go keep her company. Roland just got back from his break, so if it's okay with you, I'll close up now. You can bring your empty tanks back in the morning."

"Will do," I told him. While I'd been chatting with Stewie, Liam had retrieved our dive suits and gear bags from the employee storage lockers adjacent to the shop. I picked up my bag and my tank, and Liam and I walked down the pier to the *Tranquility*.

Once we'd stowed our gear, I started the engines and Liam unhooked the line. I headed out a short way into the cove and then put the boat in idle. "Where to?"

He raised his voice to be heard over the noise from the motors. "Dolphin drop off work for you?"

I nodded and set the course for the site off West Bay. I pulled up near the mooring and Liam hooked the ball with the long handled gaff and tied us off. We geared up, and when we'd gone through the usual equipment set up, Liam turned his back to me, and I tied a glow stick around his tank valve. He did the same for me.

The glow sticks wouldn't provide enough light to see any of the details around us, but they'd enable us to keep track of each other while focusing on the undersea sights. We'd use our powerful underwater flashlights to light up our surroundings.

I picked up my camera, and then we stepped off the aft platform to descend side by side along the anchor line. We were several yards away from the drop off at the edge of the reef, so we swam toward the wall, where the depth dropped precipitously from about sixty feet to thousands of feet.

As soon as I was immersed in the water, I felt all my worries recede, as they always did when I dove. They'd be back as soon as we returned to land, but for now, I was in a magical happy place with my favorite person in the whole world. I couldn't help smiling, even with the regulator in my mouth.

As we meandered along the top of the reef, shining our light at the vibrant corals and nighttime reef inhabitants, we saw several Atlantic trumpetfish hanging vertically among the gorgonians and sea grass, their mottled colors a near perfect camouflage. I took a picture of a princess parrotfish sleeping in a mucus cocoon she'd spun to keep herself safe from predators and parasites. By then, we were at the edge of the wall, so we dropped down to about seventy-five feet.

The current was strong, so we swam hard against it for the first part of the dive. We didn't go far, taking our time admiring the brilliant colors of the corals and the tiny fish and crustaceans that made their homes here.

When it was time to turn back, we barely had to make any effort to swim because the current carried us along at a comfortable speed. We passed by a small school of black durgon, huddled together to stay safe through the night. We rose slowly along the wall until we'd crested the rim, then we kicked our way over the reef top toward the boat. We used the mooring line as a guide until we'd reached fifteen feet of depth, then we stayed suspended under the boat, shining our lights below us to see what we could see while we waited out our safety stop.

I grew melancholy as I climbed the ladder, knowing that all my problems would still be waiting when we got back to shore. I racked my tank, then helped Liam by taking his fins so he could climb the ladder unimpeded. He shrugged out of his BCD and slid his tank into a slot behind the bench. Then he crossed the deck and kissed me.

I closed my eyes, thinking maybe my life wasn't so tough after all.

Chapter 26
Another Victim

THE NEXT MORNING, after I'd finished training with Christophe, I stopped by Joely's office to say hello. The lights in her office were off and it didn't look like she'd been in to work yet. Her computer was dark, and the surface of her desk was clear.

My blood ran cold. I looked at my watch. It was mid-afternoon.

I poked my head around the corner to peer into June's office. "June, have you seen Joely yet today?"

She was on the phone, but she looked up and shook her head.

I bit my lip. This was not good.

I called Benjamin, demanding to know if Joely was with him.

"No, I haven't seen her since dinner," he said, sounding puzzled. "What's up?"

"Nothing. I'll explain later," I said, my heart pounding with fear.

I hung up and called Dane. My hands were shaking so badly I could barely hit the numbers.

Dane answered. "What's happened now?"

"Joely was alone at Ray's Place last night, and now she's missing. We have to find her." I could hear the terrified tremor in my voice.

Dane groaned. "Why was she alone? Didn't you warn her to be careful?'

"No, I didn't. I should have, but she hasn't been here very long, and I've been very busy. Why haven't you put the word out in newspapers and online?"

He paused a moment. "Well, for one thing, I'd probably lose my job. Tourism makes up a big chunk of the island's economy, and the powers that be would not like me announcing that it's unsafe to come here. But you're right. I should have found a way. My job is nowhere near as important as the safety of those women. I haven't been as sharp as I usually am lately. I'm so worried about Maddy…" His voice trailed off.

"I understand. I haven't been at the top of my game either. But now with both Joely and Diana missing, we need to step it up. I want to go to the *Golden Kelp* to confront Seb Lukin."

"Please don't," he said. "It's not safe."

"It's safer for me than it is for the women I believe he's already captured. His yacht could leave at any time, and then we'd never find them. There's no time to waste. I'm going."

Chapter 27
Postcard from Hell

I WAS FRETTING about Joely while contemplating a huge stack of mail that someone had placed in the middle of my desk. This looked like an entire week's worth of junk. Usually, Genevra went through it before it came to me, so I only had to worry about the important stuff. I hoped she wasn't letting her work slide because she was spending so much time with Christophe.

Well, if I had to go through all this junk, I needed a break before I started, considering the long morning training with Christophe and my worry over Joely. I turned my chair to look out at the ocean for a minute. The sun glittered on the waves, and the graceful boats bobbed with the tide. It looked so peaceful and serene. I sighed. I wanted to be on my boat.

"Hey," said Maddy, "Everything okay?"

"I'm fine. Just resting my eyes. Christophe put me through a tough workout today and I'm a little beat."

I didn't want her to think I couldn't handle things in her absence. If she did, she'd force herself to come to work every day no matter what effect it had on her own health, and I couldn't let that happen. She needed rest and time to recuperate.

"If the freedive training is too much for you, we can skip the documentary this year. I'm sure the sponsors would understand." She sounded concerned.

"I'm fine," I lied. "Why are you here anyway? You should be home resting."

She bit her lip. "You'd tell me if it was too much, wouldn't you? We don't need the funding so badly that it's worth grinding you into the ground."

"No, we can't skip it," I said. "We missed the last few. They'll start to think we're unreliable and we'll get a bad reputation. Besides, RIO needs the sponsorship funds."

She sat in one of my guest chairs. "Okay. Actually, I wanted to talk to you about something else."

Now I was on the alert. "You're okay, right? Your health? The cancer…"

She held up her hand to stop me. "My health is fine. There's nothing to worry about there. As you said before the surgery, we are the luckiest people in the world, and that proved true once again. I guess I never did tell you I filed for a divorce from Newton, but I did, quite some time ago. And the divorce is final now. I just got the word today." She looked down at the floor.

While the news wasn't unexpected, it still threw me for a loop. This was the second time my parents had been divorced. After being apart for more than twenty years, they'd remarried just to expedite Oliver's adoption. Their remarriage had put an abrupt end to Maddy's romantic relationship with Dane. I swallowed. "Does Newton know?"

She was twisting her hands in her lap. "Yes, he does. He knew our second marriage was only temporary. He's okay with it."

Privately I doubted Newton was okay with a divorce from Maddy, but he'd have torn his own tongue out before saying anything to spoil her happiness, so I let it go. "Does Oliver know yet? And Dane?"

She nodded. "I was on the phone with Oliver when the papers were delivered, so he knows. I called Dane to tell him, but I chickened out before he answered. I'm afraid he's probably moved on. A wonderful man like Dane Scott…"

"I will never move on from an amazing woman like you," Dane said from the doorway of my office.

Maddy turned scarlet and looked at the floor.

Dane walked in and sat next to her at the table. His eyes were shining with hope and happiness.

Knowing that three is a crowd, I gathered up the scattered mail on my desk. "Gotta take care of this stuff," I said. "See ya."

I rushed off down the hall to RIO's café, where I went through the line and picked up a large lemonade and quite a few warm chocolate chip cookies. I sat at a tiny table in a corner away from the crowds. The first bite of cookie was heavenly. I chewed blissfully for a minute, and then I tackled the mound of mail.

I made three stacks. Junk mail that I could throw away, business mail that needed action, and other. The junk mail pile was by far the largest of the three. I'd whittled the original bundle down to just a few more items when an old-fashioned sepia-toned postcard reached the top of the stack.

The card was picture side up, and the image was of Hell, a popular tourist attraction in West Bay. Hell consists of a couple of acres of jagged limestone and ironshore formations surrounded by trees. The only things there are the giftshop and a post office where tourists can send mail postmarked "Sent from Hell."

From a casual conversation I'd had with the store's proprietor at a Chamber of Commerce meeting a few months ago, I knew this particular card was one of the more popular items they sold in the shop.

Curious, I flipped the card over. It was addressed to Fin at RIO, so whoever had sent it must have been in a hurry. Kudos to the Postal Service for getting it to me with only that for an address.

The writing on the card read "What's 18.986, -80.953? Your friend, DJ"

It looked like a math problem or some kind of riddle. I had no idea what it meant, so I put the card aside and went back to reading mail and eating cookies.

I had just finished the last cookie when a shadow blocked the sun streaming through the tall window next to me. Newton stood beside the table, looking sadder than I had ever seen him.

"Got time for your dad?" he asked.

"Always," I said. "Want me to get you some of these amazing

chocolate chip cookies?" My father has the metabolism of an athlete, although I've never seen him do much in the way of working out. He loved junk food almost as much as I did, but even at his age, he stayed slender and svelte.

He shook his head and sat down across from me. As usual, Newton looked like he had stepped off the pages of *GQ*. He was wearing the RIO "uniform" of cargo shorts and a polo shirt, but his cargo shorts had more than likely been a bespoke order from an Italian tailor's workshop. They were not made from the same canvas or polyester as run-of-the-mill shorts, but rather some lovely, soft fabric that draped beautifully and dried quickly. His RIO-branded polo shirt was exactly like the one I wore, but his had been tailored to fit him precisely and then perfectly pressed by his housekeeper before he wore it. His flip-flops were Italian leather, and I knew they'd been custom made for him. His silver hair was impeccably cut, and every strand was in place.

Honestly, I don't know how he does it. No wonder he was a perennial on *Human Magazine*'s Hot Male list.

"I assume Maddy told you, but in case she didn't, we're divorced again."

I nodded. "You okay?"

"I'll live. I knew it was coming." He reached over and picked up the postcard. "What's this?"

"I wish I knew. It came in the mail. Looks like a math problem to me," I said.

He tapped the card on the table while he thought. "Who's your friend DJ? Maybe you could ask DJ what it means."

I turned my palms up and shrugged. "No idea. I don't think I know anyone with those initials."

He raised his eyebrows. "Aah, but you do. What about Davy Jones? From the *Golden Kelp*."

Davy was the submarine pilot on Seb Lukin's mega-yacht. He'd taught me how to operate my personal sub, and at the time, he'd strongly hinted that he'd rather work at RIO than aboard the *Golden Kelp*.

"Well, that's true. I do know Davy, although I wouldn't say we're exactly friends. But why would he be sending me a postcard from Hell? Or a math problem?"

I took the card from Newton and stared intently at the writing on the back. When I freed my mind from the tyranny of my math hatred, I recognized the numbers for what they were.

"They're longitude and latitude numbers. Not complete because that might be too obvious if anyone saw it. Or maybe he's moving around a little or he didn't have access to an accurate GPS system. But it's close enough that I should be able to find whatever he's directing me to…"

Newton interrupted. "I think he's telling you where the *Golden Kelp* is."

I nodded and stood up. "Right. He must want me to intervene in whatever scheme Lukin has going on right now. Let's go figure out where this location is. We can look it up in my office." I sat down again. "Uh, maybe we could look it up here on your phone instead."

He smiled a sad smile. "I take it Dane and Maddy are in your office. That must be why you're working here instead of at your desk. It's okay. I can handle it. I lived through a divorce from Maddy once before and I can live through it again. Let's go. Dane will want to see this. It's an important clue."

I threw my junk mail in the nearby recycling bin and gathered up the rest. Newton and I walked down the hall to my office. It was empty, so I guessed Dane and Maddy had gone someplace more private to finish their conversation. I breathed a sigh of relief. I didn't want to be a witness the first time Dane and Newton came face-to-face after the divorce. "Let's track them down later, once we know what we're dealing with," I said.

I put my computer on the table, angled so we could both see the screen, then I entered the numbers from the postcard. Because they were only part of the coordinates, they covered a huge area, but I was able to ascertain that they corresponded with an area off West Bay, about thirty miles out, over one of the deepest parts of the ocean.

I slumped and put my head in my hand. "I hope that's not where they are. That's outside territorial waters. Dane has no jurisdiction that far out. We're back to square one. We'll never find Joely and Diana out there. But I won't give up trying. Not ever."

Newton stared at the image on my computer for a moment. "Keep working the problem. You'll figure it out."

Chapter 28
Deeper

THE NEXT MORNING, I hurried to the locker room to get ready for my training session with Christophe. I pulled on my bathing suit, zipped up my hoodie, and ran out to the pool deck.

He was already there when I reached the dock, pacing impatiently along its length with his hands behind his back. "You're late," he said.

I looked at my dive watch. It was quarter past six. In the morning. And he thought I was late. Yikes.

"Let's go. Today we're working on increasing your depth. How deep had you planned to go for the documentary?"

"Um, maybe two hundred feet," I said.

"Ridiculous. The current women's world record is 114 meters... Let's see, that's about 375 feet. You need to show the audience what you're made of. Unless you want them to think you're scared because of what happened to Ray..."

I swallowed. "I am scared. And I don't need to set a world's record. I've done 200 feet before. I'm comfortable with that depth."

He glared at me. "Exactly. You're comfortable. You want to show the audience something daring. Exciting. Not something comfortable, because that's boring. Let's say 100 meters."

I did the calculation in my head. 328 feet. "Okay. I can do that."

He nodded. "Good. We'll try to get to eighty-five before we end this morning." He picked up the case that held the monofin. "Let's go."

We hurried out to the *Tranquility*. I started the engines while he cast off. We covered the short distance to Training Site Two in minutes. Once we were securely attached to the permanent mooring, I came down from the flying bridge. Christophe was already deploying the life ring we used as a base for the dives.

We both dove off the *Tranquility*'s gunwales and swam to the nearby life ring. Christophe submerged and checked the position of the monofin on my feet. When he resurfaced, he said "Fifty meters. Dolphin kick. Wet equalize."

I nodded, slipped on my low volume swim goggles and metal nose plug, and began preparing my body for the dive. Christophe floated calmly beside me, one arm over the life preserver and the other holding his timer. I floated on my back, took several deep breaths, and tried to relax. When I was ready, I raised my arm in the signal to start the timer and then bent from the waist to begin my descent.

I was comfortable that I could do this depth, so I concentrated on becoming accustomed to wet equalization. It still seemed odd and slightly dangerous to allow water to flood my ear canals and sinus cavities but having them filled with water eliminated the need to equalize my ears.

Because there was no differential between the pressure in my inner ears and the water pressure surrounding me, I could dive and reach depth quickly without any ear pain or potential for damage to my eardrums. I had to admit it made diving simpler because I could go fast and stay in my hydrodynamic posture without worrying about blowing out an eardrum, although the risk of a sinus infection was pretty high.

Still thinking about the benefits of wet equalization, I reached the heavy metal weight that marked the target depth, turned, and headed back to the surface.

"Good," Christophe said when I surfaced. "Relax a minute and catch your breath." Surface time would help dispel any lingering brain fog from the dive.

He watched me closely for a few minutes, then he let some line out on the life preserver. "Fifty-five meters. When you're ready."

Fifty-five meters—about 180 feet. I took a few deep breaths to prepare, then I did my dive.

When I surfaced, Christophe watched me closely until I'd caught my breath. Then, wasting no words, he said, "Again."

After a few more dives to fifty-five meters, he let out more line. "Sixty," he said.

I nodded, did my breathing prep, and made the dive. Then I did it again—five more times, increasing the depth a few meters each time. We ended at ninety-three meters, slightly over 300 feet.

"Enough," he finally said. "Let's go back."

I was relieved to hear those words. My muscles were starting to shake, my head felt fuzzy, and I was cold. We swam back to the *Tranquility* where I zipped myself into a thick hoodie before helping Christophe haul the life preserver aboard and stow it. After filling two cups with water from the cooler, I handed one to Christophe and then climbed to the flying bridge to make the short trip back to RIO's pier.

Usually, he stayed and spent some time talking about my performance or his upcoming training plans, so I was surprised when Christophe hurried off the boat as soon as he finished tying her off. I was still below tidying up and hadn't even realized he'd disembarked.

But when I walked back onto the open deck, I saw Christophe and Genevra walking side-by-side toward the parking lot.

Chapter 29
Early Morning

BECAUSE WE WERE GETTING close to the documentary's due date, Christophe and I had been training in open water every day for the last three days. At this point, the hundred meter dive wasn't exactly easy, but I reached the depth consistently without any problems. That was one worry off my mind.

But I still had a million other things to fret about. I stayed up late trying to concoct a plan for confronting Lukin. I knew in my heart he had the missing women on the *Golden Kelp*. I just needed to find out how he was getting them there. I was exhausted from lack of sleep, and as usual, the next morning Liam and I were up before the sun.

I had a full morning of training with Christophe scheduled, and I should drop by to see Maddy at some point. I wanted to touch base with Dane today, plus, I had a pile of work from my actual jobs to wade through.

But first, I wanted to dive. Just me and the ocean. It's where I do my best thinking. I needed to be underwater, the same way I needed to breathe.

Liam had taken to leaving some of his gear on my breezeway where I keep my own dive paraphernalia. After a dive where we let everything soak in the rinse tank at my house, it made sense to hang his equipment up to dry with my things rather than to toss his wet

123

gear into his car. This morning, we went to the breezeway, selected our dive skins for the day, and packed our gear into my Prius.

It was a short hop to Rum Point, my favorite shore dive site. We geared up on the beach, and waded into the warm water, shuffling our feet as we went. When we were at mid-thigh depth, we steadied each other while we put on our dive fins. Then we stuck our snorkels in our mouths and swam to the barrier ropes.

We ducked under the ropes, then switched over to our regulators before we dropped down toward the sand below. We followed the sand chute toward the wall, searching diligently for a glimpse of Suzie Q, the resident stingray. Last time we'd seen her, we'd noticed she was pregnant, and we were both wondering if she'd given birth yet.

Stingrays usually birth five to ten babies at a time, and baby stingrays develop within an egg inside the mother. The egg contains everything the embryonic baby rays need until just before they're born. Then they break out of the egg and receive some additional nutrition from a special fluid secreted by the mother. Rays are born live, completely formed, and able to take care of themselves from the start. Most times the mother stingray lets the babies go off on their own right away, although occasionally they stick together for a few days.

We caught a glimpse of Suzie Q on the sand, and it looked as though our dive had been perfectly timed to witness the birth of her litter. We didn't want to spook her, so we covertly watched the process using our peripheral vision while hovering several feet away.

I'd brought my camera, so I discreetly filmed Suzie Q giving birth to five baby stingrays. They popped out one after another with their wings furled. After stretching a little, they swam away.

Suzie Q finished the birthing process just as our bottom time ran out. We turned to head back to shore, elated and overjoyed by the miraculous sight. It felt like we'd been given a gift to be able to watch our beloved Suzie Q and her new family. I hoped at least some of the babies would stay in the area so we could keep tabs on them as they grew.

Still on a high from the miracle we'd seen, we carried our gear to my car and stowed it in the trunk. Liam looked at the time on his watch. "I'll rinse our equipment in the troughs at RIO and stow it in the drying area so you can get right to your freedive training. You don't want to annoy Christophe. Who knows what torment he'd add to your workload if you're late?"

"Thanks," I said. "But won't that make you late for your own work?"

He laughed. "Nope. I'm the boss, remember? And besides, the media industry doesn't start their days anywhere near as early as the dive industry."

We pulled into the parking lot at RIO. I jumped out and gave him a quick kiss goodbye. "Have a good day. And thanks for taking care of the gear."

Chapter 30
Oliver

CHRISTOPHE and I had finished our daily dive training and the *Tranquility* was back in her slip at RIO. He had just finished wrapping the excess line over the cleat on the dock when Oliver came off his boat, the *Flemingo,* and stood on the dock waiting for me to join him.

I always loved seeing the clever pun he'd come up with for his boat's name. People commented occasionally that he'd spelled the name of the bird incorrectly, without realizing that it wasn't named after the pink birds at all. It was a play on our last name—Fleming. They always laughed when he explained it to them.

He'd been traveling on Fleming Environmental business, so we hadn't spoken in a while, and I was happy to see him. "Hey, Bro," I said when I hopped over the *Tranquility*'s gunwales to the dock. Then I noticed the worried look on his face. "What's up? Is Maddy okay?"

"Yeah. Maddy's fine, but I'm worried about Genevra. I can't reach her. Have you seen her around anywhere?"

I shook my head. "The last time I saw her she was at Ray's Place. Maybe she decided to sleep in a little. But this isn't like her. Normally she lets me know if she's going to be coming in late."

I turned to Christophe who had been standing a few feet away on the dock. I knew they'd been spending a lot of time together, and the last time I'd seen her they'd been together. "Have you seen her recently? Maybe last night? Did she say anything about going away for a few days or taking some time off?"

"Non," he said with his sexy French accent. "We had dinner together a few days ago, but I have not seen her recently. I do not think she would go away without leaving any word with you. She is excited about her job, and she often talks about how much she loves it and loves living on Grand Cayman." He paused a moment and looked at Oliver. "Have you tried calling her?"

Oliver gave Christophe an exasperated look. "Of course I've tried calling her. She doesn't answer."

"Are you sure she would want to take your call?" he said, earning a scowl from Oliver. "Let me try." He reached into the pocket of his gear bag and removed his phone.

We both noticed he had programmed Genevra's number into his favorites because he only had to hit one key for the call to go through. Oliver's fists were balled at his side in annoyance, but he didn't say anything. Genevra's well-being was obviously more important to him than fighting with Christophe. I was proud of his self-control.

The three of us were quiet while the call went through. Then faintly, I heard Genevra's voice mail greeting coming from nearby. Christophe dialed again so the greeting would repeat, and we followed the sound.

We found Genevra's phone on the ground in the vacant lot beyond the dive shop, an empty space with no facilities, no public areas, and no attractions. Other than her phone, there was no sign of Genevra, and since there was nothing there, no reason for her to have gone behind the dive shop.

My blood ran cold, and my throat was tight with fear, making it hard to talk. "Christophe, do you know where she went the other day? Did you see her talk to anyone else? Did you go somewhere together?"

Christophe gave an infuriating Gallic shrug. "I don't know anything. I wanted to go home. I'd had a long day of work, so I was exhausted. I invited her to come home with me, then offered to walk her to her car, but she turned me down on both. She said she was enjoying her evening."

The color drained from Oliver's face. "She decided to use herself as bait, even though we begged her not to. The needle spikers…"

"Stay calm. We don't know that yet. Maybe there's a good explanation. Anyway, Genevra's pretty tough. She can take care of herself, but I'm going to call Dane anyway." I pulled out my cell.

Dane had been working hard while still trying to be there for Maddy, so I wasn't surprised he sounded weary when he answered my call. I gave him a quick recap of the situation.

He groaned. "Get Theresa and whoever else was working last night in right away. I'll want to talk to them to see if they noticed anything. And queue up the video from the cameras. Maybe we'll get lucky and catch something in the parking lot. I'll be there in ten minutes. Meanwhile, keep everyone away from the area where you found the phone."

The three of us walked back to the pier and stood huddled in a forlorn little group. I called Theresa to tell her about Genevra and to ask her to come in.

She volunteered to call Noah Gibb and Brian Walker to have them come in early too. "Poor Genevra. I'm so sorry this happened to her," she said.

I quickly shut down that train of thought. "We don't know that anything has happened yet. Dane is on the way to investigate. Let's not panic until we know for sure she's been taken."

Oliver stifled a gasp at the word.

I understood. He loved her, and the possibility that she'd been taken against her will was horrifying in the extreme.

We were still waiting for Dane to arrive when a tractor/trailer pulled into the parking lot. It was carrying a blue personal submarine on the back. Seb Lukin, the baddest of the bad guys, had given the amazing $35 million machine to me a while ago. I had immediately signed ownership of it over to RIO.

Maddy and Newton didn't like that the sub had been a gift from Lukin, so they'd insisted we send it back to the manufacturer for a complete overhaul right away. At the time, Newton had said, "No telling what Lukin did to it. It could be booby trapped. I won't take a chance with your life."

I'd seen the sense in that, so even though the sub had seemed to be in perfect condition, we'd had it transported to the manufacturer for an overhaul. Now here it was, back at RIO, but the timing couldn't have been worse. I had no bandwidth to deal with this right now. I glared at the man crossing the lawn carrying a clipboard full of paperwork.

I lit into the poor guy. "What are you doing here? This isn't a good time. Couldn't you have called first?"

He took a step back. "Hello to you too. I'm looking for Ms. Blackthorne. I scheduled the delivery with her."

We all gasped. "When?" I asked him. "When did you talk to her?"

"It was three or four days ago. I don't remember exactly. Where is she, anyway?" he said.

"That's what we'd like to know. She's missing," I said. "And I didn't mean to be rude. It's just we're worried about her."

He nodded. "Yup. I can see that. Now, where do you want the sub?" He had a job to do, and our concerns didn't affect him in the slightest.

"Let me get someone to help you." I said. I walked back over to the dive shop and poked my head in through the open Dutch door. Stewie was in the back, filling tanks, but he smiled and shut off the noisy compressor when he saw me.

"Stewie, would you please help this gentleman with the sub delivery? Thank you." He wiped his hands on his cargo shorts and walked outside to confer with the truckdriver, and I rejoined the miserable group on the dock.

A few minutes later, I saw Dane's car pull into the lot, quickly followed by Gus and Theresa's vehicle. Noah Gibb and Brian Walker were in the back, wedged in next to Angel's car seat. Gus got out of the driver's side and unbuckled Angel. "We'll be in the café," I heard him say.

"Not too many cookies," Theresa replied, and Gus forced out a laugh.

Theresa, Brian, Noah, Dane, and Roland scurried along the path toward us, concern etched on their faces.

Dane faced the group. "Everyone please wait for me in the conference room. I'll speak to Fin out here first. Don't talk to anyone, not even each other. I'll be in to get you as soon as I can."

Christophe cleared his throat. "I have nothing to do with this sad event, and I know nothing. Am I free to go?"

Dane glared at the Frenchman. "You're free to go when I say so,

130

and not a minute sooner. Now get inside." Then Dane took my arm and walked me down the dock to the *Tranquility*, while Roland, carrying his forensic tool kit, headed toward the area where we'd found Genevra's phone.

Dane and I stepped aboard the *Tranquility* and sat side-by-side on one of the benches that lined the gunwales. He sighed. "I was hoping our surveillance plan was foolproof."

"I don't know how long she's been gone. The sub delivery guy said he spoke to her three or four days ago. Last time I saw her was also a couple of days ago. She was with Christophe in the bar at Ray's Place."

Dane sucked in a breath. "I don't trust that man. He's too smooth. And everything started when he arrived. We don't really know how long Genevra's been gone, and we need to find her right now." He rubbed his face in exasperation. "May I use your office for the interviews? I'm hoping maybe somebody will remember seeing something."

I nodded. "Whatever you need. Just find Genevra and bring her home safe."

Dane went inside to talk to Theresa, Oliver, Noah, Brian, and Christophe. A few minutes later, Theresa came out and sat down.

"Is he done?" I asked.

"No, but he wants to talk to you before he does any further interviews. He's in your office."

Dane was sitting in my desk chair, staring out the window at the ocean. I often sat like that when I was thinking, so I stood still and tried not to disturb him.

But he must have seen my reflection in the window because he turned around quickly. "Have a seat. Roland hasn't found anything helpful with his forensics. Morey reviewed the security tapes and there's nothing of interest on them. There's just one set of prints on the phone we found, so I'm assuming they're Genevra's. You wouldn't happen to have hers on file so we can confirm that?"

I shook my head. "Liam might have them though. She worked for him before she came to RIO, and his hiring practices are a little stricter than ours because of the business he's in."

"Good idea. I'll check with him when he gets here. Oliver gave me permission to search his boat, so Roland and I are headed out to do that as soon as I talk to the last two guys—Brian and Noah. And meanwhile, I'd like you to do an underwater search and recovery around RIO's cove. See if you can find anything out of the ordinary."

We both knew he meant see if I could find Genevra's body, because if she'd been under water all this time there'd be no recovery.

I didn't question his choice of words. "I'll get on it now."

Chapter 31
An Underwater Search

I WENT out the back door and took the path to the dive shop to grab some tanks for the search. This was one dive I wasn't excited about. While I was in the shop, I looked at the map of our cove, mentally creating a grid search pattern and affixing the boundary lines of each square in the grid to an underwater landmark. I started my search at the edge of the marina.

Although I was happy to be underwater, this was slow and boring work, especially because I was hoping not to find anything. The search took several hours, and I'd surfaced and changed tanks three times.

I did my grid pattern without finding anything of interest, until I approached the ledge at sixty feet, at the point farthest from shore. The terrain beneath me was a series of coral fingers jutting out into the blue. In the middle of the two longest fingers was a wide sand chute surrounded on both sides by lush corals. Directly beneath me, there were two parallel tracks about ten feet long. The tracks were so straight I knew nothing natural could have caused them, and I also knew they had been made recently, because they hadn't been there the last time I dove here. I'd been about to turn back, happy that I hadn't found Genevra trapped here underwater, until I saw the unusual marks in the sand.

I followed the sand chute back toward shore, and as I reached a depth of about twenty feet, I noticed the coral on both sides of the sand trail had been crushed and destroyed in a straight path. I knew a sub was the only thing that could have caused this destruction.

I stopped, hovering in mid water, staring at the track. Someone had brought a submarine, one very similar to mine, this way. They must have used it to take Genevra to wherever they were holding her.

I followed the trail of broken coral and found the point where I thought the sub had come to the surface. The spot was well beyond the rear of RIO's dive shop and the adjacent shore dive entry, directly beneath the middle of the vacant lot where we'd found Genevra's phone. There was even a large scrape mark on the ironshore.

I swam slowly back to my entry point, thinking so hard I barely noticed the scenery or the three squid sparkling in the sun's rays near the surface. Usually, I loved seeing squid. When the sun penetrates the water enough to illuminate them, they glow with iridescent colors, and they look a little like underwater angels. Today I didn't stop to admire their beauty because I was in a hurry to talk to Dane about how we could set a trap for the abductors.

I tracked him down on Oliver's boat, where he and Roland were finishing up their CSI work.

Chapter 32
A Second Location

ROLAND AND DANE were sitting on the bench, talking quietly with their heads together, a miasma of pure despair surrounding them.

I approached the end of Oliver's slip. "Find anything?"

Roland growled. "Nothing."

Dane said, "We're thinking about what our next step should be."

"Well, while you're sitting here thinking, I want to do an underwater search of the area around Nelson's. I'd like to see if I can find evidence of a sub in the area. Or maybe proof that Diana wasn't taken away on a sub. Maybe she went for a swim and got lost or something."

He frowned. "Not likely, and I'd rather you stayed away from Nelson's until we find the people responsible for the needle spiking. But I can't stop you from diving there or doing whatever other foolhardy thing you think of, so please do me a favor. If you go to Nelson's, take Liam or Stewie with you. Or even Benjamin. Please."

I nodded. "Okay. I can do that. I'll call Liam now."

I hurried to the café to grab a couple of my favorite cookies and a lemonade, so I'd have something to munch on while I waited for Liam. I'd been diving for hours, and I'd missed lunch. I was starved.

When Liam answered his cell, I told him I wanted to do a search pattern at Nelson's to try to prove my theory that a sub had been used to take the women. "Dane doesn't want me to go alone, so can you go with me please?"

"Let me check with Gary. We're in a meeting, but I bet he's ready for a break." There followed a few seconds of muffled conversation. "Okay, we're good to go. We'll meet you at Nelson's if you'll bring my gear and some tanks. That way we can get started faster."

"Will do. See you in a few minutes." I rushed outside to grab Liam's gear from his locker and pick up several tanks at the dive shop. I carried everything down the dock and loaded it on the *Tranquility*, since it would be just as fast for me to take the boat as it would be to drive.

I pulled up to the dock at Nelson's and tied off the boat. As soon as it was secure, I trotted down the pier to check in with Stefan Gibb. I wanted him to know what I was up to. I also hoped he'd help me out by keeping people out of the water and away from my boat while I worked.

"No problem," said Stefan. "Free drinks at the bar will keep everyone close by."

"Thanks, Stefan. Put the drinks on my tab."

"No, I've told you before, you'll never pay for anything here. Just solve this crime so we can all go back to enjoying life."

"Comping the drinks isn't necessary but thank you. I appreciate it. You don't happen to have an underwater map around, do you? It would help if I had an idea of the terrain before I start."

"I have one, but it probably won't help you. The bottom is mostly sand with just a few coral heads as landmarks, and it doesn't get deep until you're out pretty far." He rubbed his chin. "I don't know about the abutting properties though. It might be different over there."

"Okay. Thanks." I waited while Stefan found the underwater map, then I walked slowly back to the *Tranquility*. Once aboard, I checked out the map in more detail, and it confirmed that the area directly in front of the bar was shallow, and pretty much all sand with just an occasional coral head. I looked over at the properties on either side of Nelson's. Over there, where the land met the sea was all ironshore. I wondered if the water was deeper and the terrain trickier.

Within a few minutes, I saw Liam and Gary walk into Nelson's through the front entrance. Liam waved and then walked Gary over to an empty seat at the bar. Once his friend was settled, Liam jogged across the sandy beach and along the pier. He stepped aboard.

I touched his hand. "Thanks for coming. I appreciate it."

He smiled. "It's never a hardship to dive with you, but even if it was, I'd do anything to keep you safe—and to help Dane. What's the plan?"

I told him how Stefan had described the underwater terrain. "I'm wondering if Diana might have gone for a swim and got caught in a current. We should check for currents as well as entanglement hazards. But most importantly, I want to see if there are more of those parallel marks like I found at RIO. In my mind, those marks point to the use of a personal sub in the area. Plus, I want to check out the houses on either side of Nelson's beach. They look empty, and maybe the bad guys stashed Diana in one of them temporarily."

Liam nodded. "Good thinking. Do you want to split up so we can cover more ground?"

I pulled my binoculars out of my gear bag and looked at each house in turn. "They'd want to transfer their victims at a point where it wouldn't be likely they'd be seen. The shutters are closed, and the pool is covered at the house on the left. Plus, there's a thick line of bushes marking the property boundary that would help obscure what they were doing if anyone at the bar casually looked over. It might be ideal for their use."

Liam whistled. "Do you think they're bold enough to snatch someone while the bar's open?"

"Why not?" I said. "We saw them do it before. The only difference back then was that they took their victims out the front entrance."

"That's true, although they didn't know anybody was looking for them yet. Anyway, we'll focus on the left."

"Yep," I said. "But I still want to start in the central sandy area to try to check for submarine tracks and to get an idea of the currents."

"Got it," he said. "Lead on."

We donned our BCDs—our Buoyancy Control Devices— and tanks, then we did backward rolls off opposite sides of the *Tranquility* and met up underwater. I hugged the bottom to check the depth. It was only a little over five feet deep—too shallow for a sub. I motioned for Liam to follow me to deeper water.

I stayed close to the bottom until the depth meter read eight feet, which is the height of my sub. I signaled to Liam that we should begin our search here. I swam out a bit further until we were almost at the limits of visibility between us. So far, there'd been no current and no sign of anything that could be an entanglement hazard.

The bottom slope was mild, so the depth didn't change much as we got further from shore. We each made two passes in front of Nelson's without finding anything. Finally, in about eighteen feet of water, I saw two parallel gouges in the sandy bottom, identical to the ones I'd found at RIO. I tapped on my tank to get Liam's attention, and he quickly swam toward me.

The gouges were about ten feet long, completely straight and absolutely parallel. They were so perfectly aligned that I knew they couldn't be natural. We followed them toward the empty house, and every few feet the marks disappeared and then reappeared, which was puzzling at first.

I racked my brain to figure out what else could have made these gouges, but I was absolutely sure the tracks had to have been made by a personal sub like mine. I'd figured out that the pilot wasn't experienced enough to account for the ocean's surge in such shallow waters and he or she kept running aground while trying to hug the bottom.

As our path brought us closer to the ironshore area in front of the house we'd identified as the most likely target, the water got deeper and there were no more tracks. I assumed that was because if the gouges had in fact been made by a sub, the poorly skilled pilot had enough depth here to operate without hitting bottom.

I was sure the needle spikers were taking their victims and moving them with a sub. I just had to figure out where they were taking them. The sub had to have a home somewhere. Although it could dock on the surface in a marina, it would attract unwanted attention, and they needed access to powerful and complex charging equipment. That told me the sub was probably either connected with a mega-yacht or a secluded waterfront location they were using as a hideout.

The use of a sub and the deep water approach pointed to a mega-yacht as the likely lair of the crime ring, which in turn pointed to the vile hand of Seb Lukin, known to be a nasty master criminal, as well as the owner of both a sub and a mega-yacht.

I sank down below the waves and rejoined Liam. We swam slowly back to the *Tranquility* and climbed the ladder to doff our gear. I had just zipped my dive bag when Liam came up from the cabin. He plunked a broad-brimmed sun hat on my head, and tenderly tightened the sliding clasp under my chin.

"Not taking any chances with you," he said. "I have to keep you safe, and with what's going on with Maddy…"

I smiled and kissed him, then we strolled hand-in-hand down the pier to Nelson's bar trying to look like any other happy couple rather than like a pair of amateur crime investigators.

Or at least one of us was an amateur. I still had my suspicions about the nature of Liam's other role.

I raced back to RIO to talk to Dane about my plan. I'd thought hard about this situation, and in my mind, it was the only thing we could do.

"No, it's too dangerous," Dane said when I told him my idea was to go to the *Golden Kelp* to search for the missing women. "I can't take a chance on losing you too. Maddy and Newton would never forgive me. Heck, I'd never forgive myself. You're like a daughter to me. No. Nothing doing. We'll think of some other way."

Knowing Dane would eventually realize there was no other way, I didn't say anything for a few minutes so he could think. When I decided he'd mulled the problem long enough, I said "Do you have a better idea?"

He lowered his face to his hands, bending forward toward the floor. He groaned. "God help me. I don't. Not yet anyway. I need more time to think things through."

Chapter 33
Parental Advice

FOR THE NEXT SEVERAL HOURS, I stayed on the *Tranquility* working on my plan to board the *Golden Kelp*. I hadn't noticed the day growing dark until I realized I couldn't see my computer screen anymore. I'd been waiting for Dane to return and agree with me about the plan, but there'd been no sign of him. I set off on a mission to find him and argue once again for my plan. I was sure it was the best way to stop the abductions, and our only hope of getting Genevra, Joely, and Diana back safely.

I jumped lightly off the *Tranquility*'s gunwale onto the dock. As I passed the *Sea Princess* in her slip next to mine, a voice came out of the darkness. Maddy's voice.

"Fin, can you spare me a few minutes?" She was sitting on her boat's deck, alone.

"Maddy, what are you doing out here? You should be home resting. Don't you have another immunotherapy session in a few days?"

I could barely see her nod in the faint glow of the distant security lights. "Immunotherapy will be fine. I'll be fine." She stood up and held out her hand to help me board. "But right now, let's talk about you and your safety. Dane told me about your plan to confront Lukin on his mega-yacht."

"I can't just hang back and do nothing while those women are... well, who knows what. And Genevra. She's practically family."

Maddy nodded. "She is family but leave it to Dane and his team. They have the necessary skills and resources. And what's more, it's their job. Not yours."

"But..." I started.

Maddy held up her hand to silence me. "If you won't stand down for your own sake, do it for me. As you keep saying, I need to focus on getting well, and I can't rest if I'm worried about you."

"You don't need to worry. I'll be fine," I said stubbornly. "If it's Seb Lukin behind this, he won't hurt me. He likes me."

"Until he doesn't. He tolerated you when you interfered in his drug business before, and then he took his revenge out on Liam. Could you live with yourself if that happened again? Maybe this time Liam wouldn't be so lucky. Or maybe Seb would choose Oliver instead. Or Newton. It's just too dangerous. Please. Leave it to Dane."

Reminding me that Seb would hurt someone I loved if I hurt his business was like having a bucket of ice water dumped on my head. I could live with the danger to myself, but no way could I risk the people I loved. "You're right. I can't take that chance. I'll leave it to Dane."

She rose and gave me a major hug. "Thank you. I feel better already."

I helped her step up onto the dock, and we walked slowly through the rosy glow of the security lights back to the shore. She led me to one of the picnic tables outside the dive shop. Liam, Newton, Oliver, Doc, and Stewie were all seated there, looking at me anxiously.

I loved these people, and I knew they loved me in return. How could I have even considered doing something on my own that might anger Seb Lukin? My family means the world to me, and I could never do anything that might endanger them. "It's okay. She convinced me. I'll leave the investigating to Dane." The collective sigh of relief made me smile.

Liam stood up and gave me a hug. "Thank you," he whispered in my ear. "Not just for me, but for everyone here." When he broke off the hug, he said," We're heading home. Fin's had a really long day, and she needs some rest. Anybody need a ride?"

Everybody said they had their own cars, so Liam and I walked hand in hand along the shell path toward the parking lot. When we walked past it, I noticed the good times were still in full swing at Ray's Place. I caught sight of Roland sitting at the bar, pretending to be a heavy drinker, but I knew his sharp eyes wouldn't miss a thing.

The blonde woman I'd seen before was sitting on the same bar stool two seats down from Roland. I only noticed her because of the distinctive straw hat. And although it was dark and we were not very close, I would have sworn her gaze followed me as I walked away.

Chapter 34
An Ultimatum

THE NEXT DAY, I was sitting in my office after freedive training with Christophe. It had become increasingly clear that the RIO team was not up for filming a documentary. We were all too worried about our missing friends. It was highly unlikely we could finish by the contractual deadline.

I picked up my desk phone and dialed a number I knew by heart. It belonged to Will Dassault, our network connection for the documentaries. Will had been entirely sympathetic when we asked to postpone our contracted documentary the year Ray died. And he'd still been sympathetic the next year when we asked for another postponement because of Dylan Gibb's death during the filming. And again, the following year when Gus and Theresa had been kidnapped. And then again after Hurricane Willard.

I hadn't anticipated a problem when I told Will we needed another postponement because Joely and Genevra were missing, but when I made my request the lack of an immediate response from the other end of the line was ominous.

After a long, silent minute Will finally spoke. "I'm sorry, Fin. I understand how hard the situation must be for you, but I just can't do it. We've been approached by a couple of other groups that are hoping to replace RIO in our portfolio. The network bigwigs are breathing down my neck. They were understanding at first, but now they're questioning whether RIO is really committed to the partnership."

I was stunned. "Will, our research depends on the revenue from the network to keep our operation going. Newton and Maddy have been personally underwriting the costs for years, but even they can't keep doing that forever. The documentary sponsorships and the donations it brings in are our primary source of funds. What will happen to RIO if the network drops us?"

"I understand your problem, but I can't do anything about it. I'm under instructions from the suits at the top. Either RIO delivers a high quality full-length documentary by the date in the contract, or you're done. I'll be forced to sign with this other organization."

I bit my lip, not sure what to do with this news, so I decided to stall for a few minutes while I thought about how to handle it. "Are you at liberty to tell me the name of the other organization you're considering? There aren't many oceanography institutes with a stellar reputation like RIO's."

"Don't I know it?" said Will. "They approached me out of the blue, and I was lucky to find them. I can't really tell you the name, but it's a new group, and the head of this other organization has a pretty good reputation as a nature photographer. The network is thinking we shift the focus from oceanography and underwater adventures to more generalized nature stories to capitalize on his strengths."

"It's a pretty small community, Will. I bet I know this nature photographer. Are you sure you can't tell me who it is?"

"No, I can't, but you may know his most famous shot because it made his reputation. It's a picture of a petite female diver..."

I interrupted him. "The diver is Maddy, facing down a great white shark while freediving, right?"

Will sounded puzzled. "I didn't realize until you mentioned it that the diver is Maddy, but, yeah, you're right. How'd you know?"

"Because Alec Stone didn't take that photo. I did. He wasn't even there that day."

Will was clearly upset that I had guessed it was Alec. "Hold on a minute, Fin. I never said it was Alec Stone..."

"But it is him, isn't it? Trust me, Will, you don't want to get in bed with him. He's a snake."

"Look, I know you two have a history, but that's no reason to cast aspersions on a man's reputation." Will was going for righteous indignation now, and it rankled me.

"Call Carl Duchette if you can track him down. Or call Gary Graydon, the new head of Quokka Media. If you tell him I asked you to seek it out, he'll find the retraction that *Your World* published when they realized Alec had stolen my work. You'll have it in your inbox by the end of the day." At least I hoped Gary would be able to find it by the end of the day.

"But it's practically a done deal…"

"Then undo it. RIO will be delivering our annual documentary as scheduled. You can count on it." My hands were shaking when I hung up the phone. How were we ever going to complete the documentary when we were dealing with Maddy's health issues and Genevra's and Joely's disappearances?

Right now, I had no plan for how I'd get it done, but I knew that somehow, some way, I would make it happen.

Chapter 35
Planning

DESPITE EVERYTHING that had been going on, I'd still managed to put in at least a few hours a day freedive training with Christophe. I had to admit, his methods worked. I'd been a great diver before but working with him had increased my stamina to an unprecedented degree. My overall strength had improved, and I found that even on scuba, my air consumption was better than it had been, and it had already been stellar. During our practice sessions I'd made the dive to the agreed upon depth of one hundred meters enough times that it was now as routine as such things could ever be. I'd even gone a bit further a few times just to be sure nothing would go wrong on the big day.

With Gus looking over his shoulder, Christophe had been the dive coordinator for the documentary, arranging for photographers and safety divers. He not only used the cadre of top-shelf divers we had on staff at RIO, but he also called on many of his own contacts in the dive industry to fill in some gaps. He covered all the bases and put together an excellent dive plan. Then he drilled everybody on their roles and responsibilities. I learned a lot from watching him work. I wish I'd had him around when I'd planned Ray's deep dive.

Life might be so different today if I'd already had the experience of working with Christophe before planning that complex dive on my own, or if Christophe had been at RIO back then to offer some guid-

149

ance. At the very least, it would have given me more courage to stand up to Ray's demands. But Ray was a former champion freediver, and I'd assumed he knew what he was doing. Although to be fair, nobody could have anticipated what happened that day.

We'd learned another lesson from the last time we'd filmed a free-dive for our annual documentary. We didn't invite donors, industry leaders, or island luminaries to join us on the *Omega* during the dive. It's just too hard to keep track of them. Nobody would be on the *Omega* with us unless they were directly involved in the dive or the filming.

But we were planning a special rough cut screening of the documentary footage a few days after the filming in place of the galas we'd held in the past, and we were charging a hefty ticket price for that event to make up the shortfall. We all had our fingers crossed that we'd have found Joely and Genevra and brought them home safely by then. Otherwise, we wouldn't be in much of a celebratory mood.

At least the dive planning was going well. The safety and photography team for the dive consisted of ten people. Liam, Doc, and Alec were assigned to film the dive at various depths. Christophe had been adamant about inviting Alec to participate—against my better judgment—since he felt Alec's talent and reputation outweighed his awful personality.

I continued to question including Alec until finally, Christophe asked me to trust him, just as I had during training. "He has a name and a reputation. And if he works on your documentary, he won't be able to deliver his own film to the network. I will arrange the dive so you will be safe even if he tries to interfere."

"How?" I asked. "The man is a snake."

Christophe nodded. "Yes, he is. But trust that I have your safety as my primary goal, and the success of your film as a secondary goal. I will make this work."

And he did. He arranged the teams so that Alec and each of the RIO photographers was paired with one of Christophe's recruits, all of whom were experienced scuba divers and freedivers. Christophe's divers would be responsible for all the safety protocols.

Stewie and his partner were assigned to be surface support. They would be covering the last few meters of the ascent, the time when any potential problems were most likely to occur. They would be breathing Nitrox, a blend of regular air with extra oxygen added to help extend dive times without as much concern for decompression sickness or nitrogen narcosis. They'd dive down to sixty feet and follow me up when I came back into view. But Stewie and his partner could not go below ninety feet, or they'd risk oxygen toxicity reactions, which could lead to death.

Alec and his partner would start on the surface and follow me down to between ninety and 100 feet. They would be breathing regular air, and they would meet up with Doc who would initially be deployed at ninety feet. Doc and the safety diver with her would be breathing Trimix, another gas blend, and they would follow me down to 200 feet.

Liam and his safety diver partner, both also breathing Trimix, would pick up the responsibility for filming and dive safety at 200 feet and they'd be with me to the hundred meter mark. Liam would ensure he filmed me grabbing the ticket off the weight we would deploy at one hundred meters, and he'd capture my turn and the start of my ascent. This duo would follow me until I met up with Doc again, at around 200 feet. At that point, Liam and his buddy would begin a series of decompression stops as recommended by their dive computers.

Meanwhile, Doc and her safety diver partner would follow me up to around 100 feet and then pass responsibility back to Alec's team before she and her partner began their own safe ascent as recommended by their computers.

At around sixty feet, Alec's team would meet up with Stewie's, who'd take over for the remainder of the ascent. Stewie and his buddy would also be the divers responsible for ensuring I had oxygen to breathe after the dive. Once I'd performed the "okay" protocol at the dive's conclusion, they would guide me back to fifteen feet for a brief safety stop. They'd stay with me while I recovered by breathing pure oxygen for a few minutes.

Maddy and her partner would be free diving, and their job would be to follow me up for the last fifty to sixty feet. Neither of them would touch me unless there was a problem. They'd simply offer encouragement. Maddy would be using the dolphin kick in case I forgot how to

151

do it, since it was at this point that my urge to breath and the brain fogging effects of apnea and narcosis would be strongest.

During the dive planning meetings, many of the experienced scuba divers, including Alec and Stewie, insisted that I couldn't get nitrogen narcosis or decompression sickness from a freedive. Christophe explained that some scuba divers had been taught that nitrogen narcosis is caused by breathing compressed air. That statement does imply that freediving couldn't cause narcosis because there's neither breathing nor compressed air involved.

But Christophe showed us the research from AIDA, the international governing body of the freediving sport. AIDA warns its divers that nitrogen narcosis happens on almost every deep freedive. And unlike nitrogen narcosis on scuba, it's probably caused by excess CO_2, and it doesn't always dissipate as the diver ascends. I was also surprised to learn from Christophe that contrary to popular under-standing among recreational divers, freediving can cause decompres-sion sickness too.

It broke my heart that I'd been unaware of these dangers and safety measures when I'd planned Ray's deep dive. I found myself getting angry with him because he hadn't told me any of this or corrected my naïve assumptions. And I was angry at myself for not doing my own research, but I hadn't thought Ray would take unnecessary chances with his own life, especially because he was the expert, and he hadn't been in competition.

For this documentary, I was only in competition with myself and my memories of Ray's disastrous dive. Christophe had insisted I should breathe pure oxygen after I surfaced and gave him the okay sign. He'd made me breathe pure oxygen after my final training dive on deep training days, and it was good to know he wasn't taking any chances with my safety during the filming either.

Gus had joined us for planning meetings whenever he could break away from his work at Fleming Environmental Investments, and he confessed that after listening to Christophe's lectures that he'd learned a lot. "I didn't know what I didn't know about freediving," he told me, his voice full of regret. He too missed Ray, who'd been his best friend for many years.

Chapter 36
Deep Dive

EVERYTHING WAS in readiness for filming the deep freedive. I was sitting on a bench on the *Omega*'s deck, trying hard to stay calm amid the semi-controlled chaos around me. Christophe had rigged a curtain around the bench, so I'd have a little bit of privacy during my pre-dive preparations. The dive was scheduled to commence in a few minutes.

Liam, Doc, and Alec were standing next to their dive gear and their video equipment compulsively checking and double-checking everything. The safety divers stood next to them, chatting quietly, and appearing relaxed and at ease. Vincent was filming the commotion on deck, and Maddy was fluttering around him trying to make sure he caught everything of interest.

Gus and Christophe were next to the winch that raised and lowered the weighted line I would follow during the dive. The large bottom weight had several tags loosely attached to it. I was supposed to grab one when I reached one hundred meters and bring it to the surface with me as proof that I'd made the dive to the correct depth.

I was trying hard to stay calm and ignore the activity, but I had to admit I was nervous. I tilted my head back and closed my eyes, breathing deeply and trying to immerse myself in meditation, the way Christophe had showed me. The hot sun felt scorching on my shoulders. My heart rate slowed as I sought the calm center of my being, but I jumped a mile when I felt a hand touch my arm.

I opened one eye. "Alec. Go away and leave me alone."

He smiled his most angelic smile, so I knew he was up to something. He held one of RIO's stainless-steel insulated mugs in his hand. "I brought you some water. Nobody else seems to be looking out for you, and it's so hot I thought you might want something to drink before you dive."

He held the mug out to me, and suddenly, he was right. I was hot and thirsty. The mug looked so inviting, slightly frosty with condensation. "Thank you," I said, reaching for the cool drink. But I wasn't dumb enough to accept anything from him without checking it out first.

I popped the plastic cover off the mug and looked inside. Nothing but water and ice cubes. I drained the fluid, then handed him back the mug. "Thanks."

"Good luck on the dive." He smiled and walked away.

I went back to meditating, feeling even more relaxed now that I'd had something to drink.

A few minutes later, I heard the winch creak into action as it lowered the weight. Then came two splashes when Liam and his buddy did their entries. Another pair of splashes meant Doc and her buddy were in. Alec would be going in within another minute or so.

I was breathing deeply, trying to saturate my body with oxygen, when Christophe came to fetch me for the dive. He offered a hand to help me up. "You're going to kill it," he whispered in my ear before leading me to the *Omega*'s stern.

I stepped down onto the dive platform and lost my balance for a second. Christophe grabbed my elbow. "You okay?"

"Never better," I said. "Let's do this."

We slid into the water, then Christophe ducked under to make sure the monofin was positioned correctly. While he was doing that, I looked up at the *Omega*. Stewie was watching me. I waved and smiled. He waved back, but he wasn't smiling. In fact, he looked concerned.

Of course he was concerned. Ray had been one of his closest friends, and Stewie had been partially to blame for Ray diving without a safety crew following him. I knew the guilt had practically destroyed him back then.

Christophe popped up, finished with my monofin. "Ready when you are. Take your time."

"Okey Dokey," I said with a big smile.

A frown crossed Christophe's handsome face. What a spoilsport.

I sucked in a breath, jackknifed from the waist, and headed down. My dolphin kick felt a little harder to execute today than it usually did, but I put that down to nerves. I smiled and waved at Alec who was filming me. He and his safety diver followed me down. At the one hundred foot mark, Alec pulled up and hovered to wait for my return. I smiled again and waved goodbye.

His safety diver reached out to take my arm, but I pulled away and swam down between Doc and her safety diver. I love Doc so much. I stopped swimming for a minute to give her a hug.

That's the last thing I remember until I woke up in the infirmary back at RIO. Doc was standing next to my bed, checking my blood pressure. Liam was across the room in the chair. He looked like he hadn't slept in days.

"What's going on?" I said. Even to me, my voice sounded fuzzy.

"You were roofied," Doc said. "You blacked out during the dive. Luckily, I was right next to you when it happened, and I towed you to the surface."

"How did I get roofied?" I asked.

"An excellent question," she said. "I checked, and I didn't find any needle marks, so you must have ingested it. But we all ate and drank the same things, and no one else was affected. I tested everything on the buffet and didn't find any traces of drugs."

"I'm confused. How else could this have happened? And how long have I been out of it?"

"You've been asleep for about eighteen hours," she said as she touched my hand. "I know you were nervous about the dive, and you've been under a lot of stress lately. You can tell me if you took something to help you calm down."

"You know me better than that. I'd never take drugs. And the only thing I had was a cup of water a few minutes before the dive started. The sun was so hot that Alec brought it to me...Oh."

"Oh, indeed," said Doc. "I think we've found our answer."

Liam stood up. "I'm going to kill that man. You might have died." He strode out of the infirmary, clearly on the hunt for Alec. I was too tired to try to stop him.

"Now that we know what happened, if you're up to it, let's get the team in here to decide what to do next," Doc said. "After I call Dane Scott and report this, of course."

Ninety minutes later, the documentary team had started gathering around my bed in the infirmary. Newton and Dane were huddled together in the far corner, quietly conferring about how to prove Alec had knowingly given me the drugs. Doc was checking my patient monitor and making notes in a chart. Maddy was sitting beside me, holding my hand.

Christophe rushed in and took my other hand. "Mon Dieu, you could have died. It would have been all my fault. I knew there was something wrong when you stumbled. I should have called off the dive."

"It's not your fault, Christophe. I should have known better than to eat or drink anything Alec offered me. I know what a weasel he is."

Liam walked back in. "You've got that right." The collar of his RIO polo shirt had been partially torn off, and the knuckles on his hands were red and swollen.

Christophe moved aside, and Liam sat on the bed, wincing when my hand closed over his.

Dane piped up, "Roland and Morey are looking for Alec. They have a warrant for his arrest. Attempted murder. They'll find him."

"Shouldn't be hard to track him down. I just dropped him off at urgent care," Liam said.

Dane and Newton both pretended not to understand the implications of Liam's words coupled with his appearance. Dane quickly sent a text—I assumed to let Roland know where Alec was.

"Did anyone see Alec hand you the drink?" Newton asked.

I shook my head. "I don't think so. I was behind a curtain, remember?"

"What happened to the mug?" Dane said.

I shrugged. "I don't know. I handed it back to Alec after I drained it."

Dane's fingers flew as he sent another urgent text to Roland. If he was telling him to pick up the mug, I could have saved him the trouble. Vincent's crew would have cleaned everything up as soon as we'd departed. By now, the mug had been washed and put away with the dozens of others just like it.

"Obviously," Maddy said, "we'll have to cancel the documentary again this year. I knew it was too dangerous to let you freedive, and now you're in no condition…"

I held up a hand to stop her talking. "Doc, how long until I'm fit to dive again?"

She bit her lip, clearly at war with herself. She cared about me and wanted to keep me safe, but she couldn't tell a lie, especially about a patient's condition. "Couple of days," she finally said. "But I don't recommend it."

I nodded. "I understand. But I'm still gonna do it."

Chapter 37
A New Team Member

As Liam had predicted, Roland and Morey had no trouble finding Alec. He'd been just leaving urgent care when they arrested him for attempted murder. Unfortunately, he was set free when his lawyer argued that there were no witnesses to attest that he'd given me the tainted water.

And there was no mug with his fingerprints on it because as I'd predicted, the *Omega*'s highly efficient crew had quickly cleaned up her deck after I was taken to the infirmary. They'd had no way of knowing there'd been foul play involved in my accident, so they'd followed their usual procedure to ensure the boat was shipshape.

Newton, Dane, Liam, and Oliver were not happy that my rabid weasel of an ex had seemingly gotten away with attempted murder, but I was more sanguine. Living with Lily for the past few years had screwed Alec up even more than he'd been while he and I were married. I knew it was only a matter of time before he was caught in a jam that he couldn't worm his way out of, and in the meantime, I'd be sure to steer clear of him.

But I wasn't forgiving or stupid enough to let him continue to work on the documentary with me. I asked Newton to send him legal notice that RIO was severing his employment contract. I breathed a sigh of relief when the notice had been served.

We rescheduled the dive. Maddy and Christophe had both volunteered to get one of their friends to replace Alec, but I wanted someone I had a personal connection to. I knew I'd feel a lot safer when I did the dive if I was certain I could rely on at least one of the divers in each buddy pair.

I picked up the phone and called Benjamin Brooks. I'd be safe with Benjamin on the team. We weren't together anymore, but I knew he'd never let anyone or anything, hurt me.

There was a moment of stunned silence when I invited him to join the crew.

"I'd be honored," he said at last. "I'll do everything in my power to keep you safe, and I'll do a good job with the videography too. Thank you for asking me."

I thanked him for accepting and gave him the details about the dive date and the practice times.

I breathed a sigh of relief when we hung up. I felt better about the dive than I had since Christophe had insisted on including Alec.

Chapter 38
Filming

THE MORNING of the second attempt at filming, the *Omega* was anchored near Training Spot Two, floating over the deepest part. Once again, I was seated on a bench on the deck, but this time there was no privacy curtain shielding me from view. Nobody, least of all me, wanted to take a chance with my safety.

Vincent Pollilo, *Omega*'s captain, was filming the hustle and bustle on the ship's deck as everybody finished their final dive prep. The entire dive team, including Benjamin, plus Doc's most trusted EMTs, were aboard. The portable recompression chamber on *Omega* was fired up and ready in case I needed it.

We'd learned our lessons well. Between Ray's fateful dive and my own near miss, we were taking no chances. This time, the dive was as safe as we could possibly make it.

I was wearing a sweatshirt over a lightweight silver colored dive skin with a hood. Of course, the RIO logo adorned the dive skin and the sweatshirt because this dive was being filmed for the documentary. Everybody who would be in the water today was wearing a similar skin. Our names were emblazoned in a variety of bright fluorescent colors on the right leg of our dive skins so we could easily identify each other during the dive and so our viewers could do the same while watching the film.

Because his heart condition precluded diving, Gus had been assigned to guard the winch that governed the depth of the dive to ensure nobody tampered with it. He and Christophe made a final check that the guide rope and weight had been deployed to the correct depth. They exchanged a few words. I was too far away to hear what they said, but the big smiles on their faces were reassuring.

Christophe caught my eye and signaled it was time to begin final preparations. I nodded and went to a corner away from the other divers to breathe deeply and relax. It was important not to get tense because that would increase my need for oxygen, potentially preventing me from completing the dive.

Christophe joined the divers on the platform, clapping everybody on the shoulder or shaking their hands. When he'd finished greeting everyone and offering words of confidence and encouragement, he lined up the buddy pairs in the order they would make their entries.

Since they had the farthest to go to get into position, Liam and his buddy stepped off the dive platform first. Christophe used his stop-watch to mark the time until it was Doc's turn for her and her buddy to make their entries. In another minute or so, Benjamin and his buddy started their dive. Then Maddy, Stewie, and the rest of the surface team got in the water and formed a rough circle around the guide rope float.

Christophe walked over to the quiet corner where I was sitting. "Ready?" he asked. He held out a hand to help me to my feet and we walked to the edge of the platform together. We both stepped off the edge. I pulled my low-volume goggles over my eyes and positioned the nose plug. Then I floated on my back, breathing deeply through my mouth while Christophe checked the monofin's position. "We're ready when you are," he said softly.

I took one more deep breath, then jackknifed from the hips. I held my arms over my head with my hands together and began to dolphin kick my way down as strongly as I could. I put my tongue against the roof of my mouth to prevent the sea water from entering my lungs, but let the water flood my ear canals and sinuses. I was using the mouth fill equalization method to prevent ear pressure problems, so there'd be no delay or slowdown to equalize. I was so focused on my objective that I was barely aware of the divers following me as I made my descent. I didn't notice when Benjamin and his buddy stayed behind, or when Doc's team took over traveling with me.

I was moving fast, and by now the pressure from the ocean itself was helping to propel me down, even with minimal effort. I kept doing the dolphin kick, but I didn't need to put as much muscle behind it now to maintain my speed.

In the blink of an eye, Liam took Doc's place and filmed the rest of my descent. As I neared the weight, I had to maneuver a little bit to be able to reach the tag, but still I grabbed it without delay. I turned back to the surface and tucked it into my hood for safekeeping as I swam.

At this depth, I had to work very hard to escape the ocean's pull. I put every bit of strength I had into my dolphin kick. Christophe's training had really paid off, and I felt strong and in control. Liam and his buddy were right alongside me. Liam was filming.

Then Liam stopped swimming, and Doc and her buddy took over. I knew that meant I was at 200 feet. I'd covered two thirds of the dive's distance, but the remainder of the dive would grow increasingly tough as my muscles tired, and my body began to run short on oxygen. Even so, I redoubled my efforts.

Now Benjamin was beside me with his camera, keeping pace with me as I swam for all I was worth. It felt like an eon passed before Stewie and his buddy joined the group surrounding me, although I'd only traveled about thirty feet since Benjamin had taken over filming.

And now Maddy swam facing me, dolphin kicking to remind me of what I was supposed to be doing in case the narcosis had caused me to forget.

I let a tiny stream of bubbles escape from my mouth to prevent any lung problems and smiled as I kicked up the last few feet. I was going to make it this time. My head broke the surface. Before I reached into my hood and extracted the tag I'd retrieved, I took a few seconds to gulp in precious, sweet air. "I am okay," I said, as required by the dive protocol. Then I smiled at Vincent behind the camera and let Stewie stick a regulator attached to pure oxygen into my mouth. He took my hand and led me down to fifteen feet for decompression and recovery.

Stewie and I hovered there a little longer than the minimum recommendation because he wanted to be sure I was all right. I grinned at him around the regulator mouthpiece. He grinned back and gave me a high five. We'd done it.

Chapter 39
Wrap Party

I WAS ELATED that the filming for the documentary was finally over, and that it had gone off without a hitch. Of course, we were feeling melancholy because the deep dive reminded us of Ray's death, and we were anxious and afraid with Joely , Genevra, and Diana still missing. We weren't really in a mood to celebrate our achievement.

But everyone on the team had worked hard, and they deserved a reward for that. I'd known that depending on how my dive had gone, we'd either be celebrating, or we'd be distraught and possibly grief stricken. Whichever it turned out to be, I wanted the entire team to be able to let their hair down in the open bar extravaganza we'd traditionally held after the documentary filming wrapped. I'd asked Theresa to close Ray's Place to the public this evening so we could have the wrap party there.

Vincent had given the *Omega*'s crew time off to join us at Ray's Place, so in addition to all the land-based RIO staff, Christophe's team of support divers, and everybody's significant others, the bar was crowded. Every seat was taken, and although I'd known and worked with many of the people here for years, some of the faces were unfamiliar.

After we'd come back from the dive, I'd gone to the locker room to shower and take a moment alone. When I came out, Liam was on the bench waiting for me.

"Sit a minute," he said. "Take a breath. You were amazing today, and you deserve a chance to savor it."

I dropped down to the bench beside him and exhaled forcefully, making my bangs fly straight up. "It just feels so wrong to be celebrating when we don't know where Joely, Genevra, and Diana are, or what's happening to them, or…"

He took my hand. "I know. I feel the same way. I don't know what I'd do if I ever lost you. I'd move heaven and earth to find you and bring you back. But I know you'll find them and bring them home soon. I have faith in you."

I tried to smile, but I knew my effort fell short. I squeezed his hand to let him know I was doing my best. With heavy hearts, we got up to join the celebration at Ray's Place. "C'mon. We have a job to do."

Because it was a job. We were all acting, trying to project the same sense of a job well done that we'd always shown in the past.

We stopped by the bar to pick up some drinks, then Liam and I split up to mingle with the people who had worked so hard on the planning and filming. Even though we weren't open to the public today, Roland was sitting on his usual stool at the bar, pretending to drink himself into a stupor while actually keeping a sharp eye on everything around him.

I was standing at the far end of the restaurant chatting with a few of RIO's researchers who were asking me about the training I'd undergone to be able to freedive like that. I started to tell them about Christophe's regimen when I became aware of the creepy feeling you get when someone is staring at you.

Casually looking over the shoulder of the older of the two female scientists, I saw the blonde woman who'd been staring at me several times before, sitting on her accustomed stool, two down from Roland. She had a fruity-looking drink in front of her, and she'd tucked its paper parasol behind her ear. As usual, she was watching every move I made.

I thought I knew every RIO employee, by sight if not by name, so I was puzzled that I couldn't place her. But I was sure I knew her. When

I'd mentally run through all the departments and all the employees I knew, I still couldn't identify her.

Interrupting a spirited discussion about the causes and effects of coral bleaching, I said, "Who is that woman sitting at the bar?"

Instead of acting casual, all three scientists immediately turned to see who I meant, but when I followed their gazes, the woman was no longer there. She must have left while I'd been lost in thought trying to figure out who she was.

"I don't see anyone," said one researcher.

"Me either," said her assistant.

"Nobody there," said the third.

"Sorry. I must be imagining things," I said. I smiled brightly and tried to reignite the conversation, but all the while my mind was trying to solve the puzzle of the mysterious woman.

And more importantly, how to rescue the three women who'd been taken. I pretended to be enjoying myself at the party, but I was just going through the motions the entire evening. My mind was wholly focused on finding a way to board the *Golden Kelp*.

Chapter 40
A Trip to the Golden Kelp

I CALLED a meeting early the next day. Maddy, Newton, Dane, Oliver, Roland, and Liam sat around the table in RIO's big conference room. Although none of us knew exactly how he was doing it, we all thought Seb and his henchmen were behind the abductions. I announced that I intended to find a way to board the *Golden Kelp* and search for the missing women, and I wanted this group to help me find a way to do it.

"I know I agreed before not to go aboard the *Golden Kelp*, but we're not getting anywhere with this investigation. Genevra, Joely, and Diana have been gone too long. They could have been moved out of the area already, beyond our reach. They could be hurt or bearing unspeakable abuse. We can't wait any longer. Unless one of you has a better idea, I'm going."

When I finished speaking, everyone in the room was silent for a moment while they tried to think of another solution. There wasn't one. At least, not a good one.

Newton stood up. "We can't let you do this alone. If you're determined to board the *Golden Kelp*, I'll go with you."

I gaped at him. My father is handsome, brilliant, and rich, but he's no action hero. "Newton, you'll only make things worse. I'd be worried about you the whole time, and if I'm distracted—well, that could be dangerous for both of us."

"Nonetheless, I'm going, even if I have to rent a boat and follow you on my own."

I was surprised when Dane spoke up in favor of Newton accompanying me. "It's a good idea. You can't take Liam with you after what Seb did to him the last time, and you can't take someone from the police, or they'll never let you board. But you definitely can't go alone, and Newton is smart, observant, and a good negotiator if you find yourself needing to strike a deal with Lukin. In my opinion, Newton will be a big help to you. And taking him with you is the only way I'm letting you do this."

I was about to refuse, when I remembered what Liam had said when he'd arrived at my house after Seb Lukin had tried to kill him. Liam had been severely injured and could barely speak. I'd told him I was going to call the police, but before letting me call Dane for help, he'd said "First Newton. Safe house." It had puzzled me at the time, but now I was starting to wonder.

Since then, I'd figured out Liam was more than simply a good businessman and a tech billionaire. He kept a low public profile, and people sometimes underestimated him because he seemed so easy going. But even though he wouldn't discuss it, I was sure he was involved in some sort of undercover work. I wondered if Newton was also part of whatever Liam's mysterious secret activities were.

Although Newton had a more visible public persona, was it possible there was also more to him than first met the eye? He was my father, but I had only known him for a few years. Maybe, just maybe, he was into something secret too. I decided to go for it. "Okay. Newton can come with me. But nobody else. And I'm in charge."

I was surprised they didn't argue about me leading the initiative. Their frozen faces and averted eyes said they didn't want to put up a bunch of objections that might possibly provoke me into doing something rash. After a moment of silence, everybody nodded.

"It won't take me long to gear up the *Tranquility*, and I need detailed coordinates of the *Golden Kelp*'s location by the time we're ready to get underway. I don't want the coast guard helicopter nearby while we're approaching his ship. It'll spook Seb, and he's dangerous enough without aggravating him."

Dane whipped out his phone. "I'll handle that."

Maddy said, "I'm going to ask Vincent to bring the *Omega* near enough to the *Golden Kelp* to help out in an emergency. I promise they won't approach unless it looks like things are going south." The *Omega*, RIO's primary research vessel, is a 220-foot long, well equipped ship with a large crew. Vincent Pollilo had been with RIO for years, and he and Maddy were close friends.

I was stunned. Somehow, everybody had agreed to the plan. "C'mon, Newton. Let's get to the boat," I said. "There's no time to delay."

"I'll meet you there in a few minutes. I have something I need to take care of first." Newton's voice was casual, and he gazed back at me innocently while I glared at him for causing a delay in our departure.

Half an hour later, I was impatiently pacing on *Tranquility*'s deck when Newton finally arrived. I'd been just about to leave without him.

"Sorry. Took a little longer than I intended." Newton was now wearing long baggy pants, an equally baggy long-sleeved Hawaiian shirt, and a plain gray hoody. He carried a bulky black canvas duffel bag slung over his shoulder. The garments and the bag were unlike anything I'd ever seen him wear. In fact, I was pretty sure the clothes belonged to Stewie. They were way too big around the middle for Newton.

"I see you took the time to change your outfit while I was waiting." There was ice in my voice when I said it. I wanted to get going fast. Who knew what might have happened to Genevra, Diana, and Joely while Newton attended to his attire.

"Yep," he said cheerfully, ignoring my ire. "It can get cold out there on the water."

Other than a nasty glare, I didn't respond. I just climbed the ladder to the flying bridge and started the engines. "Can you get the mooring line please?" I called down to him when it seemed he was just going to sit there on the gunwale.

"Aye, aye, Captain." He stood and started to unwrap the line from the cleat on the boat neatly coiling it the way he'd seen us do.

I was just about to back out when Dane came racing down the pier waving a page of lined paper that looked like it had been torn out of the small notebook he always carried in his pocket. "Wait, wait. I have the complete coordinates of the *Golden Kelp*'s location."

I slipped the engines into idle while Newton held the boat at the dock by gripping the rope coiled near the cleat. He reached up with one hand, grabbed the slip of paper from Dane, and then dropped the line. He waved his arm in the air, letting me know it was okay to back out of my slip now.

By the time the boat was facing open sea, Newton had climbed the ladder. He handed me the tattered piece of paper, and I quickly entered the coordinates into the GPS system, which showed it would take us a little over two hours at top speed to reach our destination. We took off.

Because of our speed, the wind was fierce up on the flying bridge. Newton watched me pilot the boat for a while, then he went down the ladder. Newton isn't usually a good sailor, but I didn't see him hanging over the side, which was a nice change. I crossed my fingers hoping that he wasn't seasick and just wanted to get out of the wind.

It wasn't long before I could pick out the mega-yacht on the horizon. I kept going, until we were no more than a few minutes travel time away from the *Golden Kelp*. I shut off the engines and went down to talk to Newton.

I was surprised to find him standing in front of the daybed, the now empty canvas bag lying crumpled at his feet. A selection of guns and other weapons had been arrayed across the Caribbean blue bedspread, and Newton stood, hands in his pockets, assessing this armory.

I put my hands on my hips and sighed. "What are you doing with all this stuff? You know you won't be able to take weapons aboard the *Golden Kelp*. Seb will have us both searched before he lets us off the landing platform," I said.

"Yep," said Newton. "He might, but he needs to know we mean business." He handed me what looked like a typical wrist-worn dive computer. "Please wear this. You can communicate with me anytime by pushing this button on the side. It's secure—nobody can listen in. And this button's a rescue beacon. Push it, and I'll find you wherever you are."

"Okay," I said. I strapped the device to my wrist in place of the one I usually wore.

Next, he handed me a small revolver and a pocket holster. The gun was similar to one I'd used before, but I didn't want to carry it.

I handed it back. "No thank you. I won't need it."

He handed it back to me again. "Better to have it and not need it than to need it and not have it. Just carry it. For me, please."

I sighed and slid the holster into the capacious pocket of my cargo shorts. I watched as Newton put a similar gun in his own pocket, and then a larger, more lethal looking pistol into his waistband. He fluffed up his voluminous shirt so you couldn't easily see the outline of the gun, but I didn't think something as simple as a hoody and a baggy shirt would fool Seb for long. "Where did you get all this? And do you even know how to use a gun?"

He looked slightly affronted, then he laughed. "Yes, I do know how to use a gun. And as I've told you before, I know people who can help me out when I need certain kinds of equipment. Like when I got that optical transceiver we used last year, remember?"

I did remember. And I also remembered how thoroughly Seb's team had searched me l when I'd had to smuggle the tiny transceiver aboard his boat. "We'll never get away with this."

"Maybe not. Can't hurt to try." He smiled. "Ready? Let's go."

Chapter 41

Boarding

I WAS JUST ABOUT to start the engines again when the radio pinged with a call from Vincent on the *Omega*. "We'll be in the designated area in less than ten minutes. I'll stay back to avoid spooking the crew of the *Golden Kelp*. Unless you need anything from us right now?"

"We're good to go. But thanks for the support," I replied.

"No problem," he said. "You sure you don't want me to send over a team?"

I smiled at his bravery and concern for me. Vincent and his crew were sailors and oceanographers, not warriors. I would never lead them into potential harm. "No thanks, Vincent. Just relax. Newton or I will holler if we need you."

"Got it," he said. "Good luck."

I started the *Tranquility*'s engines, and we putted slowly toward the massive ship ahead of us. I put the engine in idle a few feet from the mooring platform. Seb had given me his private number last time I'd been aboard this ship. Before I could complete the call asking for permission to board, two crew members came down the steps that ran along the boat's side and waved me in.

We moved forward slowly, and I stopped when we were alongside the platform, which was long enough to handle two or three additional boats the size of the *Tranquility*. Newton threw the crew members a line, and they fastened the *Tranquility* to the platform. I shut down the engines and joined Newton on the deck.

One crew member held out a hand to assist me in boarding the *Golden Kelp*. "Welcome back, Dr. Fleming," he said.

I smiled at him. "Thanks for the hand. And please call me Fin."

The other crew member offered Newton a hand, but my father hopped nimbly off the boat without assistance. "And you can call me Newton," he said.

The crew member nodded. "This way, please. Mr. Lukin is waiting for you."

They led us to the open air staircase that ran along the outside of the ship. Just as we had the first time I'd been aboard, we climbed all the way up to the pool deck. The massive swimming pool glittered in the sun, and more than a dozen chaises dotted the surrounding tile surface. Several café tables stood near the entrance to the ship's interior under huge umbrellas tilted to provide shade from the hot sun. Nobody was swimming in the pool or sitting anywhere on the deck.

"Please have a seat," said the taller of the two crew members. "Would either of you like something to drink?"

"Bottled water for both of us," I said. "And we'd like to open the bottles ourselves."

"Of course." He went to the refrigerator and brought us our waters and two crystal tumblers on a silver tray. He placed an ice bucket and a small bowl of lemon and lime wedges on the table. When he had arranged everything to his satisfaction, he asked, "Will there be anything else?"

Newton smiled at him. "Thank you, but no. This is perfect."

He nodded. "You're welcome. Mr. Lukin will be with you in a minute."

But it was a lot longer than a minute before Seb Lukin hurried out of the boat's interior. Newton and I stood to greet him.

Seb put his hands on my shoulders and planted an air kiss near each cheek. "So good to see you again, my dear." Then he turned to Newton and held out his hand for a shake. "The legendary Newton Fleming. Nice to finally meet you."

Newton shook hands but didn't offer any return compliments about meeting Seb.

Seb watched Newton's face, and after a few seconds, he burst into laughter. "So, it's going to be like that, is it?"

Then he turned back to me. "How did you like your little gift?" he asked.

"The sub?" I said. "I love it, but it was a very extravagant gift. I shouldn't have accepted it, but you didn't leave me much choice. Are you sure you don't want it back?"

Seb moved his dark glasses to the top of his head. "No thank you. It's yours to keep. I have a new one. Bigger. Better. The latest model. All the bells and whistles. You actually saved me the trouble of disposing of the old one, so I thank you for that. Now, what can I do for you two today? As pleased as I am to see you, I'm a busy man." He smiled, but his snakelike eyes were cold and empty.

Newton's face was as guileless as a newborn baby's. "I'm thinking of buying a mega-yacht of my own. Fin's told me so much about this one that I wanted to see it for myself. Maybe pick up a few ideas."

Seb narrowed his eyes. His voice was like ice. "I don't believe you. Why are you really here?"

I stepped forward. "Some of our friends have disappeared. We think they might be aboard the *Golden Kelp*. Do you mind if we search the yacht?"

He sighed in exasperation and looked away for a moment. "I have nothing to hide," he said at last. "The entire yacht is open for your inspection. Would you like a guide to accompany you, or do you prefer to wander on your own?"

Newton said, "We'd prefer to be on our own, if that's okay with you."

Seb slid the dark glasses back over his eyes and tilted his head toward Newton. "Of course. I just said it was okay, didn't I? I must warn you though, the *Golden Kelp* has many rooms and many passages. You might find a guide helpful. If you get lost, just ask anyone you meet to help you." He stepped back and waved his arm toward the entrance to the yacht's interior regions.

"Aren't you going to search us?" Newton said.

Seb shook his head. "Why would I search you? We're all friends here, aren't we?"

A cold chill ran down my back.

Chapter 42
Searching

NEWTON and I stepped through the electric sliding doors that led from the pool deck to the interior of the *Golden Kelp*. We stopped as soon as the doors shut behind us. "We need a plan. This ship is massive, and we'll need hours to cover it. I think we should split up," I said.

Newton shook his head. "I'm not leaving you alone. Who knows what he has planned."

I fumed for a minute, then came up with an idea. "If we stay together, I'm worried he'll bring the captives back to a location we've already searched, and we'd never know it. There are multiple stairways, one starboard, one port. And a centrally located elevator, so it would be easy to bypass us. But what if we work it this way?"

"We start at the bridge, and when we finish, we call the elevator but don't get in. The crew people always use the stairs, so the elevator should stay at the bridge until we call it again. Then we search from top to bottom. You take one stairway; I'll take the other. We clear each room from the hull in toward the elevator, and whoever finishes first waits until the other one of us has cleared the area. We check to be sure the elevator hasn't moved. Then it's just a matter of inspecting all the levels."

Newton nodded. "I like the way you think. You have a great tactical sense. Let's go."

I pushed the button to call the elevator, and we rode in silence to the highest level. The doors opened with a loud ding and revealed the *Golden Kelp*'s transparent high-tech bridge. The glass walls offered a breathtaking 360-degree view of the surroundings. I turned around slowly and was reassured to see the *Omega* placidly riding the waves not too far away. The *Golden Kelp*'s captain watched us but didn't say anything. I assumed that meant Seb had told him to expect us.

There wasn't much to see here, but I did open a built-in chest that snugged up against the bridge. It was too small to hide the missing women, but I thought it might have led to a hidden room or stairway. The chest was full of spare fuses and bulbs, a few paperback books, and a massive flashlight. I felt around for a concealed latch, pressing against the container's walls, but I didn't find anything. "Clear."

He nodded. "Let's go then."

We split up, descending separately by one of the stairways at each side of the ship. I popped out of the door at the next level down at the exact same time that Newton pushed his door open. We nodded at each other and commenced our search.

I counted twenty doors between me and the elevator. Most of them led to sumptuous suites, each one elegant enough to house the Princess of Wales. The suites opened into a library/den/sitting room with a big screen television and seating for ten. A discreet door to one side of the library area opened into a large half-bath. Beyond the sitting areas was the sleeping room, or in some cases, sleeping rooms. Each bedroom had at least two walk-in closets, and sometimes more, along with a mirrored dressing room, and an ensuite bathroom, with a spa shower and a soaking tub. All the finishes and fixtures were high end. I peered at the shelves in all the closets looking for latches that might lead to hidden rooms, but I didn't find any.

Midway down the corridor, between two guest suites, there was a vast supply closet filled with extra linens and glassware as well as cleaning supplies, spare remotes for the televisions, high end toiletries, and a large selection of the latest books and magazines. Anything a guest might want could be fulfilled quickly and easily from the contents of the supply closet.

When I finished, I waited for Newton near the elevator until Newton completed searching his section.

Within a few minutes, he joined me. I pushed the call button for the elevator. The location display showed it coming from the bridge level, so I felt confident it hadn't moved while we'd been searching.

I rode the elevator down one floor. As soon as I exited, I spoke into my watch the way Newton had showed me. "Ready. Come on down."

A few seconds later I heard the door at the end of the hall pop open and Newton appeared. We began our search of this level.

Most of the rooms on this deck were devoted to business. There were conference rooms, both large and small, each with a mahogany, cherry, or teak table and comfortable chairs. Between every two conference rooms was a kitchen area, with a well-stocked refrigerator full of fruit, yogurt, and soft drinks. Espresso machines and coffee makers lived on the long granite counters. The cabinets held plates, mugs, and serving platters, while the drawers held silverware and napkins. There were no meetings occurring in any of the conference rooms.

Directly across from the elevator was what might have passed for an internet café had it been on land. About twenty high-end computers with large monitors sat in individual workstations. No one was in the room.

Newton and I met up at the central elevators again. This time he rode down the elevator while I took the stairs. We repeated the process through all twelve levels of the ship. I marveled at the detailed crafts-manship and the fine finishes that proved no expense had been spared when outfitting the mega-yacht. Unfortunately, we'd been searching it for hours, and we'd seen no sign that the missing women were on board or that they had ever been here.

Newton and I entered the lowest level at the same time. The only thing on this level was the airlocked room used for docking and launching the sub. I stepped inside and felt the pressure in my ears increase. I discreetly equalized the pressure using the Valsalva maneuver and reminded Newton to do the same.

Seb hadn't lied when he said he had a new sub, and it was a beauty. It hung overhead from one of the two hoists used to raise subs and move them away from the opening in the floor they used for entry and egress. The hoists could also be used to move a sub nearer to the work-bench for maintenance or to the charging stations between trips. The controls for the hoists hung from the ceiling, near a huge panel covered with dials and gauges.

This new sub was even larger and more kitted out than the one I now owned. It was painted in shades of purples and lilacs, with the *Golden Kelp* logo on its body. It held seating for nine inside its clear domed viewing area and the interior was set up with two long tables and plush chairs, almost like a conference or banquet room. Until I heard someone calling my name, I didn't stop admiring this amazing machine.

I looked over to the control area and recognized Davy Jones, Seb's submarine pilot. "Hi, Davy. How do you like this new sub? It looks amazing."

Davy smiled at me. "It is. It's a blast to pilot."

Newton walked over to introduce himself. "Hi, Davy. I'm Newton Fleming." He held out his hand.

Davy shook hands. "I know who you are, sir. I'm a big fan."

Newton burst out laughing. "Usually when we meet people, they're Fin's fans. Not sure what I've ever done that qualified me to have fans of my own, but I thank you none the less."

Davy blushed. "It's your environmental work that I respect. Very admirable, Sir."

"You can call me Newton." Newton looked at the control panel behind Davy. "What's all this?"

"Charging and system monitoring. Homing beacon monitor. Just a lot of technical stuff." Davy waved his hand at the complex board covered with dials and electronic readouts.

Newton turned back to me. "Shouldn't we have a similar set-up at RIO?" he said.

I rolled my eyes. "Focus, Newton. Focus. We're on a mission." I looked at Davy. "Several women we know have gone missing. We thought they might be on the yacht, but we searched and haven't found them. Do you have any idea where they might be?"

"No idea," Davy replied, looking at the floor and not meeting my eyes.

Newton covered the few feet between him and the control panel. He reached into his pocket to hand something to Davy. No sooner had

Davy tucked away whatever Newton had given him than the elevator's airlock doors opened with a hiss.

Seb entered the area, smiling pleasantly. "Find anything?" he asked.

"Not a thing," I said, "except a reminder of how stunning the *Golden Kelp* is. Thank you for letting us search. I realize it was an imposition."

"Yes, it was. But I allowed it because of my esteem for you, Dr. Fleming." He nodded his head slightly toward Newton. "And you too, Newton, of course. But Fin, I actually hoped seeing the *Golden Kelp* again might change your mind about coming to work for me. There's always a place in my organization for you."

I tried to make my grimace look like a smile. "Thank you, Seb. That's very flattering. But I'm happy where I am for now."

"For now," he repeated ominously.

Chapter 43
An Alternative Idea

NEWTON and I went outside to the docking platform and boarded the *Tranquility*. The two crew members who'd helped us dock were still on duty, and they assisted us in casting off. Once we were far enough away from the *Golden Kelp* that my wake wouldn't have washed over the platform, potentially wetting their feet, I revved the engines up to full throttle.

Newton got on the radio to let the *Omega* know we were off the *Golden Kelp* and on our way back to RIO, having found no trace of the missing women. Then he radioed RIO to let them know the same thing. Stewie was monitoring the marina's communications. I heard Maddy in the background saying, "Thank God," when Stewie announced we were safely on the way back, but I wondered whether it was Dane or Oliver whose fist pounded the wall when Newton went on to tell them we hadn't found Genevra, Diana, and Joely.

A couple of hours later, we were gliding into my slip at RIO. Newton tossed a line to Oliver, who wrapped it around the cleat and coiled the excess. We hopped from the *Tranquility*'s gunwales to the dock where the group was waiting for further news.

We commandeered an empty picnic table on the lawn and told them how we had searched every inch of the *Golden Kelp* without seeing anything suspicious.

Dane rubbed his face. "We must be missing something. Either that or we're completely off base about how they're pulling off the abductions." Between Maddy's health issues and his worry and frustration about the missing women, he was obviously worn out.

My mind raced as I tried to connect all the clues. There was a missing piece to this puzzle. I stood up and walked across the lawn along the ocean's edge. I stopped, staring out to sea. I retraced each crime the way I imagined it had happened. Each time, it ended with the unconscious victim being loaded into a sub.

But a personal sub—even Seb's new model—didn't have the necessary range to bring them all the way to the *Golden Kelp*. Besides, after today, we knew they weren't being held on his opulent mega-yacht. Where could they be, and how had they been transported?

A large sloop skimmed gracefully over the waves, far out to sea. It looked to be brand new, and I estimated it at about 120 feet long. And then it hit me.

The sub didn't have to transport the victims all the way to the *Golden Kelp*. It only had to meet up with a boat anchored somewhere just outside of territorial waters, but still within the sub's range, which was about thirty-six miles. If a boat was just outside the twelve mile radius of territorial waters, the sub could easily transport the captives to it and still get back with power to spare.

I jogged back to the picnic table, where the group sat glumly staring at each other, out of ideas and out of energy. "Dane! Newton! We've been looking at this all wrong. Seb's too smart to keep his victims on land. It'd be too easy for us to find them. They're on a boat, but not one that's openly connected to Seb. It would have to be fairly large, and it would be staying out to sea somewhere between twelve and fifteen miles from the coast. That leaves the sub plenty of range to transport the victims, and still get back safely."

Everybody perked up and started trying to identify which of the multitude of large, expensive boats that entered and left Cayman waters every day could be the one where the women were being held.

Newton shook his head. "That can't be it. How would they recharge the sub's batteries? They'd need a control panel like the one we just saw Davy Jones tending. There's nothing like that near RIO, and I doubt that there's one near Nelson's. It's a great thought, Fin, but I don't think it's the one we're looking for."

Newton's words instantly deflated my joy. He was right. Besides which, we'd seen Seb's new sub right there aboard his yacht, so it obviously wasn't being used to haul kidnap victims from the island. My shoulders sagged. I'd been so sure.

Chapter 44
Night Diving Class

NEWTON, Dane, and I were wracking our brains and glumly watching the last rays of sunshine dancing over the water when June came out of RIO's back door. When she caught sight of me, she walked over to the table where we were sitting. "Fin, your night diving students are assembled in the classroom. What shall I tell them? Are you coming in or not?"

I let out a deep breath. With everything going on, I'd forgotten about the class. Months ago, it had been arranged directly with me by one of our key donors, an avid diver. He and his group were only on Grand Cayman for a few days, and I'd given my word that I'd personally teach the class. I couldn't back out without making him angry—maybe angry enough to stop his hefty donations, which would be another huge blow to RIO's operations.

No matter what was going on, I had to keep my promise. "Please tell them I'll be right in." I jogged along the path to RIO's back door to pick up my training materials and gear from my office.

I rushed into the classroom. "Sorry I'm late. It won't happen again, I promise." Then I jumped right into the training. "Hi. For those of you who don't know me, I'm Fin Fleming, your instructor. I assume you've all completed the required e-learning for this course, right? Can you show me your confirmations, please?"

I walked over to each of the four divers in the class and looked at the electronic confirmations showing that they'd satisfactorily completed the required classroom training. "Excellent. Thanks. And before we begin, does anyone have any questions?"

Nobody had questions, but I still did a review of how underwater hand signals changed when night diving. "Remember, shine your light at your hand, not at your buddy's face. You don't want to blind him or her."

"Now, who wants to explain the importance of having a strobe light when night diving?"

The group's leader spoke right up. "Underwater navigation at night can be very tricky, so hanging a strobe on the boat or at the exit point makes it easier to find your way back."

"Exactly. Any other reasons?"

"A strobe or a glow stick can make it easier to see and locate the other divers," he said.

We went through the more complex aspects of the training material, and then we discussed the necessary gear. It's extremely dark during a night dive, and if a light goes out for some reason, having a backup stored in a BCD pocket can be a lifesaver. "Everybody should have at least two sources of light for the dive. If anybody needs an extra light, we have some spares at the dive shop."

The group confirmed they'd come prepared with all the required gear, so we filed out the back door and continued on to the *Tranquility*. My boat is pretty famous in her own right, so everybody in the group was excited that we were using it for the dives. I helped each diver aboard, and then I showed them where to store their gear and explained the boat's safety and recall procedures.

Newton and Dane had walked down the dock to help me cast off. They uncoiled the line and tossed it to me. I wound it neatly and stored it in its assigned location. Then I scurried up the ladder and started the engines.

It was a short hop to Training Site Two, the deeper of the two sites we used for class dives. The reef starts at about sixty feet, but there's a drop off to a sheer vertical wall that descends to more than 1,000 feet. Of course, we'd be staying on the upper reef for this dive. There was plenty to see, including the occasional reef shark, although they usually stayed near the wall.

When we arrived at the site, I used a long gaff to pull the mooring ball over and made the *Tranquility* fast. I shut down the engines and dropped a strobe light over the side. While the class geared up, I drew a map of the site on a dry erase board and hung it from two hooks embedded in the cabin entry's overhang.

The students sat down to listen to the briefing. I told them what the terrain at the site was like and what they could expect to see, which included sleeping parrotfish, small octopuses, and green moray eels. I emphasized that they should follow me and stick together. We would be spending our time on the upper reef, near the boat. I made it clear that absolutely no one was to descend the wall.

I finished my lecture with, "Divers don't usually cover as much territory on a night dive as they do during daylight hours. Navigation is trickier, so we won't be going far, but there are a lot of interesting sights you'll never see on a day dive. Now, everybody show me your two lights. Make sure they both work before we get into the water."

Everybody had both a large, heavy but powerful dive light, and a smaller light that fit in a pocket or dangled from a D-ring on their BCDs. Satisfied, I went from student to student and tied a glowstick to the nozzle of their tanks so we could easily find each other in the inky depths. I tied a glow stick to a spare regulator on a long hose, then dropped it over the side, where it would drift at about twenty to thirty feet in case anybody ran out of air before finishing their safety stop. Then I hoisted the distinctive red and white "diver down" flag and lit it up with a spotlight. We were good to go.

I entered the water first. One by one, the students made their own entries. They surfaced and stayed in a circle around me. When the last diver was in the water, I gave the thumbs down signal that to a diver means descend.

I led them across the coral and shone my light on a pair of French angelfish moving slowly across the reef top. A huge Atlantic trumpet-fish nestled vertically in the growths, waiting for his fish dinner to swim past so he could pounce out and grab it. A Caribbean spiny lobster watched us from under a small coral overhang, his antennas blending perfectly with the nearby sea grass, making him nearly invisible. A Caribbean reef octopus scuttled across the sand, scooping up clams in two of his tentacles. He hurried back to his den before eating them.

We moved on to a sleeping queen parrotfish, hiding in a small crevice and wrapped in a mucus bag she'd spun to keep predators from sniffing her out while she slept. We found a very long spotted moray eel swimming along the top of the coral, looking for something to eat.

So far, the students had done a good job of sticking together and not shining their lights in each other's eyes. That lasted until one of them caught a Caribbean reef shark in the beam of his powerful flashlight. He squeaked, losing his grip on his regulator mouthpiece, and dropping his flashlight to the bottom.

I speedily swam to him and reinserted his mouthpiece, pushing the purge button to prevent him from inhaling a lungful of water. I dove down the few feet to the reef top to retrieve his flashlight, and then I signaled for all the students to gather around me. The first few students were already at the turn-around point for air consumption anyhow, so I led the way back to the mooring line where the strobe light I'd deployed was flashing. We ascended along the line and hovered at fifteen feet for our safety stop.

The diver who'd seen the shark was hyperventilating and kept making the signal for a shark—a flat hand placed on the top of the head to represent a shark's fin. His panic caused the other students to begin hyperventilating one-by-one until they were all breathing hard, especially when the flashing light of the strobe caught the shark swimming along the reef below us. I was relieved when the three minute safety stop was over without anybody getting into a major panic. I directed them to climb the ladder, while I stayed below to make sure nobody was left behind. When the last person had moved off the dive platform, it was my turn to climb aboard.

I racked my tank and removed my mask, stowing my fins under the bench. Now that the perceived danger was over, the class was absolutely thrilled to have seen the shark. They couldn't stop talking about how fearsome he was, and as they told and retold the tale, the shark morphed from a six-foot reef shark to a twenty-foot great white, making me smile while I passed out water and fruit. We talked quietly until our surface interval was over.

When it was time for our second dive, I untied the *Tranquility* from the mooring and started the engines. I planned to do the second dive on RIO's Training Site One site because it would be quick to get back home when the dive was over. I was too focused on recovering the missing women to spend unnecessary travel time, and it was close to home.

I untied the *Tranquility* from the mooring and started the engines. The site consists of a flat, mostly sandy surface. At the far edge of the site, a gently sloping wall drops down to one hundred feet, but we would not be going below fifty feet on this dive.

Once I'd moored the boat and dropped in the strobe and the spare regulator, I erased the white board and drew a new map of this site. Along with briefing them on the terrain and the possible sea life they'd find here, I repeated the instructions about hand signals and not shining lights in each other's eyes.

The diver who'd first seen the shark raised his hand. "Will the shark be at this site too?" he asked.

"I have no way of knowing. The shark doesn't keep me updated on his itinerary." I paused while they laughed, then continued. "Seriously, part of the fun of diving is never knowing what you'll see. You can dive a site hundreds of times, and it will be different every time. But most of what you see down there won't bother you if you don't bother them first, so you have nothing to worry about. Just relax and enjoy the dive." I hoisted the diver down flag, turned on a spotlight to illuminate it, and then we were good to go.

We geared up and entered the water just as we had done on the last dive. At the bottom, the group started out staying very close together, probably because they were nervous about the reef shark we'd seen earlier. But soon, everyone was enchanted by the soothing water and the vibrant colors of the coral under their lights.

The marine life here is abundant. We saw a school of longspine seeking out crabs for their dinner. One diver unexpectedly came face-to-face with a hawksbill turtle. The diver was startled, but the turtle simply ignored her and swam away.

Hundreds of small common reef fish—damselfish, butterfly fish, sergeant majors, blue chromis—were tucked away in tube sponges or crevices in the coral, rather than darting about as they normally did during the day. Nocturnal feeders like glasseye snapper, blackbar soldierfish, and adult spotted drums were out hunting.

The only shark we saw was a small nurse shark sleeping under a ridge. When the divers shone their flashlights on him, the nurse shark turned his head away, and you could almost see him thinking "Go away. Can't you see I'm trying to sleep?" We left him in peace.

It wasn't very long before the first diver hit the turnaround point on air, so I signaled to the group that it was time to return to the boat. We all swam toward the strobing beacon hanging from the *Tranquility*. After our safety stop at fifteen feet, we climbed aboard and headed back to RIO.

Normally, when we complete a dive class at RIO, we hold a party for the newly certified students. Genevra usually handled this detail, and I'd been so distracted that I'd forgotten to make the arrangements. I knew nobody on staff was in a party mood anyway, so I crossed my fingers and hoped the class wasn't familiar with our tradition. But my hope was short-lived.

The group's leader said "Where's the party? Will it be at Ray's Place or in the café like it usually is?"

Dang. He'd been with us so many times that I should have known this man would be familiar with our usual practices. "Ray's Place. I'll go make sure our table is ready while you guys rinse your gear and change." I hurried across the lawn to the restaurant.

When I rounded the corner of the bar, I saw that someone had known I'd need to throw a party for the group because Theresa had set up a large table in an out of the way corner. I almost fainted with relief when I saw the "Reserved for Fin Fleming" sign on the table. There were seats for sixteen.

"Thank you," I whispered in Maddy's ear as she passed me on the way to her seat.

"Thank Doc," she whispered back. "She did it, not me."

I didn't know who the other seats were for until I saw Newton, Gus, Liam, Stewie, Oliver, and Doc headed my way. All our celebrity divers would be in attendance, and although Newton isn't a diver, he is an internationally famous person. The guest list was stellar. I could relax.

By this time the newly certified night divers had made their way to Ray's Place and taken their seats. Theresa served several pitchers of drinks. Some contained alcohol and some didn't, and each pitcher was clearly marked. Brian followed behind Theresa with heaping plates of appetizers for the table.

None of the RIO team was in any sort of mood for partying, but we tried to put on a good front. Even so, the party ended early when after an hour, Doc rose and asked Maddy to walk her to her car. I realized they had prearranged this so that Maddy wouldn't be stuck staying out late. Newton and Stewie took that as their cue to leave as well.

Then a few minutes later, Gus rose and said, "I need to get home to relieve the babysitter." The students got the message, and they thanked me for a terrific class on their way out. Liam and I were alone at the table. Neither of us felt like talking, so I went behind the bar to pay the bill and to thank Theresa and Brian for their hard work. I left a huge tip for each of them and dragged my weary body into my office to pick up my things.

Chapter 45
Another Mega-Yacht

EARLY THE NEXT MORNING, I was working on the *Tranquility*'s deck when a magnificent mega-yacht came into view. Her graceful form glowed in the soft light from the rising sun, and her wake glittered as though she left a trail of jewels as she passed. The yacht looked new, and I estimated her to be about 200 feet long. She'd probably set her owner back a cool $50 million plus.

Instead of passing by or heading out to sea as I'd expected, the yacht anchored just beyond the mouth of RIO's cove. A few minutes later, her crew launched an eighteen foot Zodiac RIB—a rigid inflatable boat—over the side. There was only one person aboard, and he inexpertly steered the boat into RIO's marina and tried unsuccessfully to dock in one of the visitor slips. The Zodiac lurched and bashed against the dock. Undaunted, the boat's driver backed out and tried again with the same result.

After the two failed attempts, I took pity on him. I walked over to the slip he was trying to enter and said, "Toss me a line. I'll guide you in." The man's face was backlit and shaded under the broad brim of his captain's hat, so I couldn't make out his features.

He tried to toss the line to me, but it fell short and landed in the water. 'Oh no. Now what?" The voice was familiar.

"Newton? What are you doing?" I pulled the long gaff off the *Tran-*

quility and used it to snag the line. Once I had the rope in hand, I easily pulled the Zodiac into the slip and made it fast to the cleat.

Newton looked sheepish when he stepped onto the dock. My father is extremely talented in so many ways, but water, especially ocean water, is often his nemesis.

I couldn't believe he'd tried to pilot a boat, even one as simple as the Zodiac, on his own. "Whose yacht is that you came from?" I asked him.

"A friend's," he said. "Isn't she a beauty? I'm thinking of buying one like it.'

"Stunning. But you're not really comfortable on the water. Why do you want to buy a yacht? Especially one that big. What about your environmental principles?"

Newton smiled. "I haven't actually bought one yet, although I chartered this one short-term from my friend. I thought it might be useful in the search for the missing women, since you think they're being held on a yacht. I'll learn to run the Zodiac better, and the yacht already has a very experienced crew, so I should be alright."

I held out a hand to steady him as he stepped out of the Zodiac onto the wooden dock. "Uh-huh. And how do you plan to use this yacht in the search?" It wasn't like Newton to go off half-cocked. He must have some idea about how he'd use the boat to find Joely, Genevra, and Diana.

Newton smiled at me. "I thought we could brainstorm a bit about that, but I was thinking that with the yacht and your sub we should be able to travel around the island and investigate any suspicious looking boats in the area. I haven't thought it all the way through yet. Maybe you could help me flesh out the details."

"Okay. Let's go figure out a plan." I took his arm, and we walked over to an empty table on the patio of Ray's Place. The restaurant wasn't open yet, but Theresa and her team were already setting up for the day.

Theresa came over with two mugs and a carafe of fresh coffee. "You two looked so serious I figured you needed some java to fire up your brain cells." She placed a mug in front of each of us and set the full carafe in the middle of the table. "Let me know if you need anything else." She winked at me and went back behind the bar.

"First things first. How did you envision the submarine and the yacht working together?" I asked him.

"This yacht has a door on the left side. You can't see it from here," he said when I craned my neck to check out the yacht in detail.

"If you're going to pretend that's your yacht, you need to get used to saying port instead of left," I said. "And that door is called a drive-in tender bay."

He waved his hand in the air. "I'm not planning to pass myself off as a modern day Magellan. I'll just be the prototypical pretentious rich guy and rely on the crew for any actual nautical knowledge." He smiled. "And I'll rely on you, of course."

I thought for a minute. "Okay, if there's a tender bay, I assume there's a crane in there that can lift and lower the sub. That's good. But how do you plan to recharge the sub between uses? My sub's got a lot of range, but it can't run forever on a single charge. You saw the setup on Seb's boat. We'd need something similar."

"That's the best part. My friend has a sub on order that hasn't been delivered yet. But she worked with the shipbuilder to design the yacht and specified the charging and control panel in the chamber. All that stuff has already been installed, so this boat is a perfect setup for us."

"Okay, good. Now let's figure out how we can use all this to find our friends. And we'll need a cover story."

Newton and I brainstormed for nearly two hours before we came up with a plan that we both thought would work. By now, we'd finished the first carafe of coffee and were well into the second. Along with the second jug, Theresa had brought us a platter loaded with donuts and pastries from the café off RIO's lobby. We'd eaten them all, and we were now poking at the crumbs looking for edible morsels.

She came back to pick up the empty plates and shook her head. "You two must have amazing metabolisms." She shook her head as she walked away carrying the tray laden with our used cups and plates.

"Okay, let's recap," I said. "We sail around the island at about twelve miles out, assuming that if the bad guys have the women on board a yacht they'd want to stay in international waters or at least be close enough to get away quickly. Maybe we'll meander in and out over the line a little, so it isn't obvious we're focusing on the territorial boundary. If we see a likely looking boat, I take the sub out for reconnaissance. If it seems like they might have a sub of their own, we invite ourselves aboard. From there we wing it. Have I got everything right?"

"You do," he said. "That was an excellent summary. You captured every detail."

We both laughed nervously. There were no details.

Our strategy was in place, so Newton and I asked Liam, Maddy, Dane and Oliver to come to the conference room for a meeting. We wanted to go over our idea with them to see if we'd missed anything. Our expectation was that they'd almost certainly hate the plan and come up with all kinds of reasons why it wasn't safe for us. We thought that hearing their objections would help us to make the plan better and safer.

Half an hour later, we were sitting at the table in RIO's main conference room. We'd just finished outlining the plan. Dane said, "Good. I like it."

Maddy agreed. "I like the plan too. I'll ask Vincent to patrol nearby with the *Omega*. The ship is always around somewhere, so it won't look out of place. And he can keep track of any yachts he sees and give you the coordinates to aim for."

"Even better," said Dane.

Newton and I looked at each other, completely puzzled by the unexpected acceptance of our admittedly inadequate plan.

I mulled it over for a minute. "What's the catch?"

"No catch," said Dane. "I'm sure you'll be safe, especially because we'll all be on the chartered yacht with you. Along with Roland and Morey, of course. I assume you have plenty of room for us. That boat looks like a floating hotel."

"That wasn't at all what we had in mind," I said. "We don't want to put any of you in danger. We had planned to call the police in only when and if we found a likely target. And Maddy, you have to be nearby for your treatment…"

"Nope," she said. "I only need to be around for one day every three weeks to receive the immunotherapy. And in between, I feel fine."

Dane added, "And this way, you won't have to wait for my team to arrive."

Oliver stood up. "If there's any chance Genevra is out there, I want to do everything I can to find her. I'm going too."

Liam nodded. "Me too."

Everybody in the meeting picked up their phones and began making the necessary arrangements to carry out our plan.

Dane had pulled out his phone to contact Roland and Morey. "Plan on being at sea at least a week. Trust me, it won't be any hardship. Wait till you see the boat we'll be on." He disconnected. "They'll be here in a half hour."

Newton got on the phone with the yacht, instructing them to bring on provisions for eight to ten people for a week. Then he called Gus to let him know he'd be in charge of Fleming Environmental Investments while he and Oliver were both away.

Liam called Stewie and asked him to feed Chico and Henrietta.

Maddy called Vincent on the *Omega*. The ship was out with several researchers who were monitoring water temperature and coral growth, but they were due to return to port later today.

He told her he'd begin looking for likely yachts immediately after dropping the scientists off at RIO. "I should be able to begin searching later this afternoon."

Then Maddy called Doc to let her know she was leaving her in charge of RIO for a few days.

"What about Fin?" Doc asked. "She should be in charge of RIO. And you should be at home resting." Doc didn't like anything to pull her away from either her patients or her research.

"It's important that I go. And June will take care of almost everything anyway. Please, Annie. Don't argue with me about this."

We all stared at Maddy, open mouthed. No one ever called Doc anything but Doc. Most people didn't even know Doc had a first name.

Seeing there was no way we'd be undertaking the plan to seek out the yacht without this entourage and that everything was now well in hand, I left my office to check out the sub and make sure it was fully charged.

Chapter 46
Launching the Plan

ALMOST EVERYONE who was making the trip had spare clothes in their lockers at RIO, so it was easy enough for us to pack quickly. Dane kept a small bag with a change of clothes in his car, but he stopped by the gift shop to supplement his wardrobe with a few extra shirts, another pair of cargo shorts, and a bathing suit. Newton called his housekeeper and asked her to bring him a bag.

I was outside the dive shop, gathering up my gear, when Roland and Morey arrived with their duffle bags of clothes. They stood on the shore, staring out at the yacht.

Morey's eyes were shining. "Oh my God. Is that the boat we'll be on?"

"Wow! This will be like an all-expense paid vacation," said Roland. Then he saw Dane's glower, and he quickly added, "Even though we'll be working hard the whole time."

Stewie pulled one of our rental Zodiacs up to the dock. "Transport will go faster if we have two boats." Then he hopped out and began loading tanks and luggage into the Zodiac.

"I'll drive the yacht's tender out," I said.

Newton grinned. "Thank God. I was hoping you'd say that."

When everyone had taken a seat on one of the boats, I started the tender's engines and headed out of RIO's cove to where the yacht was anchored. Stewie followed a few feet behind in the Zodiac loaded down with the luggage.

As we sped away, Maddy pointed out the flying fish leaping out of the water alongside us. Everyone smiled because they are so much fun to watch, even though it's believed that the fish fly to escape predators, not to entertain passengers in passing boats. And the smiles didn't last long because we were on a serious mission. It was imperative that we find our friends before something even more awful happened to them.

I brought the Zodiac up to the docking platform on the yacht. A member of the crew caught the line I tossed her and made the boat fast. I introduced myself and we shook hands, then we both extended a hand to my companions on the boat.

Stewie pulled his Zodiac up behind the one I'd been piloting. The docking platform was huge, with room enough for at least four more boats.

The crew person helped Stewie tie up, then she spoke into a radio attached to the shoulder of her uniform. Within a few minutes, three other crew members were on the platform to carry our luggage to our rooms. Stewie had been planning to head straight back to RIO, but I asked him to wait a few minutes because I needed a ride back to get RIO's sub.

Stewie seemed delighted to spend an hour exploring the fabulous yacht. "Need an extra hand on the team? I wouldn't mind spending a few days on this tub."

"Sorry," I said. "You and Doc have to keep RIO going while we're looking for our friends. Next time."

His smile faded quickly, and he nodded. "Getting them back is the primary objective. I get it."

As soon as the docking platform was clear of our belongings, the crew leader offered to show us to our staterooms. Newton was in the owner's cabin, which was opulent to the point of overkill, but Newton didn't bat an eye at the luxurious suite. "We'll meet in the conference room in half an hour, okay?" Then he thanked her for her help.

She led the rest of us down the hall. Dane and Maddy had adjoining suites as far from Newton's cabin as it could be and still be on the same boat. Morey and Roland had rooms across the hall from them. Liam and I were in adjoining suites in the center of the boat, and Oliver had a single room across the hall from us.

The ensuite bathroom in my stateroom was fully stocked with high end toiletries, fluffy white towels, and silk robes lined with terry cloth. I assumed everyone else had similar amenities in their rooms. None of us had much to unpack since we'd pulled our belongings together in such a hurry. The doors to all our rooms opened almost simultaneously, and we all stood in the hall wondering where the conference room Newton had mentioned might be.

We didn't have to wonder long. A crew member popped out of a stairwell at the end of the hall. "I'll show you to the conference room. Mr. Fleming is already there."

The conference room was down one level from the deck we were on, but we took the elevator instead of the stairs. We were told the stairwells were 'too utilitarian" for us to use.

The elevator certainly wasn't utilitarian. Large enough to hold at least fifteen people, the elevator's walls were covered in a lush brown suede-like fabric, interspersed with gold-veined mirrors. The floor was Italian marble.

Clearly, no expense had been spared in decorating this boat, and there were no concessions to traditional nautical décor or materials. The owner hadn't worried about water damage, energy efficiency, or even safety when choosing flooring or wall coverings. The overall effect was more opulent floating palace than boat.

We didn't speak during the short ride to the lower level. When the elevator doors slid soundlessly apart, our guide held them open while we all filed out. "The conference room is straight across the hall," she said.

A large magnetic map of the Cayman Islands hung on the wall. Newton stood in front of it, studying it intently. He'd already placed blue x-shaped magnets on some key locations, one at RIO, one at Nelson's, and a red one in the ocean where he and I had met up with the *Golden Kelp*.

Maddy joined him in front of the map and placed a blue marker on another spot in the open water. "The *Omega*. I take it you're using blue for the good guys; red for the bad."

Newton nodded. "That's right."

It only took a few minutes to work out the pattern. Vincent would move the *Omega* counterclockwise around Grand Cayman, moving in and out about five miles on either side of the twelve mile boundary that marked the edge of international waters. He'd stop periodically and send some divers out when he stopped so it would look like the *Omega* was still doing some research in case anyone was keeping tabs on him.

The yacht we were on, the *Sea Cindy,* would stay closer in, right along the twelve mile range, and we'd anchor or change course periodically while the *Omega* was moving so it wouldn't look like we were in lock step with them. While we were anchored, our passengers could swim or dive, as long as they stayed within hailing distance in case we had to move quickly.

Dane would check out the ownership of any boats that seemed large enough to keep Diana, Genevra, and Joely prisoner while we headed toward each yacht's last known location. When we were within a reasonable distance, I'd take the sub and check out the yacht in question to see if it could be equipped for docking a submarine.

Once we had the plan in place, it was time to get RIO's submarine out to the yacht. I rode back to RIO in the Zodiac Stewie had been driving. When we pulled up to the marina at RIO, Stewie and I went to the boat house so we could launch the sub. Stewie had made a trailer for it, with a small crane to lift and lower it over the ironshore, so it could be easily launched.

It only took a few minutes to get the trailer hooked up to the small ATV he used to move our boats and equipment around. At the launch point, I climbed through the sub's upper hatch, and Stewie sealed it before he backed his ATV up to the edge of the ironshore, where the water was about twenty feet deep. When the sub and I were suspended over the water, I gave him the okay sign and started the sub's engine. He gently lowered the sub into the water.

I set my course for the yacht and went full speed ahead. If it weren't for my missing friends, I would have enjoyed the ride because driving the sub was so much fun. Despite my worries, I couldn't wipe the tiny vestige of a smile off my face while I sped along.

As I approached the *Sea Cindy,* the massive drive-in deployment door in the *Sea Cindy's* hull slid open. I brought the sub to the surface, and the crew used the crane to quickly lift it into the bay. The doors slid shut before I'd even unlatched and opened the sub's hatch, so I guessed that Newton had told them to move quickly whenever the sub might be visible to the bad guys.

I exited the deployment bay and took the magnificent elevator to the conference level. The whole team was waiting for me with barely suppressed excitement.

"Vincent's found our first suspicious yacht. We'll be underway to its location as soon as the crew finishes securing your sub and hooking it up for recharging," said Newton.

I smiled. "I didn't expect our plan to bear fruit so fast. This is great."

Dane made a 'slow down' gesture. "Let's not get our hopes up. This may not be the yacht we're looking for,"

I didn't let his caution temper my enthusiasm. "But it might be. I can't wait to find out."

Vincent had sent us the coordinates for the yacht he'd identified, and Newton and I highlighted its location on the large map on the conference room wall. My excitement level rose when I realized it was positioned on a straight line between Nelson's restaurant, where one of the women had been taken, and Seb's mega-yacht, the *Golden Kelp*. That had to mean something.

It didn't take us long to get near the yacht in question. Newton, Liam, and I were in the drive-in docking bay, making a final check of the sub. Satisfied that everything was in order, I climbed the stairs to the entry platform so I could go through the hatch, which is on the top of the sub. I climbed down the inside ladder and set to work.

Liam dropped into the sub behind me and sealed the hatch door.

I bit back my surprise. "What are you doing? Did something happen?"

He smiled his glorious smile. "Nope. But I'm going with you. It's about time I got a ride in this thing."

Occasionally that smile was enough to ensure he got his own way, but not this time. "No, you're not coming with me. You'll double the weight and air consumption, and that'll reduce the safe dive duration. You can climb right back out the way you came in."

Liam opened his mouth to reply, but before he could say anything, the sub started moving.

I waved frantically in front of the glass cockpit. "Who's on the controls? Do they even know what they're doing?"

"Gosh, I sure hope so," Liam said dryly, "because it feels like we're going in."

A quick falling sensation made me giddy for a second, and then we were sinking as the ocean water closed over the glass viewscreen and the hatch at the top of the sub. I turned to the controls to make sure the engines and life support systems were operating properly. We began a controlled descent.

I didn't take the sub down very deep. We stayed at about fifty feet of depth until we were near the yacht. I circled it from below, and I didn't see any sign of an underwater airlock like the one on Seb's mega-yacht. I ascended slightly, so we were only a few feet under the waves. If anybody had been looking, they might even have been able to see us through the clear Cayman waters.

We weren't very far away from the boat when I deployed the periscope. I circled the yacht twice, but I didn't see any sign of a drive-in tender bay even on the second pass, and there was no underwater entry like the one on the *Golden Kelp*.

When we'd finished circumnavigating the yacht, I said, "Doesn't look like this is the one we're looking for. Agreed?"

Chapter 47
The Surprise

I STEERED the sub into a U-turn and headed back to the *Sea Cindy*, piloting the sub through its ascent until we broke the surface, just outside the yacht's drive in deployment bay. The crew members had been watching for our return, and the massive doors opened at our approach. As soon as they saw us, they extended the crane and lifted the sub onto the tracks on the bay floor. The tracks began to move, transporting the sub further into the bay.

The movement stopped when we were near the back wall, beside a small platform. I pulled down the folding stairway and climbed up to open the sub's hatch. I was able to step right out of the hatch onto a small, elevated platform. On the far side of the gray metal platform was a short staircase to the floor. I waited until Liam had exited the hatch, then we went down the stairs together.

I noticed the crew had already plugged the sub into its charging station, and they were busy taking status readouts on the life support systems. I was impressed at how efficient they were. Whoever owned the *Sea Cindy* had a highly professional, well-trained crew.

Liam and I left the deployment bay and went back to the business level of the mega-yacht. Our team was still gathered in the conference room, waiting for our report.

I shook my head as soon as we entered the room to end the

suspense. I poured two glasses of water from the pitcher on the sideboard and handed one to Liam. He thanked me and took a seat at the long, polished table, while I stood at the front of the room facing the team.

I put my water glass on a marble coaster on the table. "That's not the yacht we're looking for."

"What now?" Maddy asked.

"Now we wait until Vincent finds another yacht," I said.

Newton stood up. "There's nothing we can do right now. Let's go up to the sun deck. I believe they're serving drinks and hors d'oeuvres before dinner." He opened the door and led us out of the conference room and across to the elevator. We rode up in silence. None of us was in the mood for idle chit chat. We wanted action.

The sun deck was lovely, with lots of awnings shading the chaise lounges and umbrellas over the tables surrounding the sparkling pool. Soft music played from hidden speakers while a handful of waitstaff circulated with trays of hot and cold appetizers. A small bar was situated near the door to the boat's interior, shaded with its own awning. Another team from the waitstaff offered champagne or took drink orders.

In case we needed to take the sub out again, Liam and I both drank lemonade at a small table beside the pool. Dane and Oliver each had a local microbrewery IPA, and Maddy had ice water with lemon. The three of them found a table shaded from the sun, and they all sat down. Roland and Morey had soft drinks and sat together at a table off to the side. I was surprised to see that Newton held two glasses of champagne, one in each hand. He was usually not much of a drinker.

I was just about to comment on this to Liam when the sliding doors to the boat's interior opened and a stunning woman strolled across the deck. She smiled when she saw Newton. Her smile was breathtaking.

She wore a sea blue bikini top with a matching sarong wrapped around her waist. Her eyes were so pure a blue that they stood out even from twenty feet away. She wore multiple bracelets on her wrists and several gold chains around her neck, and her long honey-colored hair was pulled back into a curly ponytail. She looked a little older than me, and she was stunning.

We all stared wide-eyed when she walked directly to Newton and kissed him on the mouth. She took a glass of champagne from one of his hands and raised it toward us. "Welcome aboard the *Sea Cindy*. I'm Cindy Cooper. Please let me know if there's anything I can do to make this voyage more pleasant for you."

She reached over and took Newton's free hand. "Introduce me to your friends, Newt."

Newton walked with her to each of the tables and introduced her to the people sitting there. When they approached the table where Liam and I were sitting, she held out a beautifully manicured hand. "You're Fin. I'd recognize you anywhere from the pictures Newton carries. And I feel like I already know you because he talks about how amazing you are all the time. I'm so glad we finally have a chance to meet."

I shook her hand and smiled. "Nice to meet you too." I was staring at Newton. Who was this woman to him?

Liam rescued me. "And I'm Liam Lawton. It's so nice to meet you. Your yacht is amazing. Thank you for letting us use it." He smiled that glowing Liam smile.

She smiled back. "Nice to meet you too. And welcome aboard. I'm glad to have you here. But now I need to circulate." She and Newton walked to the final table—the one where Oliver, Dane, and Maddy were seated.

They were too far away for me to hear any of their conversation, but everybody seemed cordial enough. Liam and I were both watching with our mouths agape. I had never thought I'd see Newton with any woman who wasn't Maddy, but here he was, seemingly on very chummy terms with Cindy Cooper.

So why was I so perturbed by her? I believed with all my heart that Newton had every right to move on from Maddy. I didn't think it was a childish desire to have my parents together that made me so uneasy.

"Liam, what did you think of Cindy?"

"She's undeniably gorgeous," he said. "But there's just something…"

"Exactly," I said. We both kept a close watch on Cindy as she and Newton circulated among the guests.

After a few minutes spent in conversation, she nodded to the bartender. He pulled out a small silver chime and struck it softly. The tone was clear and pure.

"That's the signal that dinner's ready," she said. "If you'll all follow me to the small salon, Chef has a lovely buffet set up. I'm sorry we didn't have time to put together anything fancier for your first night aboard, but I think you'll find the food is more than adequate."

She and Newton walked to the sliding doors, and we all obediently rose and followed them. When Cindy had said the "small" salon, I was envisioning a room that could seat maybe ten to fifteen people, but the room we entered had space for twenty-five or so. Small tables with seating for two or four people were scattered around the room, and the center was taken up by a massive table. The feast started with a carving station and moved on to a vast variety of hot and cold foods.

Cindy stood aside and directed us to the buffet as we filed in. "Sit anywhere you like when you're ready," she told us as we passed her. Roland and Morey floated by her looking like they were having a great dream and didn't want to wake up, but the rest of us took the opulent display in stride. Maddy, Ray, and I had never lived in such luxury on a day-to-day basis, but I'd been to enough formal events, galas, and fundraisers not to be awed by the overdone extravagance of the table.

Liam and I filled our plates sparingly and found seats in a softly lit corner of the room. Neither of us was surprised when Newton and Cindy asked to join us. I was pretty sure they wouldn't want to join Maddy and Dane, and their presence would more than likely make Morey and Roland uncomfortable, so we were the most neutral table they could choose.

My father was always charming company, and Cindy's personality seemed a great match for him. After a few awkward moments, the conversation and the laughter flowed freely. I found myself liking Cindy very much indeed, and I could tell Liam did as well. And yet, there was that little inner voice saying, "watch out."

After dinner, the waitstaff brought around dessert, coffee, tea, and mints.

Cindy waved away a refill on her coffee and stood up. "I need to mingle. I've been focused on having fun, but I should be seeing to my other guests. Thanks for letting me join you, Fin. And you too, Liam. It's been a pleasant evening. I enjoyed it."

She went over to chat for a few moments with Roland and Morey.

Newton stayed seated with us. "Well? What did you think of Cindy?"

I put down my dessert fork. "She's stunning and very charming. But when you said this yacht belonged to a friend, I didn't realize you meant a girlfriend. Are you two serious?"

He shrugged. "I've been in love with your mother since I was six years old. I probably always will be. But Maddy's moved on, and Cindy is fun. Nothing wrong with us spending time together."

I raised my coffee cup in his direction in a sort of toast. "Nothing wrong with that at all. I like her very much."

I did like her. I just didn't trust her.

She was too perfect. Too fake. And trying way too hard.

By this time, Cindy had moved on and was chatting with Maddy, Dane, and Oliver. Dane and Oliver were clearly entranced, but Maddy seemed slightly subdued. I didn't think she was bothered by Cindy's presence, so I was afraid she might have overexerted herself. As brave as she was, I knew the surgery and the stress of her treatment had taken a lot out of her.

Newton noticed it too. "Help me break this evening up. Maddy looks tired."

I nodded and held Liam's hand. We strolled to Morey and Roland's table to say goodnight, then ambled over to the table where Maddy sat. "It's been a long day, and we're both exhausted. We're heading to our cabins. Anybody else ready to call it a day?"

Dane stood, and patted Maddy's shoulder. "Fin's right. This has been a long, eventful day, and you need your rest. Ready?"

We all thanked Cindy again for her hospitality and then the four of us left the salon. When we exited the elevator, Maddy said, "Do you have a minute, Fin? I'd like to chat."

"Sure," I said. "See you in a few, Liam." I turned away from my door to walk with Maddy.

Chapter 48
Mother and Daughter Chat

"I'll meet you for breakfast if you like, Dane," Maddy said when we arrived at the door to her suite. "Fin was right. Today has been a long day."

Dane kissed her cheek and said, "Text me whenever you're ready."

Maddy nodded and opened the door to her rooms. Her suite was very similar to mine, except hers was decorated in a medley of light purples, while mine was all blues. She walked over to the sideboard in the small seating area, where an electric tea kettle, two cups, and a box of assorted teas sat next to a plate of her favorite lemon cookies. There's only one way the *Sea Cindy*'s staff could have known about Maddy's tastes. Newton.

Newton had obviously given Cindy instructions on Maddy's habits and likes. I realized that he might have thought he'd moved on, but Maddy's happiness and comfort were still a high priority for him.

Maddy and I sat at the small table. I admired the print of the table-cloth—sprigs of purple lilacs on a creamy white background—while I waited for Maddy to be ready to discuss whatever was on her mind. She offered me the box of assorted teas. I'm not a tea drinker, and I had no idea what I was looking at, so I selected one of the sachets at random. When the tea kettle whistled, she poured hot water into two cups.

Maddy nibbled a cookie while she waited for her tea to steep. She didn't say anything until after she'd taken her first sip. "I'm worried about Oliver. What if we never find Genevra? Or what if she's been hurt? Oliver will blame himself, and he already carries enough guilt about his mother and his sister. Ray's death weighs on him too. He's not strong like you are."

I took a sip of my tea and tried not to grimace. Whatever herbal concoction I'd randomly chosen tasted vile, but I swallowed the mouthful stoically. "He's stronger than you think. If the worst happened, sure, he'd be upset. But after a while, he'd go on."

I pretended to take another sip of tea before putting the cup down on the small table. "Anyway, you don't have to worry. I will find her, and I will bring her home."

She reached across the table and touched my hand. "I believe you will." She bit back a yawn. "Now I'd like to go to bed. I really am exhausted."

I rose and kissed her cheek. "Goodnight, Maddy."

"Don't you want to take the rest of your tea back to your room?" she said impishly.

I'd been thrilled that our chat had been so short because I wouldn't have to drink any more of that awful brew. I shuddered. "No thanks. I've had enough."

She laughed. "That kind really tastes nasty, doesn't it? I wondered why you picked it before I realized you had no idea what you'd chosen."

Chapter 49

Vincent

THE NEXT DAY Liam and I took out the submarine to check out two yachts that Vincent had identified as possibilities, but neither showed any sign of being set up to carry a personal submarine. It was frustrating to realize that we'd nearly completed the search zone without finding any suspicious boats.

The team met on the sun deck toward the end of the day. Liam and I were leaning against the rail, staring out to sea without talking, when I noticed a small boat headed our way. It looked like one of the tenders used by the *Omega*. I nudged Liam. "Is that *RIO Two*?"

He squinted against the glare for a few seconds. "Sure does look like it."

I pointed out the approaching boat to Maddy and Newton, and we all went down to the docking platform to meet the little vessel. The *Sea Cindy's* ever-efficient crew had already arrived to help the boat tie up.

Vincent, its only passenger, hopped off the boat and greeted us.

Maddy stepped forward. "Let's talk on the sundeck." She led the way to the stairs, and we climbed past all the lower decks until we reached the very top. The bartender on duty immediately walked over and offered Vincent a drink. He requested a diet soda.

We hovered around him. "Do you have news?" I asked.

He took a sip of his soda. "Not really. But we've covered all the search area we originally identified, and we didn't find any suspicious boats. Should we search the area again, or work on developing another plan?"

I'd already concluded that my big idea hadn't panned out. We were no closer to finding Genevra, Joely, and Diana.

Oliver looked stricken. "We have to keep looking. We have to find Genevra." After a beat he added, "And the others, of course."

Newton put a hand on Oliver's shoulder. "Let's discuss this in the conference room. We'll be more comfortable there, and we'll have the map to help with the plan if we need it."

We all trooped down to the business level and into the same conference room we'd used before. The crew had just finished restocking the refreshments, so there was a brief pause while we helped ourselves to coffee. We took our seats, but at first, nobody spoke.

Finally, Dane stood and walked to the head of the table, standing in front of the map we'd used the other day. "Okay, so this idea didn't work, but that doesn't mean it wasn't a good one. It was a very good idea, and because of that, we've eliminated one possible method the kidnappers could have been using. That's a good thing. Now we need to figure out what method we investigate next."

"They could be keeping the women on shore somewhere," I said. "Maybe the sub was a red herring."

Everyone groaned at the pun.

Morey put down his coffee cup. "We can't search every empty or unused building on the island. We'd never get a warrant for that, plus it would take forever."

I stood up and joined Dane at the front of the room and picked up a marker. "What characteristics would the hiding place need?"

"Empty," said Morey.

"Well, duh," said Roland. "That's obvious."

I wrote the word 'empty' on the white board. "Emptiness could be an essential characteristic."

Oliver put his head in his hands, his frustration and fear for Genevra obvious in every line of his body. "There must be hundreds of places for them to hide on the island. We're no closer to solving this."

"Not yet, but we've only just started. What else would make a location ideal for their purposes?"

"Secluded," said Dane.

I wrote it on the board.

"Near water," Maddy added. "I still believe there's a boat involved in this somehow."

I wrote that on the board too.

"Restaurant or bar nearby," Newton said.

"Lax security at the nearby venue," chimed in Roland while I was still writing Newton's suggestion.

I gave him a sharp look, but then I realized he was right. No matter how hard I worked at it, there always seemed to be holes in RIO's security systems.

Now the ideas were flowing so quickly that I could barely keep up as I tried to capture them all on the dry erase board. Crowded. Music. Food. Tropical drinks. Connection to RIO or to RIO employees. Diver hangout. Beachfront. A dock. Visitor slips. Shore diving. Woman alone at the bar.

We were getting confused, mingling ideas for what the location of the spiking events had in common with the likely characteristics of the hideout. I held up a hand. "Let's get back on track." I erased all the ideas that related to the locations of the original crimes, leaving just the hideout ideas.

But something nagged at me. I was sure we were missing an important point—one that would have helped us to quickly find the missing women,

Liam stood up and took a picture of the board with his cellphone. He texted it to everyone in the meeting. "We're getting nowhere right now. Let's split up for a while and get back together later in the day."

Dane said, "I have a better idea. As much as I hate to leave this amazing floating resort behind, I think we're agreed that the focus of the investigation has moved back to land. I suggest we thank Cindy for her hospitality and then head home. The travel will give us time to gather our thoughts, and we can regroup at RIO late this afternoon."

We all agreed this was a good next step. Vincent assured us he had enough fuel and plenty of room on the *RIO Two* for the entire team and their bags, so we wouldn't have to borrow the *Sea Cindy*'s tender to get home.

I did some careful calculations and determined that the sub would have more than enough power to get back to RIO from our current location, so Liam and I planned to travel back in the sub. Newton went to let Cindy know we'd be leaving, while the rest of us headed to our staterooms to gather our things.

Chapter 50
Land Ho

LIAM and I entered the sub through the open hatch door, then gave the waiting crew the okay sign so they could maneuver the sub out of the deployment bay and into the water. I let the sub sink to a safe depth, and then set a course for the dock at RIO. We had several hours of battery life if we stayed below the maximum speed, and enough air to last the duration. We were enjoying the alone time.

Liam was fascinated by this mode of underwater travel. As scuba divers, it was exciting to stay as long as we wanted without worrying about depth or timing and to be able to see everything around us. Still, we were frustrated because we couldn't get as close as we usually did to the reef to see the smaller reef dwellers, most of whom usually stayed hidden in a crack or crevice. On balance, we both agreed we'd rather scuba dive, but the sub was an intriguing alternative for an occasional jaunt.

We were about halfway through the trip home when I decided to descend a little deeper to get a close look at an unusual reef formation. We dropped slowly down to about 150 feet and skimmed along an underwater ridge. A pod of dolphins was cavorting near the edge of the drop off, so I set the sub to hover nearby while we watched them play.

One dolphin was especially curious about us, and he swam right up to the sub's dome. I swear he smiled at us, and of course, Liam and I both smiled back. My heart pounded joyfully at the unexpected encounter.

After a few minutes, all the dolphins swam away, including our special friend. For a moment, I was dejected, but then I mentally thanked them for the unexpected pleasure they'd given us just by their presence. Liam and I grinned at each other.

"Wow," was all he could say.

I nodded and turned the sub back to the heading for RIO. As we were rising, another sub came soaring over the ridge of the reef, directly above us. It was large, purple, and had the *Golden Kelp* logo on the side.

I didn't think the other pilot had seen us because the sub didn't pick up speed or change direction. We rose a few feet, and we were able to get to within a few meters before the pilot even noticed us. She gave a start and steered quickly away. I had time to see that all the other seats were empty, so she appeared to be alone in the sub. The encounter happened so fast that the only distinguishing feature of the pilot's appearance I was able to catch was blonde hair.

"Should we follow that sub?" Liam asked.

I looked at the instrument panel to check our battery power before regretfully shaking my head. Until we'd stopped to check out the reef, we'd been moving at top speed, and the speed had drained the battery. I could have kicked myself for wasting the power, but then I realized that if we hadn't been in that exact location when the sub passed by, we never would have seen it.

"We can't," I said. "We definitely don't have enough reserve power to follow her, especially if we're moving at a high speed. We've got enough power to make it to RIO, and a little left over. We need to get back before dark because if I have to turn on the lights, they'll drain the batteries even more quickly. We'd be stranded out here if we went too far too fast. Maddy and Oliver would eventually come to find us, but we'd spend a couple of hours bobbing helplessly on the surface with no controls."

Liam nodded. "Okay. You're the boss. And except for the pilot, the other sub was empty anyway, so it's not like we're leaving Joely and Genevra behind."

I nodded, but I couldn't help but feel like that was exactly what we were doing.

We passed the rest of the ride back to RIO gawking at the surroundings and pointing out interesting sights to each other, while silently fretting about where the other sub had been headed. Soon enough, we were back at RIO. I made sure the length of the sub was parallel to the ironshore and close enough to disembark without getting wet, then I brought my sub to the surface almost exactly where I'd gone in the other day.

Liam reached up and opened the hatch. We both climbed out and scrambled over to the nearby ironshore. Stewie had been expecting our arrival, and he was sitting on his ATV with his elbows on his knees. He backed up the ATV. When he was close enough, he manipulated the crane's levers, and raised the sub to deposit it on its trailer. Liam and I fastened the clamps that held it in place, then Stewie drove off to leave the trailer and sub in the boathouse.

We walked along the shell path toward the main RIO building, but we encountered the investigation team sitting at one of the picnic tables. All the other tables were empty, so the secluded spot gave them privacy without forcing them indoors.

"Took you long enough," Oliver said when we joined them. "Where were you guys?"

"We did a little bit of sightseeing, which was actually a good thing. We saw the *Golden Kelp*'s sub heading away from the island. We didn't have enough juice to follow it though, so we're not sure exactly where it was headed."

Oliver's voice was tense. "Could you see who was in it?"

I nodded. "Yeah, we could. Seb's current model has panoramic glass. The whole interior is visible from the outside, and there was no one aboard except the pilot."

"Your friend Davy Jones?" asked Dane.

"No, actually it was a woman. A blonde. That's all we had time to notice. That and the empty space inside. She was really booking it. Must have been in a hurry to get somewhere." I thought for a moment. "Seb must have two pilots now."

"Did you recognize her?" Newton asked.

"Nope. She was going too fast, and she was too far away to pick out details."

Oliver was desperate to find Genevra, and it showed in his voice. "Can you pinpoint where you saw the sub? Maybe if we follow the trajectory we can figure out where it was headed."

I nodded. "I made a note of where we were when we saw it, but I'm not sure it will be helpful in identifying where it ends up. The sub is capable of changing direction on a dime. But we can try."

We all rose and walked inside to Maddy's office. She pulled down a large wall-mounted map of the Cayman Islands and surrounding sea to help us visualize the sub's travel trajectory.

I stood in front of the map and placed a marker on the last known location of the *Golden Kelp*. Then I placed a marker on the *Sea Cindy*, and a third on the location where we'd seen the sub. "I think the sub was heading in this direction. Do you agree, Liam?"

He said, "I do, but it doesn't make sense. That heading would take her directly to the *Sea Cindy*. She'd miss the *Golden Kelp* completely. And given our own experience with battery usage, I doubt she'd have enough battery power to make it all the way to Lukin's yacht anyway. But why would she be heading toward the *Sea Cindy*?"

"You're right. Dane, can you get the helicopter team to see if another yacht moved into the area after we left?"

"Will do." He picked up his phone and went out into the hall.

We were all quiet while we waited for Dane's return. When he came back in, he looked like he'd been kicked. "The chopper is out on a rescue. They'll deploy for our search as soon as they get back and can switch pilots. Probably be late tonight—or more like early tomorrow morning. We should call it a night and get a fresh start tomorrow."

"No," shouted Oliver. "By then it'll probably be too late. Genevra must be wherever that sub was headed. We have to go there right now."

Maddy put her hand on his arm. "I know this is hard, but there's nothing we can do until we know where the sub was going. We don't even really know for sure that it's connected to the missing women. We can't just sail around the ocean at random. It's a big place."

He pushed her hand off his arm. "You can wait if you want. I'm going to look for her." He ran out of the room.

Chapter 51
Trash Pickup Day

But Oliver didn't go anywhere that night. Luckily, he'd come to his senses and realized he didn't have any hope of finding the sub on his own. We already knew the missing women weren't on the *Golden Kelp*, so we'd just have to wait until we received more information from the Coast Guard helicopter.

Liam and I had gone to bed early, sleeping on the *Tranquility* to avoid the long drive home. My phone started beeping at me way too early the next morning. I looked at the alert on the screen and groaned. I was in no mood for it, but one of the last events to be filmed for the documentary was our annual underwater trash pickup contest, and today was the day. It's usually a fun event. This year, it felt like another layer of punishment.

But our viewers always found it to be an enjoyable part of the show. Any diver could sign up, and they came from all around the world to participate. We assigned each buddy team an underwater sector and gave them each a catch bag. Their job was to pick up as much trash as they could find in their sector and bring it to shore for proper disposal. We gave out prizes for the most trash weight retrieved, the largest number of pieces, the longest dive, and more. Everybody who entered got to keep their complimentary catch bag and another 'thank you' prize for helping to keep the ocean clean.

Nobody from RIO was in a celebratory mood, but that morning when we gathered in the café at RIO, I insisted we had to hold the event regardless of what was going on. After all, many divers had flown to the island at their own expense to participate. I heard some grumbling from the staff, and several whispers that having fun when our friends were missing was heartless and cold.

Was it heartless? Maybe. Probably. But all I knew was that if we didn't complete the documentary on time, a lot of the people grumbling now would be out of work because we wouldn't have the funds to keep RIO going. I carried on, ignoring the snide comments.

Theresa coordinated the refreshments, and Liam helped with timing. Stewie had drawn the sector map and made sure everybody knew where they were supposed to go. I gave a half-hearted speech thanking everyone for coming and then sent them out to search. Then I dove in to film the teams as they went about their work.

Even though most of the water around Grand Cayman is a protected marine park, somehow the divers always found trash during this event. Thankfully, as people became more aware of the damage they did to the marine life and the environment when they didn't dispose of their trash properly, we found less and less each year.

My role was to get video for the documentary and photographs of each of the buddy teams to give them as keepsakes. I took the *Tranquility* out and followed the grid plan that Stewie had setup so I could be sure to get every team. The last grid section was part of the area we used for shore dives.

As soon as I had at least one usable shot of each of the buddy teams, I went back to RIO to print out photos for each of the participants. I'd been doing this for years, so I had a template to create the souvenir photos and mount them on the plaques. All I really had to do was type in the divers' names and send the file to the printer, so I had a plaque ready for each diver quickly.

After another hour, all the dive teams were back on land. Liam and Stewie weighed the trash and counted the items each team brought back, writing the results on a large white board we'd wheeled out for the occasion.

My head was pounding mercilessly by the time we'd awarded the prizes and I'd given out the plaques. The divers all went to Ray's Place for complimentary sandwiches and sodas. I made a quick circuit of the divers, thanking everyone for participating, and then I ducked out. I had a lot to do, and too much on my mind to spend more time socializing.

Chapter 52
Christophe's Interview

EARLY THE NEXT MORNING, I positioned Christophe in a chair set against the wall in my office. I was supposed to be videoing an interview with him for the documentary. The interview would take up no more than five minutes of the film's one hour runtime, but I'd probably need to capture at least an hour's worth of conversation to get even those few minutes of usable footage. And although sitting for the interview was part of the contract Christophe had signed with Newton, he wasn't making it easy for me.

He glared at me. "Finished?

I sighed. "We haven't even started yet, and you know it. This doesn't have to be hard on either of us if you'd just relax."

Now he sighed, a long, drawn-out, put-upon noise, and I bit my lip to keep from snapping at him. I ignored his moans, finished adjusting the lights, and focused the camera, then looked through the viewfinder.

He smiled. The camera loved him. Satisfied, I sat down in the chair opposite him to begin the interview.

I started by reading the text I'd be using as a voiceover. "Christophe Poisson is one of the foremost names in the sport of freediving. He's a champion several times over, and now he devotes most of his time to training and coaching up-and-coming freedivers. Christophe, thanks for agreeing to this interview. What brought you to the Madelyn Anderson Russo Institute of Oceanography—RIO for short?"

He smiled, and I thought that smile would be one of the high points of the documentary. He started talking. "I knew Ray Russo for many years. He was just winding up his professional freediving career as I was beginning mine. He was very helpful to me, providing tips and offering to dive with me. I was sad when he left the freediving world to work at RIO, but he was tired of the nomadic life of a professional freediver. I understood. No one could blame him, especially when he married Maddy, one of the most accomplished, famous—and beautiful—oceanographers in the world."

Maddy would not appreciate the comment about her beauty. It's hard enough for women to be taken seriously without the implication that they only make it because of their looks. I wrote a reminder to edit out the comment on the pad next to me.

"You've been working on a contract basis here at RIO for a few weeks now. What's that about?"

"Newton Fleming, a great environmental advocate and RIO's largest individual donor, asked me to come out here and train his daughter in freediving. I'm a big admirer of the work Newton does on the global stage. Since I knew Maddy and Ray when she was just starting to get RIO going, I wanted to see what they'd made of their institute. I agreed to the engagement. I wasn't expecting much from Newton's daughter, but I have to admit I was impressed with her. With you."

I smiled politely as I made another note to edit Christophe's comments. Interviewing him was like pulling teeth. I'd be lucky to get a minute of usable content at this rate.

"What's it like training someone to freedive? What's the hardest thing about it?" I asked him.

"The basic skills are the same at any depth, although understanding the physics and physiology is hard. Once the student grasps the theory, it gets a lot easier. Getting students to relax and trust themselves can be very difficult, but it makes a huge difference in the results. Then, once they do relax, the problem becomes keeping them from overdoing it and going too far, too fast. After that, it's just a matter of adapting to each depth increment, slowly and carefully."

"Interesting," I said. "Anything else you'd like to add?"

"Yes," he said. "Bring Genevra home."

He stared hard at me, and I shivered. He'd seemed to be so focused on the dive that I hadn't realized Christophe had even noticed she'd been taken.

He continued looking straight at the camera, but he was no longer speaking to me. His voice was hard and cold. "Whoever you are, you know Genevra doesn't deserve whatever you have in mind for her. Set her free at once. And know this—if you hurt her in any way, I will hunt you down and kill you myself."

For a moment I was too stunned to do anything, but I finally remembered to turn off the camera. While it had been running, Christophe had continued staring at it, his usually soft brown eyes glittering with fire.

As soon as he knew he was off camera, he said, "I want a file of that last part to post on my personal website. It's crazy that you haven't been able to find her yet. It's time for me to step up and take stronger action." He rose and left my office.

Chapter 53
The Deadline Approaches

IT WAS LATE THAT NIGHT, but tomorrow was the deadline for submitting the finished documentary to the network. I'd worked the rest of the day on finishing and polishing the documentary, and I was still at it. I'd made a lot of progress today, but I knew I'd be up all night working on it even though I only had a few segments left to complete.

I was reviewing the interview with Christophe. It wasn't easy editing out his remarks about how beautiful Maddy is and about what he would do to Genevra's kidnappers, but I finally had a few useable snippets. I thought they'd work better if I inserted them into the film at intervals, rather than try to make the interview a segment of its own as I'd originally planned. I looked through the partially edited video to find the most appropriate spots.

Then I made a short segment with some of the footage I'd taken on trash day, including a shot of the pile of trash we'd retrieved and the happy divers partying at Ray's Place after the contest was over.

Last I went back over the film of my freedive, ensuring that there were no continuity breaks when Liam, Doc, and Benjamin swapped off responsibility for filming at various depths. I ended that segment with a shot of me and Stewie doing the final safety stop, with me sucking oxygen from a canister at fifteen feet. We both had big smiles on our faces.

Now it was time to add in the music and voice-over commentary. I'd done some of this work already, so I only had to dub it in for the new segments and make sure there were no breaks, dead spots, or repetition.

It was painstaking work, but it kept my mind off worrying about Genevra and Joely. I toiled through the night, and it was shortly after sunrise when I put the final touches on the film.

Just as I was cueing up the video for a last run through, Liam walked in. "I brought coffee. Do you have time for a break?"

I smiled at him, grateful for his thoughtfulness. "Not for a real break, but I'm ready for a final run through, and I can drink my coffee while I'm watching. Want to join me?"

He nodded and sat down. I took a quick sip from my mug and started the video. Liam and I each had a notebook and pen on the table in front of us to take notes in case the film needed any changes.

One hour later, the documentary was over. My notebook page was blank, and I sighed with relief. "I didn't notice any hiccups. Did you?"

"No. It was perfect. Compelling. Suspenseful. Educational but not preachy. This might be the best RIO documentary ever."

I smiled and sent the video off to the network. It was exactly fifteen minutes before the contractual deadline. I'd done it.

He kissed me. "Go home and get some rest. You deserve it."

Chapter 54

A Ludicrous Request

As soon as I'd sent off the documentary, Liam had gone to the Quokka Media offices to start his workday. But I was still sitting at my desk, too tired to move. In a daze, I was replaying the video of Christophe speaking directly to the person who'd taken Genevra, Diana, and Joely. I knew Dane wouldn't like Christophe's threat to kill the kidnappers, but I wondered what he'd think about Christophe's idea of posting the video on his own website. In my opinion, it had possibilities.

I was contemplating the potential ramifications when my thoughts were interrupted. June was standing in my office, ready to drop off the day's mail. "I already separated the junk and the routine stuff," she said. "The rest is either personal or needs you to make a decision."

I thanked her and closed the lid on my Mac. I'd deal with the mail now, while I was still too worried about my friends to concentrate on anything mentally taxing. The first two envelopes I opened were invoices for food and beverages for Ray's Place. I marked them to be paid and put them in a pile for June to process, along with a note to route them to Theresa in the future.

The next item was an invitation to speak at a diving conference to be held in La Jolla California. Because most similar invitations went directly to Maddy, I was pleasantly surprised. I pondered whether I could travel to the conference given all that was going on here at RIO.

Then again, the conference was months away. With luck, things would have settled down by then. The exposure would be good for RIO as well as for me personally. I put this one aside in a pile of things to talk to Maddy about.

I picked up an envelope that was hand addressed to me and used my letter opener to slit its seal, but before I could remove the contents, I was interrupted.

Alec Stone was standing in the doorway. "I came to get my check. The salary you owe me for participating in the documentary filming. Can I have it now?" he said.

I immediately sent an email to Fred to remind him that Alec was permanently banned from RIO no matter what credentials he showed or what story he told. Fred texted back.

> He had an employee badge

I bit my lip in frustration as I responded.

> Under no circumstances is he allowed entry, even to public areas. Post his picture on the guard podium. Label it dangerous."

When I heard the second sent message sound, I looked up at Alec with exasperation. "You've got a lot of nerve asking to be paid after what you did, but sure. Just go to HR. They have it all ready and waiting for you. Leave me alone."

I pulled out the contents of the envelope I was holding. It was a photograph of a house by the sea, taken from offshore with a telephoto lens, and I could see a ladder embedded in the steep ironshore. A boathouse stood off to one side of the lot. I stared at it, puzzled about why someone would send it to me.

Meanwhile, Alec was still standing in my office. He cleared his throat. "I thought you'd have the check. I need the money right now."

"I know it's been years since you actually worked here, but surely you remember how we do things. If you want your check, just go get it. It's in HR."

He still didn't leave. Instead, he sat down in one of the visitors' chairs in front of my desk and slumped to one side. "Actually, I wanted to talk to you. Ever since she's been dyeing her hair, Lily's like a different person. Please, will you talk to her?"

I couldn't believe his nerve. He'd recently tried to kill me, and now he was asking for my help. "No. I won't."

I was still holding the photo of this unknown house, and I flipped it over to see if there was a message. The initials 'DJ' were scrawled in pencil. There was no other writing.

But when I'd turned the photo over, Alec suddenly sat up straight. "What are you doing with a picture of Lily's house?" he said.

Now I was the one on alert. "Are you sure Lily lives in this house?"

He nodded. "I should know. I'm paying the mortgage on it."

"Where is it?" I said tersely.

He blurted out the address. It wasn't far away.

"You said she started dyeing her hair. What color is it?" I asked.

He looked wistful. "I always thought she was gorgeous with her dark brown hair, but I have to admit, she looks even better now. It's a beautiful honey blonde."

He kept on talking but I'd stopped listening after I heard the word 'blonde.' Now I realized who that woman I'd been seeing everywhere really was. It was Lily. And it had been Lily piloting the sub the day Liam and I saw it heading out to sea. I rushed out of my office toward RIO's rear exit.

Behind me, I heard Alec shouting. "I'll just stop by HR to get my check, shall I?"

I didn't bother to answer, just pushed open the back door and raced down the path to the dock.

Chapter 55
A Mission

As I ran by the dive shop, I shouted to Stewie. "Call Dane. Tell him to meet me off the coast near Hell. I know where the missing women are."

I didn't stop running until I vaulted onto the *Tranquility*'s deck. I quickly unfastened the lines, pulled in the bumpers, and started the engines. I was away from the dock not more than two minutes after Alec had given me the location of Lily's house.

As I approached the area where the house was located, I slowed my boat down so I could study the homes close to the water's edge. Finally, I found the one I'd been looking for. I dropped the anchor and hurried into my scuba gear.

I wasn't far from shore, so it only took me a few minutes to swim to the ladder that led to the grounds of the house. I climbed up and quickly doffed my gear, leaving it on the ground near the small boathouse.

I noticed the electrical meter on the outside of the outbuilding. I'm no electrician, but the meter seemed much larger than normal, which I believed meant this shack used a lot of power. I slapped my forehead when I realized that was the detail that had eluded me when we were listing a potential hideout's characteristics. If they were charging the sub there, the location had to use a ton of power, and they'd have a huge electric bill. We probably could have located the location easily by looking at power consumption. Now I was sure this must be where Lily was docking the sub.

I walked around the boathouse, trying to peek into the windows to see if, as I suspected, the building had been set up as a charging station for a sub. The tiny windows were high up off the ground, and very dirty. Luckily, I'd been doing pullups as part of my freedive training, so I hoisted myself up to the window.

I rested one forearm on the windowsill and dug my bare toes into the wall for balance, using my other hand to clear the grime away. It was so dark inside the boathouse it was hard to see anything. I cupped my hand over my eyes to block the glare. It was then that I felt a sharp poke in my back.

I dropped to the ground and spun around. Lily was standing less than two feet away, holding the point of a spear gun aimed at my heart.

She smiled, a slow, evil smile. "Long time no see, Sis."

"I'm not your sister. Now put down that ridiculous speargun before you get hurt."

She sneered. "I hear you call Oliver your brother all the time. He and I are twins. Ergo, I must be your sister."

"Think what you like," I said. "I'll do the same. And I think you're a nutjob and no relation to me. The only thing you and Oliver ever had in common is your looks. Now take me to wherever you've stashed Genevra, Joely, and Diana. I've come to bring them home."

"Have you now?" she said. "I'm betting you don't know what you're getting into. Turn around so I can tie your hands."

She poked my belly with the point of the speargun. Not hard enough to break the skin; just hard enough to remind me of its potential to cause injury. I turned around and put my hands behind my back.

I knew Lily would have to put down the speargun to tie my hands. As soon as I saw the spear tip on the ironshore beside me, I whirled around.

My quick move startled her, and she jumped back. Whenever I'd stood up to Lily in the past, she'd backed right down, so I took a step toward her, and as I'd hoped, she took a step back. Now she was right on the edge of the ironshore. Without taking my eyes off her, I bent down and picked up the speargun. I waved the point menacingly, although we both knew I would never use it on her. I still had nightmares about the one and only time I'd shot someone with a gun, and this felt even more personal. "Game over, Lily. Where are you stashing the missing women?"

She sneered. "They're on the *Golden Kelp*, you fool. You can't imagine how hard we laughed when you and Newton were searching for them."

"Who is 'we'? You and Seb?"

I waved the spear's point again, and she teetered on the edge of the ironshore. The fall would only be a few feet; there was plenty of water below her; and we were near the ladder. She was a good swimmer and wouldn't be in any danger if she did fall in. It made me wonder why she acted so afraid of going over the edge.

It was almost like she was killing time. But why?

Her eyes darted past me to my right, and I turned my head to see what she was looking at. Cold metal touched the left side of my neck.

Cindy was holding a pistol to my neck. "Put down the spear. We all know you're too soft-hearted to use it anyway."

Slowly and carefully, I bent down to place the speargun on the ground.

"Good girl," said Cindy. "Lily, tie her hands."

Lily opened a door into the boat house and emerged with a short length of rope. This time, I put my hands together in front of me, and she tied them.

When she finished, I said, "Where are the women you took. I told you I came to bring them home, and I meant it." I wasn't worried about these two hurting me, but now I was the one hoping to stall for time until Dane arrived. If Stewie had called him right away when I was leaving RIO's dock, Dane and his team should be arriving at any minute.

Ignoring me, Cindy pointed the pistol at the boathouse. "Lily, prepare the sub."

241

Lily went inside and opened the wide doors that faced the ocean. I heard the groan of the davits as they moved the sub slowly toward the sea.

I figured it wouldn't hurt to get some answers while we waited for the sub to deploy or for Dane to arrive, whichever came first. "Where were Genevra and the others when Newton and I were on the *Golden Kelp*? I was so sure they'd be there."

Cindy gave a hard, sharp laugh. "They were there, right up until we recognized the *Tranquility* approaching. We gave each of them another hit of ketamine and loaded them into the second sub before you arrived. I took the sub out through the underwater deployment port while you and Newton were waiting for Seb on the swim deck. I brought them to the *Sea Cindy*. Then I brought them back when you and Newton had finished your search. I had just enough time to get back to the *Sea Cindy* to meet Newton for our rendezvous."

I thought a moment. "Now I get it. I should have known when I saw the two hoists and duplicate charging setups on the *Golden Kelp*. You really were using two yachts and two subs, so you had enough juice in the first sub to make it to the *Sea Cindy*, then you used the second sub to finish the trip to the *Golden Kelp*. You just reversed the process to get back here. My mistake was not suspecting you were using the *Sea Cindy* as the halfway point. I bet there's a full charging and maintenance setup inside this boathouse. Am I right?"

"On the money. Too bad Newton was so besotted with his new gal pal that he never suspected I'd be involved. None of you ever even considered that the *Sea Cindy* was the interim holding spot. Course, when you and Liam saw Lily on her way to my boat, I thought for sure you'd figure it out. But Lily was right. You're too dense to catch on no matter how obvious the answer is."

I nodded. "True. I never like to think badly about my friends. I guess Newton and I are alike that way. But tell me, how did you get involved in all this?"

"Lily's mother, Cara Flores, was my mother's sister, so Lily and I are cousins. Cooper was my mother's married name. Cara introduced me to Seb years ago, and we all worked together from time to time. I brought Lily in when Seb and I sketched out the plan to get back at Newton."

"Uh-huh. I'm really not clear on the plan. Exactly what was the goal?" I said.

"I wanted payback for the way Newton treated my aunt Cara. He used her, and all the time they were together, he was still in love with your mother. He threw Cara aside when Ray died, hoping to get Maddy back. Now he's going to lose his precious daughter. Too bad the last laugh's on him."

I was getting anxious. Where was Dane? What could be taking so long? I needed to keep stalling. "That's not exactly the way it happened. Newton and Cara were over years before all this started."

Cindy growled, a nasty guttural sound. "Liar. That is exactly what happened. Cara wouldn't have lied about that. Newton and Maddy have to pay. And so do you."

I was honestly puzzled. "Me? What did I ever do?"

"Nothing. But Seb has a beef with Newton. He thought the best way to hurt Newton was to hurt you."

I was astounded. "Seb and Newton know each other?"

She waved her hand around in an 'I don't know' gesture. "Some business thing to do with Maddy."

"If the goal was to hurt Newton, why take Genevra and Joely? And Diana? None of them even knew Cara, and they barely know Newton."

"Didn't matter. We targeted Ray's Place, figuring Newton would have to stick his nose in and get involved to protect his precious Maddy. We messed up pretty bad the first time when we accidentally killed the woman we selected. We dumped her behind the bar with some little jerk she'd been spending time with." She shrugged, like Polly's death meant nothing to her.

That made me angry. Seething, I looked her in the eye. "You should know something about the people you murdered. Neither of them deserved what you did to them. Her name was Polly Peterson. She was an only child, and her elderly parents are devasted. He's a good friend of mine. I call him Chaun, but you aren't good enough to call him by his nickname. You should call him Mr. Chaunsey."

She shrugged. "Whatever. So, to continue…we took Joely for practice, and we chose Genevra because Lily wanted to stick it to her pious twit of a brother. Taking Diana was a red herring, so you fools wouldn't catch on. We'd planned to take you next."

"Well, you have me now. Why not let the others go?"

She shook her head. "No can do. They know too much."

By now, Lily had finished deploying the sub from the boat house. It bobbed just off the ironshore, secured with a line. The hatch was open. "Ready," she said. "Do I look okay? I want to look good when I see Seb. He's so dreamy."

Cindy's mouth gaped. "That's creepy. You do know he's your father, don't you?"

Lily turned pale when she realized Cara really had lied to her about who her father was. I thought immediately of how this knowledge would hurt Oliver, and I vowed to keep it from him forever if I could.

Cindy laughed when she saw Lily and I were processing her revelation. She waved the gun at me. "Get in."

I held my arms up in front of me. "I can't. My hands are tied."

She laughed again, an evil sound. "Nice try. But no way you're getting untied. Now move." She pointed the gun at me. The steel gleamed with the same cold light I saw in her eyes.

Slowly, I took the few steps across the yard toward the waiting sub. Lily had placed a short wooden plank leading from the ironshore to the sub's open hatch. The board was narrow, and it pitched slightly with each wave, making it hard to stay balanced as I tried to cross it. I considered jumping into the water and making a break for it. I was sure that even with my hands tied I could reach the *Tranquility* before either woman could physically stop me, but I wasn't sure I could outswim a bullet or a harpoon. I hesitated.

Cindy was impatient. She walked up behind me and gave me a push. I stumbled forward and fell heavily through the hatch. I landed with a painful thud on the floor.

A few seconds later, while I was still dazed from the fall, Lily lowered herself through the hatch, the speargun slung onto her back with a strap. She put the speargun on one of the seats in the first row and sat in the pilot's seat. After starting the motor, she began checking the instrument status, ensuring the battery was fully charged, the oxygen tanks full, the CO_2 scrubber operational. Satisfied that all was in order, she flipped the switch that irised the hatch closed, sealing it tightly.

As soon as she was seated, I felt the sub begin to move. Cindy must have removed the gangplank and untethered the sub while Lily did her checkout. Lily was working the controllers, but it took her a minute to gain mastery over the sub's movement.

Chapter 56
Adrift

THE SUB PITCHED AND ROLLED, gave a little lurch, and then settled into a smooth and steady pace, heading to deep water. Lily didn't notice that the sub's erratic motion had repositioned the speargun, but I did. Its point now protruded toward me from between two of the front seats.

She was concentrating on the controls, intent on staying on the right course. I leaned forward, looking over her shoulder.

I rubbed my bound hands carefully on the spear's razor sharp tip while I spoke, hoping the conversation would distract her from what I was doing. "What's our ETA?"

She waved a hand in the air. "Shut up. I don't want to talk to you."

I was still trying to sever the knots without letting her notice. "Okay. Suits me," I said.

The sub tilted slightly and the speargun moved, the tip slicing into my hand. I couldn't help but give a little yip of surprise and pain.

She looked back at me and realized what I'd been doing. "Bad girl. That'll cost you." She picked up the speargun and stowed it on the floor in front of her where it was out of my reach.

I settled back in my seat, working on a plan B. I knew if I boarded the *Sea Cindy*, I was a goner. I had to find a way to escape from the sub before we arrived at the yacht. The problem seemed insurmountable.

I looked over her shoulder at the gauges. We were cruising along at about one hundred twenty-five feet of depth. If need be, I could easily reach the surface from there without scuba gear, especially with all the freediving training Christophe had recently put me through. But I would never be able to lift the hatch against the pressure of the sea.

Then I remembered watching Lily seal the hatch before we left. Unlike the hatch on my sub, which had a mechanical lid that had to be manually lifted up, this sub's hatch was a series of overlapping electronically operated panels that moved horizontally rather than vertically. Lily had simply pushed a lever to close the hatch, and the panels came together and sealed against each other.

I was certain the sub must have a safety mechanism that would prevent anyone from accidentally opening the hatch at depth. I wondered if the safety also had an emergency override.

There was only one way to find out. I'd have to trick her into telling me what I needed to know. "You're a pretty good pilot. Smooth, but of course, this sub is so advanced it practically drives itself. I guess a monkey could pilot it as well as you do."

She made a stop motion with her hand. "Shut up. I'm concentrating."

I was leaning forward over the front row of seats, my head near hers, my words emerging only inches from her ear. "Too complex for you? Need some help?"

She pointed to a large red button near her left knee. "I'm warning you. Keep it up and I'll jettison you. You'd be gone in seconds. Then I'd just pump out the water and be on my way. You'd be dead, but nobody would care."

She moved the lever that controlled the sub's depth. "I think I'll make this trip a little deeper than I usually do just to be sure you don't try anything stupid."

I watched the numbers on the depth meter increase. We were now cruising at 250 feet. Still feasible for me to make it to the surface if only I could get out of the sub.

I tried to sound scared. "Is that depth safe? Won't we run out of air or be crushed?"

"Honest to God, I don't know why people always rave about how smart and brave you are. I have plenty of air for the trip, even if I have to pump out the water after I toss you out. If you keep annoying me, I might just decide to throw you out like yesterday's garbage. It takes less than a minute to reseal the sub and completely clear it of water."

She pointed to a small tank attached to the cockpit. "And meanwhile, I have my spare air here if I need it, so I'd be fine alone down here for fifteen minutes or so anyway. Plenty of time to reach the surface. Unfortunately, you don't have one."

Just like that, my plan crystalized.

"Aren't you afraid you'll accidentally open the hatch if it's that easy to do? It seems dangerous to have the control right there in the open." I tried to sound like I admired her bravery.

She took the bait. "Nope. It's like one of those childproof caps on a medicine bottle. You have to push and turn the lever at the same time."

"Like this?" I said, reaching across her and pushing and twisting the lever as hard and as fast as I could.

The hatch panels began to slide apart, and water rushed in through the rapidly widening opening. While Lily gaped at the inrushing torrent, I pulled the spare air canister off its mount on the cockpit and tossed it over my shoulder. It rolled under one of the empty seats in the back row.

Now Lily looked panic stricken.

I stood up and slogged over to where the sea was rushing into the sub. "Better hurry and find it. Water's coming in fast." I took a deep breath and jumped, grabbing the edge of the hatch with both hands. I pulled myself up and off to one side, kicking as hard as I could to make it through the torrent. I was out of the hatch and in the open ocean in less than two seconds.

My hands were still tied together, but that wasn't a problem right now. I put my arms out straight over my head, so I'd be maximally hydrodynamic, and began to dolphin kick my way to the surface.

Because I wasn't wearing my monofin, I didn't move anywhere near as quickly as I did during my dive for the documentary, but I was still confident I could reach the surface without a problem. I'd figure out my next step once I was free and in the open air.

The water grew lighter as I neared the surface, helping to keep me focused on my goal despite the lack of air. My head popped out of the water, and I took a deep breath. I'd made it.

But now I was in the open ocean with my hands tied together. My dive training had taught me how to stay upright on the surface for long periods without using my hands to help, so I wasn't worried about drowning.

But hypothermia might get me. Sharks might get me. Heck, even Lily might get me, and if she did, she'd be in no mood to go easy on me.

But first things first. I had to get my hands untied. I held them up in front of me and saw that while rubbing the ropes against the speargun, I'd managed to fray the knots more than halfway before Lily had caught on to what I was doing. But even so, my hands were still bound tightly together, so I couldn't use them to work on the knots.

I tried pulling the rope apart by pushing my hands in opposite directions, but the rope didn't budge. I took stock of my assets. I was wearing only a bathing suit. No place to stash anything. And no BCD with a helpful cutting tool in the pocket. I was going to have to do this on my own.

I brought my hands to my mouth and bit the rope, gnawing, chewing, tugging with all I had. It tasted disgusting, and sea water rushed into my open mouth, but I just spit the water out and kept going. It was my only hope.

The sun was heading toward the horizon by the time I'd managed to fray the rope enough that I thought I could separate my hands. With one last tug, I was free.

While my hands were in front of my face, I realized I was still wearing the dive watch Newton had given me before we searched the *Golden Kelp*. He'd told me I could use it to communicate with him. I didn't know what its range was, but it was the only tool I had. I prayed it would work.

I pushed the button with my waterlogged and wrinkly fingers. "Newton? It's me. Can you hear me?"

There was no response. I tried again. And a third time. No answer.

I must be out of range. The watch had several other dials and buttons. I tried each one, but most of them were just standard dive watch functions. I pushed on the dive watch's face, and the pressure activated a strobe light. A message appeared on the screen.

Beacon activated. Four hours estimated operational time.

I turned in a circle. I was miles from land. But I couldn't just float here while the watch's battery drained away. I used its compass function to find the way home, and I began to swim.

Chapter 57

Pickup

MUCH LATER, I was beginning to regret my impetuous plan to effect my escape by flooding Lily's sub. My arms felt like lead. My legs ached. I was hungry and thirsty.

And cold. Very cold.

Night had fallen.

The ocean was dark and lonely.

When I saw a spotlight scanning across the water's surface, I didn't know whether to hide or hope for rescue. If she had managed to save herself—and she wasn't too embarrassed to admit how I'd bested her —Lily had already had plenty of time to reach the *Sea Cindy* and get Seb to deploy a search team, so this could be a boat full of Seb's henchmen. But it could also be Dane and Newton, finally responding to the SOS I hoped my watch was emitting. I pressed the watch face tight against my belly to hide the light until I was sure who was coming.

The boat's searchlight swept the area around me, getting nearer with each revolution. I debated whether to hail the rescuers or duck underwater where they wouldn't see me. The correct response would differ depending on who was on the boat, and I still couldn't tell. Then again, my energy was flagging, and it might be better to be picked up no matter whose boat it was. At least I'd be alive.

My dilemma was solved when a dim figure on the boat's flying bridge hailed me with an electronic microphone. "Fin, where are you? The homing signal says you're nearby, but I can't see you. Give me a shout if you can hear me."

I was overjoyed to recognize Liam's voice. I waved my arm above the water's surface, and the watch's light shone out across the darkness. I shouted, "Over here!"

"Gotcha," he said through the megaphone. "Hold on. I'm coming for you."

Within a few seconds I saw him dive off the boat's bow, carrying a life ring. Someone on the boat swiveled the spotlight to guide him as he swam toward me. It only took us a few strokes to come together.

He embraced me when I touched his shoulder. "Thank God Newton gave you that homing device. What are you doing way out here anyway?"

He didn't wait for an answer, just slipped the life ring over my head, and kissed my ice cold lips. "I love you. I couldn't stand it if anything happened to you." Swimming easily through the gentle waves, he towed me and the life ring toward the boat.

As we got closer to it, I recognized the *Flemingo*. Oliver was standing on the stern, and he reached down to offer me a hand up the ladder. I would never admit it, but I was glad for the help. I was frozen stiff.

As soon as I was on deck, Oliver wrapped me in a warm towel. He squeezed my hand, but he was so overcome with emotion he couldn't speak.

"I know, Oliver. I feel the same way. Thank you for finding me."

Liam swept past us toward the cabin. Within a few seconds, he brought me a cup of hot fresh coffee and a handful of cookies. "Come inside out of the wind," he said. "Catch your breath. Then you can tell us what happened."

I nodded, wrapping both hands around the mug hoping to absorb a little of its warmth. Unfortunately, it was one of the ubiquitous RIO-branded insulated stainless steel mugs, and no heat reached my hands. Drat. But at least the coffee inside was piping hot. I drained the cup and scarfed down my cookie.

Liam led me into the cabin and wrapped a blanket over my shoulders. He used the towel to wring some of the excess moisture out of my hair. Then he slipped my arms into the sleeves of a hoodie and zipped it to the neck.

Oliver came in and rummaged through one of the drawers. He handed me a pair of heavy socks. "They're clean," he said.

"I wouldn't care if they weren't. I'm freezing." I put down my mug, took the socks and slipped my feet inside. Heavenly.

Oliver refilled the mug and handed it back to me. I took another sip of hot coffee and a big bite of my second cookie. "Where are Dane and Newton? You should let them know you found me so they can stop their search."

Liam and Oliver looked at each other for a beat before Oliver said, "They already know. I radioed while Liam was retrieving you. Meanwhile, you must be starving. I'll make you something more substantial to eat." He went to the galley kitchen and started scrambling some eggs. They smelled delicious.

In a minute, Oliver brought me a plate heaped high with scrambled eggs and toast. "Eat now, and then you can tell us what's going on."

I was shaking from hunger after my ordeal, so I figured he was right. I couldn't help Genevra and Joely if I was too weak to help myself. I took a bite of the eggs, then a bite of toast. I didn't stop until the plate was empty.

I handed the dish to Liam. I was ready to tell him what I'd discovered, but before I could start, he pulled a warm blanket over me.

"I know..." I said.

"Hush, Love. We'll talk later. Sleep now."

Chapter 58
Wake Up

I DIDN'T MEAN to fall asleep, but it was like Liam's words had put a spell on me. I don't know how long I slept, but when I opened my eyes, the sky was still full of stars and darkness. Liam and Oliver were sitting at the galley table with their heads on their arms, both snoring softly.

"Did you get them?" I asked, sitting up and rubbing sleep from my eyes.

Liam sat up. "Get who?"

Was he daft? "Joely and Genevra, of course. And Diana. Did you get them?"

He came over and put his arm around me. "I think you've been dreaming, sweetheart. We still don't know where they are."

"But I do know. They're on the *Golden Kelp*. Lily and Cindy told me." I stood up, ready to go chasing the bad guys all by myself.

Oliver looked sleepy. "When could you have seen Lily? And remember, Cindy is on our side." He yawned and stretched.

I practically sobbed. "No, she's not. They're both working with Lukin. They were taking me to him when I escaped. Didn't I tell you all this last night?"

They both shook their heads. "First we're hearing of it," said Liam.

"Did Newton and Dane retrieve the *Tranquility*? Are they on the way?"

Liam sat beside me. "Everything's fine. Let's get you back to RIO and then you can tell us what happened."

"Aren't you listening? We can't go home to RIO yet. I know where they are. We have to get those poor women back right now before Lukin moves them again. It may already be too late. I shouldn't have let myself fall asleep. Poor Genevra. I've let her and Joely down."

Oliver gasped. "Genevra? You found her? Where is she?"

I put my hand on his arm. "Calm down. I just told you. She's on the *Golden Kelp* with the others. We have to get them before Lily or Cindy tells Seb I know where he's holding them." I didn't want to tell Oliver I'd left his twin sister in a flooded sub two hundred and fifty feet under water. She should have been able to save herself, but you never know. The ocean takes what it wants.

"We have to go to the *Golden Kelp* right now, before Lily calls them or gets there with the sub. It's early yet. The crew is probably still sleeping. We can rescue Genevra, Diana, and Joely and be back at RIO before they know we've been there or that we even know where they are."

Liam made a 'slow down' gesture. "You've already searched the *Golden Kelp* and they weren't aboard. And why don't we want Cindy to know we've found them?"

"Because the women were held on the *Sea Cindy* while we searched the *Golden Kelp* and vice versa. Cindy's in on it with Seb. Hurry up. Set a course for the *Golden Kelp*. It's not that far away."

Oliver rushed up to the flying bridge and started the engines. He radioed the *Omega*, asking Vincent for the *Golden Kelp's* latest position. He made a sharp turn and floored it. I realized we'd been anchored overnight, so we weren't that far away.

After a short trip, Oliver threw the *Flemingo* into neutral. We must be approaching the *Golden Kelp*. I was already attaching a spare regulator and a full tank to a buoyancy control device I'd taken from Oliver's equipment locker.

I shrugged into Oliver's BCD, grabbing his fins on the way to the *Flemingo's* stern. "You coming, Liam, or do I have to board that yacht alone? Either way, I'm going." I took a compass heading to the

Golden Kelp, just now becoming visible on the barely brightening horizon.

I checked the pocket of the BCD to make sure I had a dive knife or scissors and a light. "I don't know what kind of shape the women are in. Lily told me they've been drugging them to keep them docile. They may not be able to swim. Oliver, I'll signal if I want you to bring the *Flemingo* closer.

"Wait," said Oliver. He was holding a dive scooter, one of the small, sleek, professional models we used at RIO for exploration. "Use this, it'll help you conserve your energy. You need every advantage you can get."

I nodded. "Good idea."

I stepped off the dive platform. Oliver handed down the scooter. I flipped on the power, descended a few feet, and headed toward the *Golden Kelp*. I hadn't gone very far when I noticed Liam beside me, using a scooter of his own. I gave him the okay sign and revved my machine to top speed.

My plan was to approach the *Golden Kelp* from below and use the sub deployment port for access. I knew the sub port would most likely be empty because Lily had a sub at her location, and the other would have been waiting aboard the *Sea Cindy* to allow her to switch subs and make it the rest of the way to the *Golden Kelp*.

My assumption was that the missing women were being held somewhere near the sub control room, since it would be easier to move them back and forth from the sub when necessary to keep them more isolated from visitors.

The powerful scooters covered the distance to the mega-yacht in just a few minutes. Through the still dark water, I could see the light from the open sub-docking area shining down. I signaled to Liam to slow down and wait while I checked out the situation.

My head broke the surface of the water in the deployment port. As I'd expected, neither of the subs were here, but that didn't mean they couldn't arrive at any moment. I spun in a circle to make sure the control room was empty. The only person visible was Davy Jones, the sub pilot and mechanic. He was sitting in the corner, watching me.

Davy left his seat by the control panel and walked across the floor, making a scraping noise as he walked. I didn't have time to figure out

259

what was making that noise right now. I needed to get my friends back.

Davy took my scooter and placed it in a nearby rack, then he held out a hand to help haul me up out of the water since there were neither stairs nor a ladder. He held a finger to his lips in the signal for silence. I nodded my understanding and stowed my fins on the rack near my scooter.

After taking the flashlight out of my BCD pocket, I waved it in a circle underwater to signal Liam to come aboard. A few seconds later, I saw him approaching from below, so I stowed the flashlight back in my pocket.

Liam rose through the water. I took his fins and the scooter from him and placed them on the rack beside mine while Davy gave him a hand getting up on the deck.

I was afraid Lukin had the room bugged, so I pulled the dive slate out of my BCD pocket and scrawled "Where are they?" I held it up for Davy to read.

Davy limped over to the sub's maintenance and control panel, which took up most of the far wall of the room. He pulled down a lever on the left side, turned a dial on the right, and then entered a code in the keypad. Soundlessly, a panel in the wall swung open. Whatever space was behind the panel, it was in complete darkness.

I raced over to the opening, Liam a step or two behind me. After pulling the flashlight out of my BCD pocket again, I shone the light into the small, dank cell. I saw a jumble of bodies against the back wall, and I recognized Genevra's bright hair. None of the women moved, and my heart sank, thinking I was too late to rescue them.

But then Genevra slowly lifted her arm to shield her eyes from the light. "No more, please. We're being as quiet as we can."

Next to her, Joely sat up. She shook the person lying beside her, who I assumed was Diana. My assumption was confirmed when the person sat up and I heard the clicking of the beads in her braids.

"Genevra, are you tied up? Chained? Can you walk?" I said, as quietly as I could.

She was slow to answer. "Dunno. We haven't been upright since we've been here. The ceiling's too low to stand. We can't even crawl."

My heart broke, but I would have time to cry for her ordeal when we had her safe on the *Flemingo* and we were on our way back to RIO. I held out my hand. "C'mon. I'll help you."

Genevra shook her head. "Diana's in a bad way. Take her first."

She pushed Diana across the small space to the cell's opening. I reached in and pulled Diana across the last few inches, then lifted her to her feet. She wobbled unsteadily.

I turned to Liam. "Take her to the docking platform and signal Oliver. We'll need the boat to come to us. They're in no condition to swim."

He put his arm across Diana's back to help hold her upright. "It's okay now, Diana. We'll get you out of here." The two of them started to walk slowly toward the exit, one baby step at a time.

I shone the light in the small area again. "Joely, you're next." I pulled her arm to help her out of the cell.

"Davy, take Joely to the platform. I'll get Genevra."

"I'm sorry. I can't do that," he said. He pointed to his foot. There was a bright steel manacle on his ankle. A short chain led from the manacle to a steel ring in the wall.

The scraping sound I'd heard when Davy walked had been the chain rubbing against the steel deck. "Lukin will kill you when he realizes you helped us. We have to get you out of here."

Davy bit his lip and nodded. "He already found out I sent you that mail. That's why I'm chained. But you go. I'll be fine."

I shook my head. "We're not leaving you. Liam, I need you over here."

Liam helped Diana to sit, then he strode back across the room. He took one look at the chain around Davy's ankle, then he picked up his dive scooter and smashed it down on the steel ring. After he'd rammed it three times, the scooter was in pieces, but the ring had finally come free of the wall. He coiled the chain and handed it to Davy. "Get Diana out of here."

When I turned back to the cell opening, Joely was still down on her hands and knees. She wobbled when she tried to stand, but I held out a hand to steady her. "Go with Liam. We don't have much time. The sub could come back at any moment."

She shuddered. "I can do it."

Liam took her weight, and they walked across the room.

261

I reached down and finally pulled Genevra out. "C'mon. We don't have much time." I put my arm around her, and we walked unsteadily across the room and through the door to the docking platform. I held my breath until we were in the open air. Liam and Davy were ahead of us, helping Diana and Joely to the *Flemingo*.

"Start the engines, Oliver," I shouted.

Genevra was still moving slowly when I heard the sound of a bullet whizzing by my head. "Can you go faster? We've got to get out of here."

She tried hard to move quickly, but she'd been locked in that tiny cell and drugged repeatedly. The movement must have been agony for her, but she kept going. Another bullet whizzed by, missing me by a hair.

Liam emerged from the *Flemingo*'s cabin at a run. He rushed across the length of the platform and picked up Genevra. "Go," he said. "Run. I'll be right behind you."

I ran, bobbing and weaving to make it harder for the gunman to hit me. Just shy of the *Flemingo*, I slipped on the wet platform and fell. Davy reached out and pulled me onto the *Flemingo*'s deck. I was still flat on the deck when the sound of another bullet made me flinch. Davy grunted and joined me on the floor. A spray of blood told me he'd been hit.

A second later, Liam reached the boat and gently lowered Genevra to the deck to keep her safe from the bullets, which were coming fast and furious now. He quickly untied the mooring line and raised his arm to give Oliver the signal to go.

The sound of a gunshot rang out. Liam fell.

I started to rise to go to him, but Davy held me back with his good arm. "Wait until we're away. We don't want to lose you too."

I shook off his hand and crawled over to Liam. I reached out to hold him, but just then the boat gave a lurch and started backing away from the *Golden Kelp*. I slid along the deck to the cabin, which would have been my next stop anyway.

I had to stop Liam's bleeding, so I crawled inside the cabin and grabbed the towel he'd used to dry my hair not so long ago. It was still damp, but it was the first thing I found that I could use to help stop the bleeding.

On my way back to Liam, I poked my head up over the gunwales to see what was going on back aboard the *Golden Kelp*. A small band of men armed with rifles stood there, aiming their guns our way. As soon as my head was high enough for them to see, they let loose with another barrage of bullets. I ducked back down and crawled to Liam. His eyes were closed.

I checked him over to see where he'd been hit. The only wound I found was in his upper arm. Blood was flowing freely, but at least it wasn't arterial bleeding. I pressed the towel to it to staunch the wound.

He opened his eyes when he felt my touch. When he saw it was me, he lifted his other arm and put his hand over mine. "Are you okay?" he asked softly.

"I'm fine. And you'll be okay too as soon as we get you to Doc."

"Anyone else hit?" he asked.

"Davy. Another arm wound. Everyone else is unhurt."

"Good." He closed his eyes again.

I grabbed a length of rope and tied the towel in place so I could check on Davy and the others as soon as we were out of rifle range. I could still hear the sound of guns firing, but the bullets didn't seem to be reaching us any longer. I stood up and walked into the cabin for the first aid kit and a blanket.

I carried them over to Davy and bandaged his wound, which had already stopped bleeding. I figured he'd be fine. I gave him a sip of water and covered him with the blanket. "I'll be right back."

I wanted to move Liam into the cabin where the light was brighter so I could do a better job of bandaging his wound. I went back across the deck to where he lay unmoving. He was so still my heart stopped.

I put my ear to his chest and heard his heart beating. I thanked the universe for not letting him die. Then I reached under his arms and lifted his upper body. I slung one of his arms over my shoulder and stood up, bringing him with me, mentally thanking Christophe for all the squats and leg presses he'd made me do. Liam groaned softly but didn't say anything. I walked into the cabin, carrying most of his weight as I went.

I sat him on the daybed, then lifted his feet so he was lying down. After I untied the rope that had been holding the towel in place and pulled it gently away, I put antiseptic on most of his arm and reban-

263

daged the wound tightly. Then I put the arm in a sling to prevent him from using it. I gave him a sip of water, but most of it dribbled right back out. Refusing to think the unthinkable, I wiped his chin and covered him with a blanket.

Joely and Diana had been sitting quietly in the captain's chairs, gulping down cup after cup of water from the cooler and watching me work.

"Will he be okay?" Joely asked.

"Yes, I think so. I need to go up on the bridge to talk to Oliver. Will you watch him while I'm gone? Come get me if anything changes. Can you manage that?"

She nodded, so I left to climb the ladder to the bridge.

Oliver was standing at the helm, one arm around Genevra and the other steering the boat.

"Let me drive," I said. "You take care of her."

He nodded and helped her over to the ladder. She was still very unsteady on her feet, so he stood behind her as she climbed down, to act as a stabilizer in case she lost her balance.

I steered a course for home.

Chapter 59
At RIO

WE WEREN'T FAR from RIO when I remembered I'd left the *Tranquility* anchored near Lily's house. I wanted to retrieve it before she damaged my beloved boat. I put the engines on low and climbed down to talk to Oliver and Liam.

The *Flemingo*'s cabin looked pretty cozy in the warm glow of the sun. Oliver had taken care of everyone, ensuring they had blankets, water, and coffee. He'd scrambled eggs for the women, who were starved since they hadn't been given much to eat while they were in captivity. Liam and Davy were resting comfortably. Oliver was staying close to Genevra, hovering over the back of her chair, a worried look on his face.

"Can you join me on the deck, please? We need to talk," I said.

He looked at Genevra for a second, then took her hand so she'd walk out with him. The two of them sat on the gunwales, shoulders touching and holding hands.

It would be a long time before he'd be comfortable letting her out of his sight. And there was no reason Genevra couldn't hear our conversation. I shrugged. "How did you know where to find me? It's a big ocean."

"Newton received the distress signal you sent out on some crazy device he has. He didn't want to leave Maddy, so he asked me to go pick you up. Liam decided to tag along because he was worried about you. All we did was follow your beacon. It led us right to you."

My heart plummeted. "Why couldn't Newton leave Maddy? Is she okay? And where are he and Dane anyway? I'd have thought they'd be with you."

Oliver bit his lip before answering. "Maddy had a bad reaction to one of her immunotherapy drugs. The doctors are giving her steroids to manage the symptoms. She was unconscious when we left, although Doc and her oncologist both say she'll be fine."

I was angry about being kept in the dark, since after all, Maddy is my mother. My voice was testy when I spoke. "You should have told me right away. I have to go to her right now."

He glared at me. "Why should I have told you sooner? You can't make the boat go any faster than it already is. And Maddy is unconscious. She doesn't even know you're not there, so all it would have done if I'd told you earlier was to make you crazy with worry."

I inhaled slowly. He was right. He'd made the correct decision. If I'd known about Maddy I might have been too distracted to successfully rescue Diana, Genevra, and Joely. I might have even put off the attempt completely and lost the chance to save them.

"Okay. I get it. Now I'm going to call Doc and let her know we're bringing in a couple of wounded and so I can check with her on Maddy's condition. I want to be there with her as soon as possible."

Oliver took Genevra's hand. "Me too. And I won't relax until Doc has a chance to check Genevra over. When I think of what you've been through…" I could see his love for her shining from his eyes. It was so intense, I had to look away.

I went up to the flying bridge to call Doc and steer the boat. A while later, I slowed down as we neared RIO's dock. I'd also radioed ahead to Stewie that we were coming in. He promised to meet us, and he was as good as his word. When I angled the *Flemingo* into the slip, he was standing at the ready to catch the line I tossed him. Christophe was also on the dock, pacing back and forth and probably annoying Stewie to no end in the process. Oliver let go of Genevra's hand long enough to drop the boat's bumpers over the side, and I shut off the engines.

As soon as the noise of the engines died away, Christophe jumped onto the *Flemingo* and wrapped his arms around Genevra. "Mom Dieu, I am glad you are safe, Cheri."

Genevra hardly reacted at all, neither returning his embrace nor stepping away from him.

Christophe's display shocked me, although it probably shouldn't have, given his ultimatum during the filming of his documentary interview. I'd known Christophe and Genevra were spending a lot of time together. Maybe things between them had progressed romantically.

I looked over at Oliver to see how he was reacting. His face had gone pale, and his mouth dropped open. I guess neither of us had seen this coming.

Finally, Christophe released Genevra and helped her off the boat. Joely and Diana walked out of the cabin together and helped each other to disembark. Liam and Davy followed slowly behind them.

Oliver and I were alone on the deck. He turned to me. "What just happened? Genevra? Christophe?"

I shook my head. "They're friends."

"Yeah," he said. "I could tell."

Flashing red lights illuminated the front parking lot, signaling the arrival of Doc and the medical team.

Doc raced from the parking lot across the lawn and down the pier. She stopped next to Genevra. "Are you okay?"

Genevra nodded. "Shaken, but otherwise fine. They didn't hurt us. Mostly gave us drugs to keep us quiet."

Doc looked at me. "Liam and the other guy? Davy?" They were both sitting on the dock.

"I bandaged them up. They've lost blood, but I think they'll be okay. No bones or vital organs involved."

"The women? How are they doing?" She glanced over at Joely and Diana huddled together near the *Flemingo*'s bow.

"Fine as well. Hungry, thirsty, and groggy, but otherwise okay."

Doc directed the first two teams of EMTs running toward us to Joely and Diana. She waved the third team over to attend to Genevra.

As the medics strapped Genevra into the gurney, she said, "Take really good care of Diana. Joely and I already knew each other, which was a comfort, but she didn't have anyone."

Doc made a low, angry sound like a growl. "Barbarians." She directed the next sentence to the EMTs. "Be gentle."

Two more gurneys rolled down the dock, their wheels rattling against the wooden slats. Doc held them back while the original three gurneys headed toward the ambulances in the parking lot. "Keep all three women together in one ambulance," she said. "Put Liam and Davy together in the other."

The EMTs nodded and went about their work. When Liam rolled by me on the last gurney, I reached out and squeezed his hand. "I'll be right behind you."

He smiled, but his skin was gray, and his mouth was taut with pain. Seeing him like this made my heart hurt.

"Coming?" Doc said. She took off at a run, easily beating Liam's gurney to the parking lot. She was fast, but not faster than me.

Chapter 60
The Hospital Again

THE HOSPITAL'S emergency staff quickly took charge of the arrivals, leaving Doc and me standing near the desk. "How is Maddy? Can I see her?" I asked.

Doc bit her lip and blew out a breath. "Yes, of course. She's fine. She woke up just before I got your call. Sorry, I didn't mention it before. I was worrying about my new patients."

The thing about Doc is that when you're her patient, she focuses on you with one hundred percent of everything she has, like you're the only thing in the world that matters. Maddy was out of the woods, and I knew Doc had turned her focused warmth on Genevra, Joely, and Diana. Plus Liam and Davy. I couldn't fault her for the slight delay in telling me about Maddy's condition.

"Lead the way," I said.

Before we took more than a few steps toward the elevator, Oliver ran through the sliding doors. "How is Genevra? And how is Maddy?" he said, sweating a little bit from the dash across the parking lot.

"They're checking Genevra over now. You can see her when they're done. We were just heading up to see Maddy. Come with," Doc said, holding out a hand to him.

We entered the elevator, and as the door slid shut, Christophe rushed into the emergency room. Oliver was staring at the floor and didn't see him arrive, and I didn't mention that he was here.

Doc led the way down the hall to Maddy's room. She was sitting up in her bed looking tired and pale, but alert. She smiled when she saw us. "How is Genevra?" she asked.

Newton was slumped in a chair beside her bed. "And Joely?" he asked.

Dane was leaning against the wall next to the window. "And Diana?" he said.

Doc answered. "They're checking them out in emergency now. They were drugged, but I don't think they were harmed otherwise."

Dane said, "Thank you, Fin. What you did was amazing. But you shouldn't have tried to do it alone."

"It was fine. I was fine." I swallowed. "Newton. About Cindy…"

He waved a hand in the air. "I knew she was working with Lukin. I just needed her to make a mistake so we could move on her."

"Who is we?" I asked.

He and Dane exchanged glances.

"Us," Newton said. "All of us. By the way, how is Liam? I heard he got shot. Thank God you're okay," he said.

"Thank Liam," I said. "And you might have told me not to trust Cindy."

Newton looked thoughtful, but he didn't speak. I assume he was mulling over whether not telling me about Cindy had been the right call. We both knew I had trouble hiding my feelings when I didn't like or trust someone, but on the other hand, I might have been a lot more careful if I'd known she'd been playing for the other team.

I fell quiet for a minute, mulling over whether I should be angry at Newton. I decided to let it go. Either way, we'd all come through it fine.

It was time for me to make my own confession. I turned to Oliver. "I need to tell you about Lily."

Dane interrupted. "Why don't you start at the beginning and tell us everything. You can fill us in about Lily when you get to that part of the story."

But before I could even start telling them how I'd found the second sub and gone out to save the missing women, Oliver's phone rang. Despite Doc's glare, he answered it.

"Oh hey, Lily," he said. "Yeah, she's with me, and she's fine. I can't talk right now. I'll call you later." He disconnected.

"That's odd," he said. "Lily wanted to know if I knew where you were. What's that about?"

"All part of the story," I said. And then I told them the entire tale.

Chapter 61
A Week Later

STEWIE HAD RETRIEVED the *Tranquility* for me while I was at the hospital with Maddy. He and Gus had checked it out thoroughly to be sure Lily and Cindy hadn't booby trapped it in any way. Once Newton and the others were convinced it hadn't been touched, I was good to go.

I needed to deliver another batch of images for the next issue of *Ecosphere,* so I was out diving alone—just me and my camera—at the dive site known as Fantasea Land.

Although I was alone underwater, I wasn't alone on the boat. Liam was with me aboard the *Tranquility*. Doc hadn't cleared him to dive yet, so he was spending my dive time sitting on the boat's platform, reading a Nick Sullivan book, with his feet dangling in the warm ocean water—just relaxing and recuperating while I captured images for my column.

By the time I was ready to finish my second dive, I had plenty of shots to choose from. Fantasea Land didn't usually offer any big or scary-looking specimens to photograph, but it was a reliably beautiful and colorful site. The coral was vibrant and healthy, teeming with reef fish in a variety of sizes and colors, and there were tons of sand chutes and swim-throughs that lent themselves to striking photographs.

I saw so many of my favorite fish. Stately purple tangs, swimming slowly over the coral. Blue chromis, schooling together and swaying in the surge. A gorgeous Princess parrotfish, munching on the coral with her sharp beak. A spotted drum, a few jacks, a pair of stately-looking queen angelfish, a gray triggerfish, and a diminutive fairy basslet. Even though I had decided that for this month's issue, I would focus more on the coral and plant life, I photographed them all.

But Fantasea Land is home to some large brain corals and tube and dome coral. Anemones, their pink tinged fronds dancing gently in the current, made a nice image, and some ancient elkhorn coral rose above the reef. A large orange tube sponge offered shelter to a dozen tiny shrimp and fish. A spotted moray eel stuck his head out of his lair below the sponge and yawned at me, his wicked-looking teeth gleaming.

This site is beautiful and calm, ensuring that every photo practically composed itself. It was easy to get all the shots I needed.

I checked my dive computer and saw I was nearing the limits of my bottom time. I still had half a tank of air, but even so, it was time to return to the boat. I had plenty of images to choose from for my column, so there was no sense in pushing the envelope by overstaying my safe dive time. I hovered over the top of the reef at fifteen feet for my safety stop.

The water was clear enough that I could see for hundreds of feet in all directions, and the bright sunshine created cones of brilliant light all around me. The water seemed to sparkle and shimmer as the gentle wash of the waves turned the sun's rays into prisms. I found myself smiling, even with the bulky regulator in my mouth.

When my dive computer signaled that my safety stop obligation had been met, I allowed myself to drift up toward the surface until I could grab the lowest rung of the *Tranquility*'s ladder. I held on and removed my fins, then climbed up a rung to hand them and my camera to Liam so I'd have two hands free to hold onto the rails.

He stowed the fins under a bench and put the camera in the freshwater rinse tank, then he quickly returned to the dive platform. Using his good arm, he lifted my BCD and tank from my shoulders and carried the entire assembly to the nearby rack.

When he returned to the *Tranquility*'s stern, I was already seated on the dive platform, with my feet in the water. It was so peaceful, warm, and sunny, that I didn't want to leave yet. Liam stepped onto the platform carrying two cups of water, handing one to me before sitting down. He placed my sunhat on my head and tightened the chin strap.

I smiled at him. I knew love when I saw it, even without words. Sometimes love looks like strawberries and a chocolate fountain, but more often it's as simple as plopping a hat on someone to keep them safe from the sun.

Either way, I always felt Liam's love for me. We sat shoulder to shoulder, not speaking, just enjoying being together for a few minutes.

"Ready to go?" I said after a while.

"Let's get married," he said.

"Sure," I replied. "If you'll tell me your big secret."

He leaned over and kissed me. "Sure," he said. "If you promise to marry me anyway."

A Sneak peek at Killer Storm

Chapter 1
8 hours ago

STORM ADVISORY BULLETIN

HURRICANE WILLARD ADVISORY NUMBER 38

NWS TPC / NATIONAL HURRICANE CENTER MIAMI FL

DANGEROUS HURRICANE WILLARD THREATENS THE CAYMAN ISLANDS. PREPARATIONS TO PROTECT LIFE AND PROPERTY SHOULD BE RUSHED TO COMPLETION. MAXIMUM SUSTAINED WINDS HAVE INCREASED TO MORE THAN 135/156 KM/HR WITH HIGHER GUSTS. THIS IS CATEGORY FIVE ON THE SAFFIR-SIMPSON HURRICANE SCALE. SOME FLUCTUATIONS IN INTENSITY ARE LIKELY DURING THE NEXT 24 HOURS.

HURRICANE FORCE WINDS EXTEND OUTWARD UP TO 90 MILES /150 KM FROM THE CENTER AND TROPICAL STORM FORCE WINDS EXTEND OUTWARD UP TO 175 MILES /280 KM.

STORM SURGE FLOODING OF 8 TO 25 FEET ABOVE NORMAL TIDE LEVELS ALONG WITH LARGE AND DANGEROUS BATTERING WAVES CAN BE EXPECTED THROUGHOUT THE CAYMAN ISLANDS DEPENDING ON THE EXACT TRACK OF WILLARD.

RAINFALL AMOUNTS OF 12 TO 30 INCHES POSSIBLY CAUSING LIFE-THREATENING FLASH FLOODS AND MUD SLIDES CAN BE EXPECTED ALONG THE PATH OF WILLARD

Chapter 2
6:30 AM

I TOSSED the storm advisory aside. It was ominous, but our preparations were well underway at this point.

Just to confirm that in my own mind, I looked out my open office window at the increasingly angry sea, watching Stewie, RIO's director of dive operations, supervising the removal of all our boats to send them to drydock. The ocean swells had grown overnight, and white-caps were licking at the top of RIO's dock. The sky was a looming grey, and there was a bite to the breeze unusual for Grand Cayman.

The smell of hot coffee made me turn around.

"Dr. Fleming, you're in early," Benjamin Brooks, RIO's CFO, said, sliding a steaming cup onto my desk. He smiled, and I realized again how lucky I was to have him as a friend and sort of boyfriend. He was more than a friend although less than a soulmate. I enjoyed his company, but I always held him at arm's length even though he'd made it clear he wanted more. Not for the first time, I wished my best friend Theresa was around so we could talk about my confused feelings. Unfortunately, she and her husband Gus were traveling in Europe on Fleming Environmental Investments business.

I returned Benjamin's smile. "More like I stayed late. I've been here all night," I replied as I popped the lid off the coffee. "Thanks for this. You can't imagine how much I need it."

"Finola Fleming, you can't keep burning the candle at both ends. It's time to tell Maddy you need an assistant."

The 'Maddy' he referred to is my mother, Madelyn Anderson Russo, the founder of the Russo Institute of Oceanography, which we called RIO for short. I'd spent my childhood in the corridors at RIO or on the research vessel *Omega*, and since everyone around me called her Maddy, I'd always called her that too.

I'd been working long hours at RIO covering for Maddy, its absent director and a world famous oceanographer on the order of one of the Cousteau clan or Sylvia Earle. I was so tired the thought of breakfast and some quiet time in my cozy home on Rum Point on the North Side of Grand Cayman made me sigh with longing.

Benjamin was always thoughtful, and he immediately recognized the depths of my exhaustion. "But right now, you need a break. C'mon. Let's get some breakfast and then I'll drive you home before the storm hits."

My official job at RIO was supposed to be VP of marketing and chief underwater photographer, but with Maddy away working with the folks at the Woods Hole Oceanography Institute on a joint project, my workload had increased exponentially. I'd been struggling to keep my head above water, and that had never happened to me before.

I already held down several jobs, each with a demanding load of details, but usually I handled my varied workload with ease. Now I was feeling overwhelmed, which was even more galling because the mountain of desk work had kept me from diving for the last several days. I was feeling the stress of being away from the ocean in addition to the work overload.

I sighed. "Sorry, Benjamin. I can't take time for breakfast. I've got to finish this spreadsheet today. And thanks for the offer, but I won't need a ride home. I'll be staying here through the storm. I have to make sure the research labs are okay."

"Fin, you've turned into a drone. You used to be fun." His words were said lightly, but I could hear the concern behind his teasing.

I looked at him over the tops of my new glasses. I'd been spending so much time on my computer lately that my eyes were feeling the strain. Then I looked back at my screen where I'd been working on finalizing RIO's budget for next year. It's a well-known fact that I hate spreadsheets. And numbers. "I have to finish RIO's budget for the next fiscal year. We need to have it ready for the board of directors meeting."

Benjamin cleared his throat. "Too bad RIO doesn't have an accomplished and highly experienced CFO on the staff to do those budgets for you."

Benjamin was RIO's CFO, and he was definitely accomplished and highly experienced. But my fatal flaw—or at least one of them—is assuming everything is my responsibility, and because of that assumption, I tend to take on too much. I realized I should have delegated this project to him weeks ago.

When he saw the realization hit me, he laughed. "And I believe I'm supposed to be the chief number cruncher around here. You're the creative genius. Don't waste your time messing around with spreadsheets instead of doing what you do best. You should be in the ocean, taking beautiful photographs, not sitting inside crunching numbers."

He walked around my desk to peer at my screen. "Departmental budgets? Piece of cake. Let me handle them." His fingers hovered a half inch above the keyboard of my Mac. "May I?"

I shrugged and swiveled the computer toward him. His fingers flew across the keys as he emailed the much-despised spreadsheets to himself. "I'll have them back to you by end of the day. Now let's go. Time for breakfast."

I'd always loved my job at RIO, mainly because it required me to dive every day, but lately, I'd felt chained to my desk. My mother had turned most of the day-to-day operation of RIO over to me last year while she'd been living in New York City. And now this new project with Woods Hole was taking up all her time, and she'd hardly set foot on Grand Cayman in almost a year.

Plus, my father, Newton Fleming, had asked me to keep an eye on the operations of his business, Fleming Environmental Investments, while he too spent time in the states. At least his assistant, Justin Nash, handled most of Newton's company's routine decisions, and my brother Oliver was working there part time when he wasn't at school in New York. That meant I only had to get involved in the really big issues. But the ocean is my happy place and sitting out my life on dry land had never been part of my plan.

Still, I had responsibilities. "There's a storm coming," I said. "It could be dangerous. I need to stay here."

"The latest predictions say the storm will miss us. And anyway, danger is your middle name," said Benjamin.

"Not so," I said, flipping the paper with the latest advisory his way. "Hurricane Willard is coming on with a vengeance."

Benjamin read the storm warning. "Yikes. Okay, I stand corrected. But anyway, I stopped by the dive shop on the way in. Stewie is already supervising the removal of all RIO's boats to drydock to wait out the storm. He's closed up the shop and put on the storm shutters. Eugene is buttoning up the main building, and per your orders, Vincent has taken the *Omega* out to deep water to ride out the storm. And since you're crazy busy here, I was afraid you'd forget about your own house. I sent a couple of the maintenance guys over to your place to put up the hurricane shutters and stow all your outdoor stuff in the cabana. You can relax. Even your home is safe. Everything is as ready as it can be. Let's go. You'll be able to relax once you get home."

"Thanks, Benjamin. I did forget about the outdoor furniture at home," I said. Now I was worried about what else I might have forgotten.

"Forgetting things isn't like you, Fin, You're usually on top of every detail. You have to get some help around here," Benjamin said. "You'll drive yourself into the ground."

"Okay, you're right." I held up my hands to stop any further arguments. "Let's get some breakfast from the café and then I'll go home." I dropped my blue-light glasses on my desk and slid my feet into the flipflops I'd kicked underneath.

When we reached the café, there was a sign on the door saying it was closed because of the storm. I'd given the order for RIO's café, gift shop, and aquarium to stay closed today when the storm seemed imminent. Another thing I should have remembered. Another oops. I rubbed my forehead in frustration.

I pulled the café's keys out of the pocket of my cargo shorts. "I guess, we'll have to make our own breakfast."

We settled for toast and another cup of coffee, then we donned the traditional sailor's yellow rain gear and walked out the back door of the RIO building onto the crushed shell paths leading to the onsite dive shop, the picnic area, and RIO's marina. I nodded approvingly when I noticed Stewie had already stowed away the picnic tables from the lawn and closed the storm shutters on the dive shop.

The team of contractors from the drydock boat storage facility was busy hauling all RIO's boats out of the water, but they paused a minute to don their own raingear before going back to work loading the boats on the carrier. It looked like they'd have all our boats out of the water in plenty of time to beat the full fury of the gathering storm.

The first drops of rain were beginning to fall, and according to the weather reports, it would be a deluge before long. The early raindrops were already big and hard and felt like angry pellets smashing into my skin. If this was any indication of the fury of the coming storm, we were in for a bad day. Despite the rain, Benjamin and I continued across the lawn to check in with Stewie, who had recently taken over dive shop operations.

Stewie's return from rehab several months ago had been a piece of unexpected good luck. He was a huge help to me now that he was clean and sober, and I hoped he could stay that way for good.

He turned and smiled at me when I entered. As I did whenever I saw him, I discreetly checked him out for any signs of a relapse, but his weathered face looked lean and healthy under the brim of the hood of his yellow rain slicker.

He pulled the last knot tight around the tarp he'd used to cover the tank compressor. "That's done," he said dusting his palms on his T-shirt. "I think the shop is ready. I'll just go check with the boat handlers to make sure they're on schedule, and then we'll be all set to ride out the storm."

"Why don't you take off now, Stewie. You've been working all night and I want to be sure you get home before the storm hits," I said. "I can take care of anything else that comes up."

Stewie looked at the lowering sky and assessed the rising wind. "If you're sure it's okay, I wouldn't mind leaving now. It's been a long night."

"Go home and stay safe. Thank you for all your hard work coordinating the storm prep. I appreciate it."

He looked pleased at my words. "Fin, you be careful out here. This storm is a monster of a hurricane. Keep inside, out of the foul weather.

And with a storm like this, conditions can change fast. Make sure you stay alert."

"Will do, Stewie."

Stewie had been one of my stepfather Ray Russo's closest friends, and he'd known me since I was a little girl. Sometimes he felt he had the right to remind me of safety rules even though I was his boss now. And I was a licensed technical diver, a certified PADI dive instructor, and a master boat captain. I do know my stuff.

But I don't mind his worrying. We've been through a lot together.

I took a deep breath of the ozone laden air. "You should go home too, Benjamin. It'll be much safer for you. You've never been through a tropical hurricane, and it can get pretty intense."

"All the more reason I should stay with you," he said. "I'm not leaving you here alone. No way. No how. Can't let anything happen to my best girl." He reached out to brush a raindrop off my cheek.

"Your car would be safer in your garage at home," I told him. "And you'd be safer there too. Since you haven't been through a storm like this, you may not realize how bad it can get."

"I do know how bad it can get, which is why I'm not leaving you here alone." Benjamin crossed his arms stubbornly. He had a habit of being a bit controlling and high-handed, reminding me unpleasantly of my ex-husband, Alec Stone. It was the reason I'd never let myself fall in love with him despite his efforts.

Or at least, it was one of the reasons. The other was Liam Lawton, but I try not to think about Liam too much.

After managing to evade the high collar of my rain slicker, an unpleasantly cold, fat raindrop slid down my neck and along my spine, making me shiver. I didn't want to waste time arguing about where Benjamin stayed during the storm, nor did I want to give in and let him stay with me.

I had no intention of going home and leaving RIO unattended, but I told him what he wanted to hear. "I'll go home if you'll go home," I said.

"Good. I'm ready." He pulled his car keys from a pocket in his shorts.

"You go on ahead. I need a minute to see Rosie and make sure everything is okay in the lab." Rosie is an Atlantic Pygmy octopus.

She'd been the subject of my doctoral thesis, but she later became more of a pet than a lab animal. I liked to think Rosie and I were friends as well as lab partners.

Benjamin looked suspicious at my change of heart, but he nodded. He and Stewie headed out to the parking lot and their cars. I watched them drive away before I went back inside, even though the rain was intensifying by the minute. On my way to the lab, I picked up my computer and rounded up a couple of flashlights from the supply closet in case of a power outage, although between the emergency generator and the massive battery backups for the lab and the infirmary, I was confident I wouldn't need the flashlights.

As I crossed the lobby, I noticed Ralph, our new security guard, biting his lip and watching the storm through the huge panes of glass that defined RIO's atrium.

"Ralph," I called to him. "Why don't you go home before the storm gets really bad? Nobody will be out in this weather. The building will be safe, and you should be with your family. I hear your new baby is due any day now, and your wife will want you with her."

"I don't know, Doctor Fleming. I don't want to leave you here all alone during the storm. Like you say, it could get bad."

"It's okay. What if your family needs you? If the baby comes, I'd rather you were at home with your wife than stranded here. You can go. And by the way, call me Fin." I smiled at him.

"Thanks" he said. "I think I will leave then if you're sure it's okay. My wife does get nervous in a storm, and now with the baby coming...." He crossed the lobby back to the guard room to grab his raincoat. "I'll see you later. And thanks for this."

I locked the front door behind him and continued heading for the research labs, a suite of windowless rooms located in the center of the building. As soon as I entered, I could tell that most of the sea creatures in the lab were edgy. They could sense the storm coming. Even Rosie didn't pop out of her shell when I approached.

I sat down at one of the lab tables and since Benjamin had volunteered to do the budget spreadsheets, I decided to do something fun. I started working on a photo collage I'd wanted to put together for a new poster to sell in the gift shop.

After about ten minutes, I realized I needed some sketches I'd left in my office, so I left the lab to pick them up. When I glanced through the slats in the hurricane shutters that covered the huge windows in my office, I noticed the team from the drydock had left the marina.

I was still watching the gathering storm when a solitary figure in yellow rain gear ran down the dock and across the lawn toward the parking lot. I couldn't see the person's face or discern anything about them under the bulky slicker and baggy rain pants. I hoped whoever it was got home safely.

It took a moment before I realized a big problem—one boat had been left behind by the boat handlers. I raced to the back door between Maddy and Benjamin's offices to see if I could catch the team before they left, but they were long gone by the time I reached the door.

Peering through the raindrops, I noticed the storm surge had gotten worse just in the short time I'd been inside. Waves were crashing over the dock, and the solitary boat was straining at its lines. With a shock, I recognized it as my brother Oliver's new boat. I wondered why the boat handlers hadn't taken it along with all the others on the list I'd given them.

With a sinking feeling, I realized why this boat had been left behind. I had forgotten to add Oliver's boat to the list. He'd just bought it from a boatyard in New York, near where he attended college, a few days ago and had it delivered so it would be here waiting when his semester ended. He'd worked hard and saved up to buy it. If I didn't get it to safety, it would be smashed to bits against the dock or the nearby ironshore. If that disaster happened, it would be my fault. Another fine example of me screwing up by taking on too much.

Without thinking about the danger, I ran through the door and across the lawn. Waves crashed up onto the grass and washed across the wooden boards of the dock. The storm was getting worse, but I kept going. I was sure I'd be able to get the boat to deeper water and still get back to shore safely. I wasn't thinking of the danger to me, only of how hard Oliver had worked to buy the boat.

I jumped aboard and raced below to start the engines. I untied the mooring lines and backed out of the slip. The ocean tossed the boat like it was made of paper, and I had to grip the wheel hard to stay in control, but I was determined to save this boat because Oliver loved it.

Gunning the engine, I headed out to sea until I knew I was over deep water and with any luck, far enough from shore to keep the boat safe during the storm. I threw the anchor overboard and let out a long line to allow the boat to ride the swells, which were already about fifteen feet high, and getting higher by the minute.

My pulse pounded when I looked back at the dock. Knowing I'm a strong swimmer, I'd assumed I'd be able to make it back to land easily, but I hadn't realized how quickly the storm was intensifying. The shoreline was only a few hundred feet away, but it might as well have been miles. Yet the only way for me to get back to safety was to swim through the mounting turbulence.

In addition to being a strong swimmer, I'm a lucky one. My brother's dive gear was all set up in one of the tank racks near the swim platform in the back.

I threw on Oliver's buoyancy control device—his BCD—slid his mask over my face and stuck my feet into his full foot fins. I checked the tank's pressure gauge, and the tank was full, but because the storm was escalating so rapidly, I probably wouldn't have stopped to change it even if it had only held a breath or two of air. I was relieved to have the full tank, but even a partial fill would normally be enough to get me to shore. I stepped off the boat, knowing I'd have to drop below the surface as quickly as possible before I became disoriented by the wild sea.

The water, normally warm and placid here in the Caymans, was like ice. As I'd expected, the waves were almost irresistible on the surface, and I was tossed around like a beach ball in the windstorm. As good a swimmer as I am, if I stayed on the surface, I knew I'd never make any headway against the ocean's might, even though the tide was coming in. My best hope was that the water was calmer at depth.

I dropped down to the bottom as quickly as I could. The tidal surge was almost as intense as the storm surge, moving me forward and backward at least fifteen or twenty feet with each pulse. Luckily, since the tide was heading in, my forward motion slightly exceeded the backward pull. I made slow but steady headway toward shore.

I held on to submerged rocks with all my strength to avoid losing ground to the ocean's pull when the waves receded, and I scurried toward shore as fast as I could when the tide surged ahead. The perilous journey was short in distance, but it seemed to take forever until at last, a wave broke over my head and I felt air against my skin. I was in the shallows.

I heaved my body up onto the dock, digging my fingers into the rough wood so the ocean couldn't pull me back. It took everything I had to stand up against the wind and the waves, but I did it. I tore off my borrowed dive gear, leaving it to the mercy of the ocean. I'd buy my brother a new rig when this storm was over, but the tank and BCD were too heavy and awkward to wear while fighting against the powerful wind. I'd need every ounce of strength I had to make it safely back to the building as it was.

If I made it back to the building.

I ran along the remains of the dock, sloshing through the rushing water sluicing over the boards. Waves crashed over the wood, pulling my feet out from under me with each step, the water trying to suck me back into its clutches. It was disorienting and made me dizzy, but to falter now meant certain death. I ran, bulling my way through buffeting winds so strong they felt like hitting a solid wall.

One more step. Another.

I felt grass under my bare feet, but my ordeal wasn't over. The waves had followed me across the dock, and they reached out with grasping fingers of cold water. My feet were frozen and numb. I pushed ahead, my bare feet sinking into sucking mud with each step. I crouched low, to make myself a smaller target for the wind and pushed ahead.

I was running as fast and as hard as I could but making very little progress. I couldn't —wouldn't—give up. I couldn't lift my head to check my position, but I knew I was less than fifty yards from the door to RIO and safety. It might as well have been miles. Each step felt like my last, but after every tortured footfall I sucked in a breath and mustered the resolve to take one more.

The visibility was terrible through the driving rain. I couldn't see even a few inches ahead of me. I stretched my arms out in front to prevent me from bumping into the building. It seemed like ages before my fingers touched the heavy, solid steel door, and I pulled it open. The wind took it from me and slammed it back against the concrete wall, knocking out a large chunk of cinderblock that must have weighed at least a pound or two. The furious wind picked up the mass of cement and carried it away before I could react. There was nothing I could do about the flying boulder except hope it didn't do any property damage or hurt anyone. I stepped inside and tried to shut the door.

The wind followed me in, pushing me back, the gusts making it almost impossible to pull the heavy door shut. After what felt like a lifetime, still shivering with fear and cold, inch by inch, I managed to get the door shut and locked.

Links to my Books

Shop my online store

Shop the Series Page on Amazon

Also by Sharon Ward

In Deep

Sunken Death

Dark Tide

Killer Storm

Sea Stars

Rip Current

Or see the entire series Fin Fleming series by following the link or using the QR code on the previous page.

If you enjoyed Hidden Depths, you can continue reading about the adventures of Fin and the gang by following the links above.

Also, nothing (except actually buying the book) helps an author more than a positive review, so please give Hidden Depths (and me!) a boost by leaving a review. Here's the link:

Hidden Depths or

And if you'd like to subscribe to my totally random and very rarely published newsletter, you can sign up here.

Link to SharonWard.com

Acknowledgments

So many people help with writing a book that it's hard to remember to thank everyone. There are, however, certain people who have been with me on this journey for years, and here they are, in no particular order.

Mary Beth Gale, my oldest (not in terms of age) writing buddy and critique partner. Your eagle eye is much appreciated.

Andrea Clark, your prose writing is like other people's poetry. It's that good. Thanks for taking the time to point out the flaws in my early drafts. I wanna be you when I grow up.

Stephanie Scott-Snyder, your job is as scary as your writing. I don't know how you do what you do. I'd be scribbling pictures of rainbows with my broken crayons if I had to spend so much as a day in your job (She's the world's best forensic psychologist, specializing in serial killers. YIKES!). Thanks for hanging out with me. I'm glad we met in Tuscany.

Kate Hohl, a brilliant writer and a tireless cheerleader. How could I do this without your encouragement?

And C. Michele Dorsey. You're a terrific writer and a true inspiration. Thanks for being my writing buddy.

Jack, I already mentioned several times you're the world's best husband. Don't let it go to your head.

And Erin Lambrinos, my beautiful daughter. Thanks for being you. You're incredible.

Scott Lambrinos, Cam Lambrinos, Taylor, and Milan Lambrinos. Love you all.

Josh, Jen, Parker, and Isaac Ward. I wish you guys lived closer so we could see you more.

Erin, Pat, Collin, and Anthony Rogers. A fun part of the family. I'm lucky to have you.

Ed and Teri Hoitt, early cheerleaders, and continued supporters. An excellent brother and sister (in-law.) Dave and Trish Hoitt and Bob and Patti Hoitt. Two terrific brothers with even better wives. Thanks.

About the Author

Sharon Ward is an avid scuba diver. She was a PADI certified divemaster and has hundreds of dives under her weight belt. Wanting to share the joy and wonder of the underwater world, she wrote In Deep, the first book in the Fin Fleming Scuba Diving Mystery Series.

Beside In Deep, books in the series include Sunken Death, Dark Tide, Killer Storm, and Hidden Depths. Sea Stars, book 6, will be out in late Summer, 2023

Ward lives on the south coast of Massachusetts with her husband, Jack, and Molly, their long-haired miniature dachshund, the actual head of the household.

.

www.ingramcontent.com/pod-product-compliance
Ingram Content Group UK Ltd.
Pitfield, Milton Keynes, MK11 3LW, UK
UKHW010622230625
6528UKWH00001B/3

9 781958 478219